I0699015

CROWE COUNTY HOSPITAL

TALES FROM CROWE COUNTY

TORY TALLBERG

CROWE COUNTY HOSPITAL

TALES FROM CROWE COUNTY

CROWE COUNTY
HOSPITAL
TALES FROM CROWE COUNTY

The following is a work of fiction, taking place in an alternate time where entities walk among us. Similarities to persons, places of business, events, and incidents, including demonic possessions, incubi births, and werewolf medical emergencies, are entirely coincidental.

Copyright © 2022 by Tory Tallberg

All rights reserved.

The scanning, uploading, and distribution of this book without permission is a theft of the author's intellectual property. If you would like permission to use material from the book (other than for review purposes), please contact torytallbergwrites@gmail.com.

Content Warning: The following work contains graphic scenes including but not limited to disembowelment, dismemberment, murder, medical trauma, and violence, Other sensitive topics include profane language, birth trauma, death, abduction, abuse of authority, and blood. Reader discretion is advised.

Cover Design | Editing | Book Design and Typesetting
Enchanted Ink Publishing

ISBN: 979-8-9861551-0-4 (E-book)
ISBN: 979-8-9861551-1-1 (Paperback KDP)
ISBN: 979-8-9861551-2-8 (Paperback B&N Press)

Thank you for your support of the author's rights.

Printed in the United States of America

For Libby, my most persistent editor and voracious fan.

*Thank you for all the phone calls, encouragement,
and for reading every. Single. Draft.*

And to my Good Witch of the Past, my brilliant Nana.

I love you both.

PART 1

PETER'S NO GOOD, ROTTEN SUNDAY

CHAPTER ONE

Crowe County Hospital is haunted.

By itself, this statement is not special.

Every hospital in the world is haunted to some degree or another. It's a fact.

But, Crowe County Hospital is *haunted*, which holds an entirely different meaning.

Peter Winsted was aware (from his infrequent jaunts to bars outside his home county and even less frequent chats with strangers in those bars) that the *hauntings* of Crowe County were what caught people's attention.

On the chance he wasn't off-putting enough to avoid these conversations, they always hit the same beats.

People craved stories about the hospital's four belfries, which stretched to the sky as the centerpiece of the cityscape. They showed him grainy photographs taken from the freeway on their trips past Crowe, noting how North Belfry sat next to its sisters' shadows at night, void of light and life.

Most of all, if Peter couldn't escape the conversation before it came to that point, they had questions about fifteen years ago.

They asked him to remember when the attack happened. When hundreds of people perished at the hands of an entity that tore the hospital's defenses to shreds. A time when Peter Winsted was thirteen years old, watching rolling blackouts consume his city.

When the *hauntings* began.

It was with these hauntings in mind, Peter began his shift.

At the very same hospital.

In the shadow of North Belfry, in a concrete bunker with a driveway that travelled beneath the hospital's East Belfry and Grand Street, was a twenty-eight-year-old Peter Winsted. He inspected his ambulance with the diligence of someone who cared deeply for their job, while being grossly underpaid to do it.

The plight of most paramedics.

A cup of black coffee balanced on his stretcher, a staple of his work space. It was scalding and newly stolen from the nurses' break room, supervising Peter as he tugged open aluminum drawers lining the walls of his rig. The routine was refined as his lithe fingers picked apart IV supplies, tested the wall-mounted suction cannister, and ensured his packs were left stocked by the medics conceding rig 415 to him that evening.

Of course, they were not.

A bead of sweat flew from Peter's twitching mustache as he stared down the orange medication box open on his stretcher. The glorified tackle box was in shambles, its posture and supplies unsteady as a barfly after a long night on the tap. Beside it, the airway bag splayed its contents like a gutted pig, if that pig lacked all essential organs.

"Lazy sons of bitches," Peter grumbled, flicking through the remaining stock with distaste.

He withdrew two vials of clear liquid labelled *Epinephrine* from the bottom of the pack, replacing them in a drawer meant to hold five.

Dammit.

You need what you need for a full moon in Crowe County. Nothing more. Nothing less.

This lesson was learned early in his career, and Peter carried it with vigor. He secured his airway bag on a bench stretching along the right side of the ambulance, leaving the medication box an open sarcophagus on the stretcher's crisp sheets.

In this moment, Peter knew he had less, which simply would not do.

We'll deal with that soon.

Ducking through the doorway between the front and back of the ambulance, he caught the sound of shoes pounding against the sidewalk three feet above the windshield.

A voice screamed from the group, "Wait! Wait for me!"

The uneven tread of flip-flops assaulted the pavement.

The paramedic bent forward, squinting at the sun through a concrete window above the windshield.

Stale summer breeze seeped into the subterranean ambulance bay with angry traffic on its back. Chain-smokers hacked from Crowe County's Emergency Department entrance at the end of the block, staining the cloudless sky with thin wisps of carcinogen.

Peter recognized the city stretching awake in the early afternoon like a dog who'd spent the day basking on the front porch.

A rabid dog who was also on a government watch list.

Seven boroughs made Crowe County. From the wealthy Sticks to the seaside suburb, each borough commanded and demanded attention from Crowe Ambulance Corps every night.

This was especially true on a full moon.

At any given time, magic users were preparing supplies for benign workings, or maybe to carve hearts from sacrificial victims, if you believed the tabloids. Families cooked Sunday dinner and discussed school while their neighbors attempted to summon greater demons. Some residents locked themselves in their basements to keep their lycanthropy at bay, while specters lurked in the shadows. Old biddies broke their hips, and forty-year-old couch warriors suffered heart attacks in front of the Game Show Network.

It was home.

A car passed, blasting heavy bass from scorned speakers, and Peter allowed it to wash over him like a salve, carefully acquiring his final preparations.

Two silver-plated vests slumped unceremoniously on the driver's seat, the remaining evidence of a slovenly preceding shift. Peter lifted both, giving them a once-over before returning to the back of the ambulance, where he slung a set onto his shoulders.

The vest strapped snuggly against his long-sleeved shirt, its pads inviting sweat on his sternum. Hands on his hips, he observed the final rig setup with a frown.

The strips of fluorescent light above twisted in his sight like ballet dancers, their electricity static cling in the space around him. The air weighed his shoulders down more than the vest, with the clutching presence of others who'd existed in the space before him remaining like imprints on undeveloped film. The bits of themselves people left behind, now bending and flexing between the cascading overhead light.

Giving him a toothache on his bottom-right molar, too early in the shift.

Peter scrutinized his shirtsleeves as the dull ache coursed through his jaw, shoving them boldly above his elbows in the safety of his rig.

Jagged tattoos stretched along his forearms and disappeared beneath each sleeve. Blasted by a bold steady hand, their deep black ink was worn by time and poor artistry. The designs were hooked like upholstery needles, writing a story of a teen with too much pocket money and no sense of growing old.

Peter tracked them delicately under his fingertips, their movement familiar and reckless. They were his safety. His family's protective sigils.

Graying memories.

"Everything in order, Ace?"

The voice was placid as an untouched lake and came from a gentleman in his late fifties who'd earned the term *gentleman* in every sense of the word. Tranquil, despite years working a rig, the man looked upon his partner with calm humor twinkling behind thick-rimmed glasses. This was not a man who rushed for much, nor a man who missed a beat.

This was Henry.

"Previous crew left it a fucking mess." Peter gave his shirtsleeves a self-conscious tug and dragged them to his wrists. "All in all, I think we're set for the first couple calls at least. Sixteen gods-damned hours."

"Control room was complaining about their sick calls," explained the gentleman, trading Peter a paper cup of tea for his own vest in a familiar exchange.

Peter snorted, retrieving his coffee from the stretcher. "Who calls out on a full moon? S'worse than Christmas."

"You don't celebrate Christmas." Henry chuckled, donning his vest.

"That's why it's worse." Peter grinned, returning the tea to its rightful owner. "Better than calling out tomorrow, I guess."

Henry took his place at the foot of the stretcher.

"That is up for debate. I would rather work a full moon than the anniversary. Any day of the week. Birchwood already has the barricades outside of Grand Street."

Peter tapped his coffee, occupying the bench beside his airway bag. "Any news on who might try something this year to celebrate?"

"Not yet. But tomorrow I'll be listening to dispatch from the comfort of my armchair."

Peter smiled.

Attempted a smile, maybe. He couldn't be certain.

His expression hitched halfway to a grimace as shards of cold wafted beneath his nose, attached to gray matter in the air like amoebae.

The tips of Peter's fingers paled as he fiddled with his cup, eyes flitting among the small ripples of burnt coffee creating concentric circles within it.

"Ace . . ."

Henry's glasses were fogged by his drink, suspended mid-sip. The needling sensation beneath Peter's fingernails amplified as he caught his partner's eye, and a hiss escaped him like a deflating balloon.

"Oh, damn . . . sorry." Peter sucked in the stale air so it filled his chest. "I think they forgot to cleanse the rig tonight. There's a lot of excess bullshit floating around. I'm having a hard time keeping it away."

"Please elaborate on 'bullshit.'"

Peter fixated on his hands, straining his eyes like a raccoon on a leash, trying to settle on one spot. Pale yellow sparks leapt from his fingertips, sparklers visible to only his eyes.

He released his breath.

And they were gone.

"The air feels heavy tonight," the paramedic said. "I'm uncertain why, but I have a sneaking suspicion the moon won't make it better."

"Even so." The gentleman squared his posture. "Cerebral sensitivity like yours is like Raynaud's. Stress and the cold make it ten times worse. And it ain't cold out, Ace."

Another pointed glance caught Peter mid-sip, risking a burnt tongue over current conversation.

But Henry was direct.

"Is there something you wish to talk through? Causing you stress?"

Peter cleared his throat, choking down the burnt coffee. "No, I'm all set, H."

The tattoos under his sleeves were uncomfortably warm with the lie, but he continued.

"I wrangled some silver and stakes. Med kit is restocked, but epinephrine is still on shortage, and it was like pulling teeth to get more from the pharmacy. Got so much bicarbonate hanging out, it's beginning to think it's important."

"Well, we can't have that."

Peter shuffled his feet as Henry sipped his tea at last.

"Who's the nurse in charge tonight?"

"J or C." Henry raised a caterpillar brow. "You're not angling to disrupt the charge nurse so early in our shift, are you?"

Peter stood, ready to be done with the conversation. "Nearly always."

Henry conceded the unspoken battle with the air of someone who knew time was the best way to wear down an opponent.

"Well . . . be smart about it."

A bouncing step and Henry's warning carried Peter off the back of the ambulance like a flea out to ruin a dog's day.

He dove into the fray of emergency personnel.

Paramedics and EMTs at scattered stages of exhaustion bustled in the cramped concrete bunker before him. They restocked supplies and extracted patients from a long fleet of vehicles pulled headlong into spaces beside rig 415. Most held the neat insignia of Crowe Ambulance Corps, a yellow CCH blasted into the side of their green-and-white ambulances. This fleet competed for space with ambulances of other towns sporting less tacky signage, who sought help from the only Trauma 1 facility in a good radius.

Fluorescence from the bunker's ceiling shed sickly light on the ragged workforce, all equipped with vests identical to Peter's, specifically for the full moon. Most were undone in the safety of the bunker, but the extra weight was worth sweat-drenched uniforms for the protection against lycanthrope jaws.

Gasoline reek and the practitioner's sweat mingled with a strong antiseptic sting permeating from the outer walls of the hospital.

A single notepad sheet was stuck to the wall's center, *Caustic: Do Not Touch* scribed in light pencil.

Day shift cleansed those walls, drawing standard protective sigils into the gray concrete. And until the sigils settled into the stone, it burned everything.

Peter discovered one slow night that this included tongues, and gave the wall earned distance.

Exchanging limited pleasantries, Peter reached the doors separating the ambulance bunker from the Emergency Department.

Runic script clouded the glass so he could only make out vague shapes of movement beyond them. And even then, he couldn't be certain they were real.

The hospital liked playing tricks. Especially on a full moon night.

When he placed his badge to the door pad, the glass opened to an empty EMS foyer, confirming those suspicions.

The room was sterile and whitewashed, only large enough to hold two stretchers at once.

If you were lucky.

Old ham and pine assaulted Peter's nose. A lonely half-eaten sandwich sat on a security desk to his immediate left. Smoke seeped from brass bowls beside the forgotten meal, piled with charred evergreen needles and cinnamon. Evidence of an ongoing cleanse.

The doors slithered shut, enclosing Peter in the room.

One person stood beside the doorway into the Emergency Department from this antechamber, leaning like a silent specter against the eggshell walls. Their outfit was casual appearing, a black button-down tucked into black slacks, transitioning into black dress shoes that contrasted in sharp relief against blue tile floors. At first glance, he could have been at home in a corner coffee shop, spewing poetry to poorly played jazz piano.

But his thousand-yard stare cut into Peter, dissecting his innards into thin slices with a single glance. The man was a living ink blot, watching with persistent silence as the paramedic held out his badge for exam.

"Chaplain. Shift good?"

The lingering taste of rotting rosemary and pine clung to Peter's tongue as the man leaned forward. He flipped the badge purposefully in callused palms engraved with sigils that scarred him fingertip to wrist.

And then relinquished it with a nod.

"As good as it can be, medic. Be quick."

Peter made no attempt at small talk, the man's endless eyes burning the nape of his neck as he proceeded into EMS hallway.

Crowe Emergency Department spread through the

bottom of East Belfry like a ladder with three rungs. EMS hall was Peter's first rung and the one he knew best. A row of stretchers hugged the wall, bottlenecking the corridor past two oversized doors to the trauma bays Peter and Henry serviced at least twice a shift.

Patients of less acuity stocked the stretcher "beds" with, as Henry would put it, "considerable ire and indignation."

Considerable ire—Peter threw a grin to a disgruntled fellow restrained to his stretcher—*is a vast understatement.*

Past the trauma rooms, the beds thinned to a no-man's expanse of barren space as numbered rooms marched along the wall.

Each of these rooms was punctuated with a faint glowing light, which traced the interior of the doorframes.

Crowe's basic security standard.

Way-lines.

They cast a dusky blush light on the Emergency Department, delicately providing entryway security, like an invisible fence in Peter's eyes. Their purpose was to deter shadows and keep in fiends, keep ghosts from congregating in negative space, protect patients from the horrors of a building with centuries of violence and death under its belt, and protect practitioners from the patients who succumbed to such a place.

The lines dispelled energy of all kinds, barriers for and from those affected by the hallowed halls of Crowe County Hospital.

They were guaranteed to work 79.4 percent of the time.

A number Peter had made up based on his personal success with them.

He proceeded down the second ladder rung with room placards counting the way.

Room 27, 28, 29 . . .

The PA crackled to life overhead. "Environmental to room 30. Environmental to room 30."

Peter stalled with room 30 in sight.

The way-line laid into the doorframe flickered like an extinguishing candle, its blush color fading to deep blood red. A seditious black mire tried to spill into the hall, buffeted and restrained inside the room by the way-line's light, as if by a pane of glass.

Peter groaned, idly looking for a place to put his coffee before two nurses in Crowe's signature plum scrubs shoved him.

"Watch out, medic!" the first snapped. "Which room?"

"Room 30!" the second replied, dragging a rattling code cart. Her shoulder collided into Peter's without apology, forcing him to the side as a doctor in their spangled white coat pursued hot on their heels.

Guttural screams echoed throughout the hall, splintering the tile as the practitioners disappeared into the chaos, and the way-line tracing room 30's doorframe plunged to black.

Peter grimaced, sipping his coffee.

The slow sip of someone suddenly watching a problem unfold that was not his to solve.

Before resuming his stride.

Room 29, 28, 27 . . .

"Hey, medic!"

A leathery man with Coke-bottle glasses shuffled toward Peter, pushing a wheelchair slowly down the hall. Contained in the wheelchair was someone Peter considered in need of embalming, making the ancient redwood of a man behind them appear youthful by comparison.

No one put it past Doc R to push a corpse around for vanity, which was a joke everyone mostly meant in jest.

Peter clocked the patient for chest rise before returning the greeting with any zeal. "Hey, Doc. What'cha in charge of here?"

The man extended a petrified hand to the ceiling. "She was causing trouble in split flow, cursing people up and down the hall. Of course, she doesn't have any power behind anything, but she's been puttin' enough people on edge. So I told J I'd take her for a walk, see if I could calm her down until we got a bed for her."

The body, a frail woman now that it had context, began to stir.

Without missing a beat, Doc R moved the wheelchair back and forth with the rhythm of conversation.

"Gives me a break from the grind, anyhow. Residents gotta fly on their own sometime, you know?" He smiled the smile of an attending who delighted in leaving his residents on a full moon night in July, whatever that was. "You bring someone in just now?"

Peter shook his head, unable to look away from the way the hospital warped around the man before him. The air flexed and played around his shoulders like an otter, keeping the jovial man in a clear bubble within the dense hospital air, like water splitting oil.

The paramedic blinked once, tightening the grip on his coffee. "Nah, just stocking up to go out. On a sixteen with my partner."

"On a full moon."

"Yup."

"Sounds like you drew the short straw. I'll be thinkin' of you." He sighed, beginning to walk away as his charge awakened in earnest.

A hasty question spilled from Peter's lips as he stepped aside. "You wouldn't happen to know where J is?"

Doc R answered with certainty, not breaking his stride.

"Holding."

The confidence was reassuring as Peter watched the pair roll down the hall, pausing before ten steps were taken to speak with practitioners gathering in front of room 30. The side of Peter's mouth twitched once.

And he continued on.

Crowe County Hospital, Emergency Department Holding, 15:17

Peter sipped his coffee on the threshold of the top of the Emergency Room ladder, looking out over an expansive room bustling with people. Stretchers were stationed along the walls, each enclosed in a set of curtains to cordon them off from their neighbors.

The illusion of privacy.

Cardiac monitors blipped a chorus of static from the wall, the electric interference from past spirits and the presence of healthcare workers causing them to malfunction more often than they worked.

Nurses in plum scrubs darted among these stretchers, and Peter observed them tending to the patients contained by their curtain-divided slots.

A bag of blood ran into a pale creature in the far corner slot as similarly gaunt figures held the creature's hand, clad from head to toe in thick clothing. Another stretcher appeared to contain nothing but air, spoken to by a social worker in a bright yellow jumpsuit who Peter recognized from the trauma bay. Another set of curtains was open just enough to where Peter could see the corner of a large white bag resting on the stretcher. The body bag was still and neatly labelled, though the softest weeping emanated from that same slot.

All the while, the room's way-line hummed along its periphery, defining the chaos of a full moon beneath the fun house gloom of fresh burning pine, which floated inches from the ceiling.

This was Holding. And Holding was always two steps away from total calamity.

In the far-left corner, a congregation gathered around the first stretcher. A woman in a doctor's white coat hunched over the head of a patient who was splayed on the stretcher. The patient's hospital gown was opened wide as a lab-coated resident rhythmically compressed his chest. A reedy chaplain paced the way-line in those unassuming shoes, muttering into his dark sleeve cuffs.

This stretcher was a beacon for practitioners, the exact reason they came to Crowe.

The thrill.

A voice broke sternly from the pack. "Fucking gods. Get it together, people."

Peter found J amidst the choreographed chaos. She was manning a code cart and scribbling vital signs on the back of a receipt. Perspiration pinned short gray hair to her forehead in clumps, making it apparent to Peter that the middle-aged woman had jumped on this fellow's chest before the residents arrived.

"Is that official documentation?" Peter said over the woman's shoulder.

J didn't lift her gaze, deftly assembling a dose of epinephrine before handing it to another nurse in the fray. "When we are *properly* stocked, I will *properly* document."

"Already a night?"

"Clearly."

The doctor at the patient's head let out a crisp command. "Suction."

A suction catheter exchanged hands, slurping red-tinged liquid from the back of the patient's throat before the laryngoscope appeared. This duckbill-shaped metal contraption lifted the patient's jaw, allowing a tube passage. Another set of hands attached a bag to the tube. A stethoscope was set against his chest. The way-line glowed steadily under the chaplain's feet as the bag was squeezed, the man's chest rising with artificial breath on both sides.

It was a dance set to the waltzing tempo of fritzing monitors, and the choreography was flawless.

"Do we have a pulse? Who did a pulse check?" J demanded.

Metropolitan Ballet, eat your heart out.

An anonymous voice answered, "I did. No pulse."

"Restarting compressions."

"Next dose of epi in two minutes."

"Communicate better, everyone," J commanded, locking eyes with Peter. "Can I help you?"

Peter stood steady under the scrutiny. "Is he an early werewolf bite? Ghoul rampage?"

"Heart attack." J snorted. "You do realize most of the time it's the mundane that kills people."

The chaplain's teeth chattered in the distance, hands planting against the wall as every light in Holding flickered off and on again.

J exhaled roughly. "I only enjoy useful people in my ED, medic."

Peter straightened his spine, unintimidating to the seasoned and burnt woman before him. "We need epinephrine on 415."

"That sounds like a pharmacy request."

"They won't give us more than two rounds with the shortage."

"Sounds like all you need to get back to the hospital," she said in a clear tone.

Convince me otherwise or leave.

Peter inhaled sharply.

"You know my partner and I run into illegal sect activities more than most, and effectively reviving ritual human offerings is high priority to avoid entity occupation on-site. Being a full moon, we will run into lycanthropy and need it for *that* protocol as well. Pharmacy doesn't understand because they have to worry about numbers, but I need a couple extra doses."

J jotted successful pulse recovery on her receipt with a thin frown.

"And," Peter rushed to add before judgment, "it's fucking hot out, J. You're telling me I'm gonna be riding with the 'open windows are good for the soul' purist on a ninety-degree full moon night short stocked? Have pity."

The woman let a smile slip, rubbing her forehead with a liver-spotted hand. Peter was certain if you could count them like rings on a tree, it would place Henry's age months from J's.

"Fine," she conceded. "I'll wrangle you a couple more doses."

Peter smiled, watching the monitor above the team read a staccato rhythm. The patient on the stretcher moved, and someone hastened to cover him with a blanket.

"Thanks, J."

"Yeah, yeah. Give H my best . . . No, he doesn't need a fucking shock! You gave him epi to restart his heart, of course it's fucking fast!"

Crowe County Hospital,
Ambulance Bay, 15:38

Peter clutched a bag of epinephrine from pharmacy in one hand and a donut from the nurses' potluck in the other, on top of the world as he stepped into the afternoon humidity.

His elation was short-lived as he slid into the passenger seat.

Peter dragged his sleeves to his elbows in a huff.

It was ninety-seven degrees, humid, a full moon.

And the windows were fully open.

"You know the only reason I got the epi was J felt bad for me, right? Air conditioning isn't poisonous."

Henry acknowledged his partner with a smile, reaching across the dash to crank the air conditioner on low, a gentle courtesy without a response. Midafternoon radio split the silence as Henry leaned into the key, the engine resurrecting with three delicate turns.

"Let's get moving, Ace."

CHAPTER TWO

Persephone Tower,
Freer Village, 16:22

The Persephone Tower apartment complex thrust from the asphalt in a futile attempt to punch the sky. Among lower complexes in the housing project of Freer Village, it crammed next to its companions with only a sidewalk's breadth between and a courtyard of sun-scorched crabgrass at its feet.

While there were many apartment complexes around the building that served similar purpose, Persephone Tower was the most distinct in Crowe's skyline. The building was five sided and twenty stories tall, six more than the highest belfry. Every cinder block laid into its frame was laced with ironwork, originally marketed as an abode that was impenetrable: "Foolproof against all ailing ghouls and spirits! You need not be proficient in arcane arts to live safely within Crowe County!"

The promises were as empty as the commercials were cheap, when those constructing the vast complexes realized iron was not only ineffective on its own, but an expense that they couldn't recover.

Cut to Persephone Tower's decay.

"This will not be like last time, Ace."

The Tower windows absorbed daylight, streaked by years of neglect, observing Peter and Henry remove their gear from the rear of the ambulance with a vacuous stare.

Available parking was slim, and Peter was determined to not look at the Birchwood Services van sitting beside rig 415.

Hulking.

Dark.

Birchwood Services was known for engines that purred like bronchitis-ridden jungle cats and tinted windows, which obscured their passengers. Their insignia was nearly imperceptible, drawn a shade lighter than the pitch-black sheen that distinguished their vehicles, but the briar of thorns surrounding a stoic *B* was a strangling presence.

Just like Birchwood.

They arrived in Crowe County the same time as Persephone Tower, with similar intention to make Crowe "safe" for its citizens.

Whatever that meant.

A skirt of chains clinging to the truck's underbelly clattered gently in the July breeze, and Peter slammed the ambulance door shut with more force than he intended. The sound echoed across the empty courtyard.

"Birchwood can do whatever the fuck they want. It's not like there's actual patient care they can obstruct this time. I have no problem leaving a spirit extraction for another rig."

Henry's hand found Peter's shoulder as the supply pack hit the stretcher. His smile did not reach his eyes.

"We will talk to them as little as possible. Get in, get our spirit, and let them process the scene. We will be okay."

Peter drifted into the wake of his partner, traversing a cracked walkway past a fading sign that read, *Persephone Tower: Luxury Living, Affordable Prices.*

Two uniformed individuals leaned idly in the threshold of the building. Peter knew the first, George, to be midfifties or so. George was well built and average in every sense of the word, with the exception of impressive whiskers and bone structure designed for contempt.

This elder came to Crowe fifteen years ago for the establishment of the Birchwood Services branch within the city. In the days following the collapse of the North Belfry, he managed to climb his professional ladder quickly and build a reputation for little patience dealing with those less than human.

In short, George hunted for sport.

The other agent claimed a brow so strong it could support a vase, and used the moniker "Cowl" with his Birchwood constituents. Peter, however, knew him as Clarence. He was Peter's height with ropy muscles that built layers onto his thin frame like clay. And with a pang of discomfort, Peter noticed Clarence's salt-and-pepper hair had been dyed a deep unnatural brown since their last encounter.

Silver buck knives were sheathed at their sides, play toys next to slender rifles slung across their chests. Identical badges hung from chains at their hips, the briar of thorns surrounding an ornate letter *B* glinting in the afternoon light.

More disturbing were their pinky rings — brass with the same insignia.

Brotherhoods wore rings.

Peter rolled down his sleeves with the subtlety of gunfire, falling a step behind Henry's approach. Automatically, he removed the silver spangles adorning his wrists, shoving them into his pockets.

His partner spoke to the pair. "Dispatch called for spirit removal."

"Yup. So let's make it quick." The bewhiskered George rocked off the entrance of Persephone Tower, making room for the two with a sniff. "Neighbors called for a missing person after not seeing Ms. Frances for two days. No obvious break-in to the apartment, but there is suspected cult nonsense intertwined with the victim. The police and ME's office will be here soon to process the scene."

Peter spoke up. "Birchwood was notified before the police?"

Clarence observed Peter with a frown, eyes wandering down his covered arms, not unnoticed by George. "It's new public procedure with grotesque supernatural findings. We get called in prior if there are creatures that might be a hazard."

"It doesn't look like Birchwood will be needed." The elder spoke, holding open the door to Persephone Tower. "I'd say we could beat feet before the cultists get wind of the discovery, but it looks like you brought one along with you."

Peter slowed to a halt, the stretcher a dividing force between him and George.

Clarence crossed his arms, mumbling, "This ain't the place, G."

"It's always the place with this one," George said, gesturing to Peter with distaste. "He's an obstructive piece of shit. And I'll call him what I want."

"Clever," Peter retorted. "Court-mandated sensitivity training did exactly what I expected it would for you."

The man white-knuckled the entry, leaning over the stretcher with enough space for a low threat. "Careful, pagan."

Saccharine breath assaulted Peter's senses, knocking him off-center. The air around them was kinetic, and the sting of it leapt onto his fingertips.

All at once, Clarence wrangled his partner with a tug on his shirt while Henry's swift guiding hand led Peter away from the Birchwood agents devolving into quiet debate in the doorway.

"Keep moving, Ace."

Peter shook the sting from his palms, crossing into the lobby of Persephone Tower.

The faint aroma of cigarettes filtered from cloudy carpets and mismatched chairs along the walls of the cathedral room, frayed to the bone. Two chandeliers dripped crystal from the ceiling, their bulbs flickering with the practitioner's step. Wood floors underfoot were worn and pockmarked through long-lost sheen. Beneath the wear of mismanagement were hints of a gilded time. Persephone Tower held the good-intentioned grandeur of a place meant to withstand, a place not initially meant to decay.

Bulletins were tacked indiscriminately into a large corkboard at the entrance.

Babysitter needed, off hours. Please contact . . .

Fortunes read! Most accurate in the Village!

Legal troubles with Birchwood? Try calling . . .

Building meetings every 3rd Thursday. Contact —

Peter led the stretcher to the most ostentatious of them all, where sloppy red paint dripped like viscera from the *Out of Order* sign tacked to one of two elevators at their left, dried in crusted puddles below their feet.

"We will be going to room 1130," Clarence said as he called the elevator. "Seeing how it is suspected human sacrifice for cult activity, you will be escorted into the apartment by me while G guards outside. Sound reasonable?"

The elevator button's pitiful flicker brought the grinding of heavy metal into the cavernous hall.

"We're professionals," Peter said. "But if your partner is still sore in the ass about last time and gonna be threatening about it, I don't want to be in an elevator with him. Or near a crime scene, for that matter. *That's* reasonable."

George watched Peter with a hardened gaze, whiskers twitching like the top of a boiling teakettle.

"The lycanthrope was in *our* care," Peter continued, undeterred. "Once they are, you Birchwood lot back off. Even the police said—"

Henry interceded, stepping placidly between the two. "I'm certain we can work this site amicably and without personal involvement. All of us. As professionals."

A pitiful ding punctuated the silence, and the elevator shambled open beside Clarence. Without a word, the group crammed reluctantly around the stretcher and continued on their way.

Professionally.

Room 1130,
Persephone Tower, 16:47

They exited onto floor eleven's dimly lit hall, an accurate representation of the other floors in Persephone Tower.

Ornate floral light fixtures bloomed from the walls, their brass scuffed from decades of colliding with new residents' mattresses and bent from children swinging on their loops. Their cracked leaves and missing petals exposed harsh lightbulbs underneath, but overall, the hallway held a similar warmth to the lobby.

The gray carpet was well trod, layered with bright welcome mats while the reek of industrial carpet cleaner fought for space with wafting dinner scents sizzling from behind closed doors. As the group of four filed past the neighbors in silence, varying décor popped from each closed entryway.

A daisy-yellow door was carved ornately with repeating sigils, a sprig of thistle tacked on the tallest part of the frame. Another was gray and covered in broad strokes of lye suds, fresh and dripping onto the fraying hall carpet.

They were familiar rituals, providing insight to the occupant within each apartment, and Peter soaked in the sights as the scent of a dozen dinners settled in his nose. The early meals of a community bracing for a full moon in Crowe County.

George interrupted the silence, slapping a meaty hand against a dull green door.

"This is it."

A large sunflower wreath hung crooked from the entryway. Simple and sweet. It held character and charm, joining the rank of its neighbors. Fat granules of pink salt lined the outer threshold, the seal dragged and broken by the activity of the door.

George turned to the pair, knocking his buck knife as he shoved gloved hands in his pockets. "Dunno what the PD will end up saying, but it seems we got a straightforward case of human sacrifice."

Peter sighed, stepping aside to allow Henry into the scene before him.

"We will need a moment alone to properly assess if the spirit is lingering for extraction," Peter requested. "If you and Clarence would remain out here."

The Birchwood two exchanged a hard look.

Clarence's skin reddened at his temples. "Still an active crime scene."

Henry spoke, and there was finality to the gentleman's words. "I have worked more spirit extractions than you probably ever will, young man. And we are trained to do this portion alone. You leave us to our job, and if we get overwhelmed, we will let you know."

He proceeded over the broken salt line, and Peter smiled, angling the stretcher clumsily through the door to get it closed behind them.

Without agent accompaniment.

"You're amazing, H," Peter whispered. "The looks on their faces—"

Henry silenced his partner with a wave of his hand, standing quietly in the center of the apartment. "I do look forward to discussing Birchwood's shortcomings as people later, but let us be respectful, Ace."

Peter swallowed his response, noticing the sweet shoebox of an apartment for the first time.

Hand-drawn flowers were scribbled on bright blue wallpaper, their delicate petals crammed around gold-framed photographs that hung askew from bare nails. A plush couch was arranged between two wilting ferns under a window directly ahead where sweeping views of Freer Village's infrastructure laid itself out before them. Factory shells stretched along blocks of neighborhood like felled giants, with scattered residential homes spotted seldom among them.

Beyond the familiar view sat another on the horizon. The four belfries of the hospital touched the sky, and with the July sun still baking the city, they looked deceptively serene.

Bright light streamed through the apartment window, rendering candles on the coffee table obsolete as the practitioners set their eyes on their patient in full sunlight.

What was left of a person lay enveloped in a gold dress. They shimmered against a worn muslin bed, pulled down from a cabinet in the wall. Their glassy eyes fixed on the door as if awaiting company, skin faded to a color of old blood.

Stagnant.

Gray.

Carefully drawn lipstick flaked at the corners of their mouth, a labor of love wasted in death.

Peter's eyes passed all this, settling on the steak knife puckering the dress through the person's abdomen, trapping them to the mattress. A gaping hole in the middle of their chest savaged apart their ribs to an empty cavity where the heart should be.

The sight was a lightning strike behind his eyes, and Peter's hand shot to his forehead. "Fuck . . ."

"Ace?"

Peter pried his fingers from his face, holding a hand up to Henry.

Beside the body was a figure resting on the edge of the mattress taking rapid form. A thin golden scrim sizzled into view, vaguely the shape of the person on the bed without any features. It shifted like a school of fish in water, sporadic movements that violently ebbed and flowed.

Neither practitioner dared to move.

Until it spoke.

"Excuse me."

The new voice fractured the silence.

Coming from the air itself, the soft tone flooded Peter's lungs with the tang of split atmosphere, electricity dancing down his throat. He fixated on the body's golden shadow, attempting to match the being to the woman on the bed, a dark-haired creature with a jaw in early stages of decay.

"I don't like foul language, if you don't mind." The detached voice spoke again, and Peter's hairline prickled in a gentle breeze coming from everywhere and nowhere. "Who are you?"

Henry placed his hands in his pockets, and the corners of his mouth formed a smile Peter had trouble deciphering.

"We can certainly restrain our language. My name is H, and this is my partner, P. We have come to offer our assistance."

"Assistance?"

"Yes." Henry treaded with care as the voice wavered around their heads. "But first things first. Maybe we can have your name?"

Another pause followed.

"I don't know . . ."

"You don't?" Peter said monotonously, his eyes drawn to the knife in her abdomen as the scrim took form.

The air around the blade pulsated black, shadowed tendrils snaking their way into the bed, the ceiling, strangling the body like vines.

Henry stepped forward, and Peter noted his divided attention, catching his eyes every few moments as the conversation continued. "It's understandable you don't know immediately. Take your time trying to remember. We will help in every way we can when you do."

"Okay."

"How are you feeling right now?"

The scrim paused, struggling with the answer. ". . . I don't know. I don't feel much."

"I'm sorry about that," Henry responded quietly. "Honestly, that is a very common feeling, and not at all odd in your circumstance. Do you remember what happened to you?"

Henry knelt before the apparition, his posture open. Peter kept the edge of his thoughts on the conversation, his skill set elsewhere in the room as he paced the perimeter, attention affixed on the weapon.

"I was cooking dinner, getting ready for company."

A shorter pause interrupted her speech while Peter looked to the sink where a pan sat in stagnant greasy water. Carefully, he stooped beside the bed.

"And then . . . I don't think I remember anything after that."

"That is fair."

The golden shadow continued to waver while its back remained to the body. A shifting shadow from the knife flickered once around the abdomen of the corpse, and their ghost bent, clutching their waist.

A long whine issued from her throat, peeling the delicate flowers from the wallpaper so they fell to the floor like snow. "I don't like feeling this way."

"What way would that be?"

"Empty . . . I feel empty. I . . ."

She gasped.

"Wait, I'm . . . M-my name is Frances!"

The memory came hard and fast, the sudden revelation turning Frances's blur into a solid golden mass on the bed. Near corporeal.

Peter could almost sense the arch to her brow as essence spilled off the spirit like mist from a waterfall, stinging his cheeks.

From behind the apparition, Peter caught Henry's wide eyes.

The gentleman was deliberate with his response.

"Frances. Wonderful."

We don't have much time.

In the bright glow of his patient, Peter returned the knife handle, its hilt crowded with detail. Sigils swirled around the wood, burned in a familiar pattern that encased a jagged elm tree, extending from the hilt to the tip. These designs connected around the tree trunk, marrying themselves with its gnarled leafy limbs.

Black tendrils splintered from the boughs of this tree, curling around the body like a morning glory climbing a trellis.

A necrotic cursed morning glory.

Peter's fingers twitched, observing the tendrils' movement as Henry spoke.

"Frances, are you able to see the uniform I am wearing?"

"Uniform?" There was a significant pause, the sheets underneath the blur crumpling, as if clenched in two fists. "You're . . . from the hospital?"

"I am."

"Why are you here . . . ?"

The question ran abruptly into another, leaving no time for an answer.

"Is that me?"

Peter's attention severed from the knife, adjusting his gaze to the golden blur that was now turned in his direction. If it had eyes, he was certain he would be staring directly into them. He looked down to the corpse and back as the golden shadow extended an arm, reaching for the hand of her body, both in slow motion and too quick to stop.

Without a word, the practitioners scrambled from the bed as contact was made.

"Why am I . . . ?" Frances's voice spilled from the walls in discordant melody as the light from the kitchen flickered and faded.

Peter's jaw ached, and Henry's dense curls stood to the sky. Electricity accumulated in the room, siphoning threateningly around the solid golden mass on the bed like mist. In a single bound, Peter abandoned the knife, hurrying to retrieve his bag.

Henry intervened first.

"Frances?"

"I'm dead . . . ?"

"Yes."

"I'm dead!"

Peter withdrew a cluster of candles bound together

with red twine and a worn leather case from the side pouch of his supply bag. The materials were haphazard, homemade. And he breathed in the stifling scent of perfumes that tumbled from the bag's interior.

"My . . . my heart."

"I know. I am sorry, Frances."

Peter affixed two candles to the end of the stretcher with medical tape, using it as a stage setting, pulling bay leaves, black salt, and cinnamon from the same small pack.

"Who did this?"

"We don't know yet. Before they can investigate the scene, we have to get you to the hospital."

Peter clasped his hands around the ingredients, allowing the electricity from the room to siphon toward his fingertips and into the herbs. They warmed beneath his palms like a perfect cup of tea, with an exception.

The paramedic watched the collection in his hands, observing the salt granules doing their best to buffet his attempt at weaving this warmth. He rolled his eyes despite himself.

Come on . . . let's not be stubborn now.

"But they'll find out who did it?"

"I hope so."

A lungful of ozone tilted Peter's world as he sucked in the charged air, exhaling it down his limbs into the salt granules with gentle force. The collection of herbs and salt flared with heat before fading to a consistent full glow. Embers after a campfire.

Delicately, he laid them around the bases of the candles.

"I can't go to the hospital."

"Okay, maybe we can talk about alternate options."

"I *can't*."

The certainty hit Peter like a punch to the gut, and his fingers lost grip on the red string as the force of her refusal stiffened them to uselessness. He hurried to retrieve it.

"This is not your fault," Henry said, his firm patience everlasting. "We will not force you anywhere, and your distress is reasonable. However, we would love to be able to assist you. And the only way we can do that is by trying to understand."

"H." Peter interrupted the conversation, waving once from his station near the door.

The golden blur's gaze landed on him like a gunshot, center mass. Henry hurried to bridge the care.

"This is my associate, P. He's here to help in some ways I cannot."

The weight of Frances's incorporeal eyes rested on Peter as he held up the string. His shaking fingers attached them to one candle, then another, bonding them with a bridge of red.

"When I was little, my nana taught me this ritual. I see the candles on your coffee table. Have you ever seen this before?"

Quietly, the specter shook her head.

Peter continued. "It was to help us break connections we did not want. Ones that weren't serving us."

"I can't leave . . ."

"But you want to?"

The silence between them was profound, the golden haze flickering as it grappled with something as complex as a *want*.

". . . Yes."

Peter sighed, releasing a breath's worth of tension from his limbs into the air, where it dissolved around his head.

"I know you feel trapped. I can see what's keeping you."

He reached for a small matchbox from his pack, letting the rattle of its contents strike the air once, twice, three times.

"But you're free to make your own choices here. No matter what was taken from you, Frances, you have a choice now."

The match smoked in a wisp of sulfur fluttering through the air. Frances was next to the stretcher in an instant, a flicker, the fire dancing against her form as she watched the flame between Peter's fingers. Black tendrils curled around her stomach, the spectral tree roots grounding her to the bed.

But, for now, she was with Peter.

He lowered the match carefully to one candle, then the next.

The golden blur stooped to watch them burn, her vacuous eyes unmoving as the candles were slowly consumed by the flame. Wax dripped in globules onto the pile of herbs, twitching the shards of cinnamon to their own end.

Peter's eyes were on Frances, how her kinetic form softened through the burn as they neared the string. The blackened shackles writhed, shrinking from the stretcher while trying to keep their hold.

"You're going to feel a big pinch," he murmured, consumed by the flame hitting the red string.

It burst in a flash of fire that reached for the ceiling, illuminating the room like a flicker of lightning. Frances gasped as the knife's tendrils fell to the floor before fading completely.

Leaving a simple ornate knife in its wake.

In the abdomen of what once was Frances.

Peter leaned against the stretcher, watching the candle's remaining fire flicker and fade in the spirit's eye.

Until the working was nothing but wax and herbs and a pile of salt.

"How are you feeling?"

"Better . . ."

Peter smiled. "That's good to hear."

Without a word, the shimmering figure floated around the stretcher, settling on its surface with the flickering echoes of its spirit having surprising traction against the material. Henry's surprise broke his placid demeanor as she did.

It was not often a spirit was so formed they interacted fully with the equipment.

In this way, Peter could tell Frances made Henry just as nervous as she made him, even in her calm state.

"We are going to move through your building to the ambulance now." Peter replaced his satchel inside the jump kit. "Is that okay, Frances?"

"You're going to stay with me?"

"Yes, of course."

The paramedics opened the door to a tepid Birchwood duo, who appeared as uncertain as Birchwood Services could in a crowd. A company of officials lined the walls outside room 1130, flanked too close for comfort and all itching to be the first to process the scene.

Four pale green uniforms of Crowe County Police Department chatted with George and two street-clothed individuals adorned with the bloodred patch of the Preternatural Crime Unit. Bringing up the rear were three crisp white medical examiner jumpsuits, whose safety goggles sat perched on their sweating foreheads, waiting for scene access.

The paramedic checked in with Clarence, who stared at the golden scrim on the stretcher.

"Birchwood Services is staying with the scene?"

The man nodded once, letting his eyes linger a moment longer on the candles melted at Frances's theoretical feet. "That's —"

"A family recipe."

"Huh . . . I'll escort you out."

Electricity strung through the group like chains of lightning, fizzling into static around the golden haze.

Pausing once to hitch up the bags, Peter wheeled Frances past the line of people, listening to his patient speak through the silence.

"When we get to the hospital, do you think someone can call my sister? I need her to know."

A sudden lump sprang into Peter's throat. "Of course, Frances. Whatever you need."

"She's going to . . . she's going to be so sad."

Neighbors flanked doorways, their eyes following the paramedics walking down the hall beside the Birchwood Services agent. Sharp gasps and indistinct murmurs flew through the air. Curiosity was consumed by sorrow but did not linger with Clarence bringing up the rear.

The uniformed group they left behind set up shop outside 1130, and Frances remained still as the elevator's down arrow flickered to life under Henry's thumb.

"Someone hurt me."

Her voice was small but certain, and Peter watched the hem of the gold dress develop a thread count. The elevator shambled open, and he took a moment to move into its depths, allowing Clarence and Henry beside him.

Peter cleared his throat. "Well . . . you don't have to worry about that immediately. Like Henry said, we are going to help you."

A detached gaze followed him from shifting angles, raising goose bumps along his spine.

"I'm cold."

Peter forced a smile, watching the back of Henry's head as the elevator hobbled its course. "I have a blanket in the ambulance. Does that sound all right?"

"Yes, thank you."

The stuttering lights of emergency vehicles flanked their exit from Persephone Tower, dancing within Frances's golden glimmer. Peter loaded the stretcher into the ambulance with bystanders clustered nearby, keeping distance with Clarence's proximity.

The Birchwood man lingered, squinting at the sunset like he was appraising its worth.

Peter did his best to ignore him.

"I'll be in, in a moment, Frances." He smiled once, shutting the doors. Henry circled to the front of the ambulance, and Peter made to do the same.

"Medic," Clarence called, keeping a small distance beside the hulking Birchwood truck.

Peter turned, observing the man's sideways stance, facing away from the conversation.

"What."

The Birchwood man sighed, twisting the signet ring on his pinky finger. It slid over his last knuckle, dancing with the tip of his nail before he placed it back again.

"Pete, you know you can't use my name at a scene."

"I won't use Cowl." Peter crossed his arms. "It's deliberately dumb. Of all the pseudonyms—"

Clarence turned fully to him, his form blocking the sun. "Then use something else. My pseudonym protects me, and you need to respect that."

Peter rocked onto his toes with a quick glance at the ambulance, putting on a show of giving it some thought.

"Fair enough."

"Thank you."

He nodded. "Anything else I can do for you, *Agent*?"

Clarence shifted where he stood, kicking a heel against the tire of his truck. "Yeah, actually. Why'd you have to work an unbinding?"

Peter's stomach knotted, choosing his words carefully. "The hilt of the knife was charmed for containment. Don't know why. I'm sure the MEs will figure the same, but I'm going to radio them the details now that Frances is settled."

Henry's voice shouted from the passenger window. "You coming, Ace?"

"Be right in!"

Clarence spared a single look at Peter before departing swiftly toward the tower.

Alone on the gravel drive, Peter tilted his face toward the setting sun with a sigh. Wrenching the side door of the ambulance open, he entered the space with the golden shadow.

Keeping his promise, the blanket warmer hit him with a blast of unwelcome heat and Peter unfolded a starched bath towel over the apparition.

The gold dress sighed in relief, the coarse fabric sinking to the stretcher below.

"Thank you."

Peter allowed his gaze to drop to the floor, swaying with the rocking ambulance as Henry sidled into the driver's seat. Without a word, the older man started the engine and began their journey to Crowe County Hospital.

CHAPTER THREE

Sunlight kissed the horizon, steadying for its dive into the night as a dusky purple sky darkened to plum.

Peter watched brass numbers count up and up and up on townhomes butting against the busy main road, marveling at Henry's smooth arrival into a cramped parallel park in front of 1437 Maplewood Ave.

"We've never picked up Bernadette together?"

Peter observed the faded townhome, resting his forehead on the passenger side window. "I haven't had the pleasure."

Four windows and a thin doorframe sagged under the weight of aged brick, their glass panes fogged in ribbons by decades of a cigarette smoker with a penchant for neighborhood watch. The mogul lawn sloped in a mountainous display, with a hairdo of balding dirt patches among lush crabgrass colonies. Aluminum pigs in an array of Christmas attire and luau skirts stared from their stations among the yard. Their reflective eyes were vacant, illuminated by a tangled system of flood lamps whose fluorescence aimed from the rusted iron picket fence to the dusky building.

They bathed the scene in sterile white light stolen from an operating room.

"Henry, I think those pigs can see into my soul."

Henry's smile was not reassuring, and he opened his door directly into traffic.

Blaring horns of passing vehicles accompanied the gentleman's bold step into rush hour. The top of his graying head bobbed along the front of the ambulance toward the sidewalk, unfazed.

Peter was glued to his seat by the mysticism surrounding Crowe Hospital's most infamous frequent flier. Calls to pick up the magic user with a penchant for hypochondria at 1437 Maplewood Ave. were dreaded, and he was fortunate to avoid them until now.

"Will you be joining me?"

Henry's glasses twinkled in the setting sun, like his disconcerting cheery demeanor.

Peter popped the passenger side door begrudgingly, sliding out of his seat.

"I heard she predicted rig 148's accident. Took Millie out of work for four weeks."

The gentleman's brow dug a trench between his eyes. "I heard that was the case, yes. But you have to remember, she doesn't will events to happen. She simply predicts them."

"Well . . . maybe she should keep those predictions to herself."

Legend preceded Bernadette.

Still, nothing prepared Peter for the creature who emerged moments later through the lopsided doorway, carrying a crowded floral suitcase the size of a small bear.

Infamous Bernadette stood a breadth taller than four feet, with a loose yellow sundress clinging to her aged frame like a second skin. A cigarette clung for dear life on her bottom lip.

Oversized pink rain boots stymied her gait, but Bernadette's eyes were fierce, latching on Peter's face the second she cleared the threshold. She flopped down the brick stairway, and Peter watched the air around her burn, leaving a trail of gray mist in her wake. Judging by the professional navigation of her suitcase over the molehill front walkway while maintaining unrelenting eye contact, the woman had a routine.

She approached with the air of a person who disapproved of breathing if it left her inconvenienced.

"I don't know you. I deliberately asked dispatch for someone I know."

Peter looked down at Bernadette, at her hair's transition from a brilliant shade of purple to gray ombre at her roots.

"Oh, um . . . Well, I'm—"

"I have chest pain." The unlit cigarette danced between her teeth. "I have ten out of ten chest pain, and I need the hospital."

Bernadette heaved the floral suitcase past Peter and onto the back step of the rig as Henry found the good grace to step into the conversation.

"Hello, Bernie."

The sprite of a woman expelled a sharp burst of air. "Henry! Why is this stranger here?"

Henry chuckled, offering an arm into the ambulance. "Even you cannot always have your preferred chauffeur."

Emotion flew across the woman's face, severity morphing to delight, ending in a furrowed brow that made Peter question the thought in Bernadette's head.

Hand on Henry's arm, she clambered into the back of the ambulance.

And Henry climbed dutifully in her wake, shutting the back doors with a snap.

Peter stood, despairing, on the sidewalk of Maplewood Ave., squinting at the closed ambulance. Pleasant chatter echoed from beyond the metal doors, which became swallowed by screeching tires and deafening horns of traffic three feet to his left. His gaze lingered on the floodlights flickering in the dusky sunset, the aluminum pigs staggered like a minefield across Bernadette's front yard.

"All right, Winsted," he mumbled. "Let's get this over with."

Instead of Henry's game of human Frogger, he slid through the passenger side into the driver's seat.

Henry's voice travelled through the opening to the back of the rig.

"Hooking you up to the monitor, Bernadette. Excuse my cold hands."

Bernadette waved away the apology. "Will we make it to the hospital before nightfall?"

"Depends. With my associate driving, we may end up in Boston."

Peter flicked on his turn signal like it meant something before gunning into traffic. The dull beep of a heart rate lingered in Peter's right ear. He took his opportunity to blast the AC, drying the sweat on his upper lip before responding.

"I take offense."

"You should take it as constructive criticism and learn to read a map better," Henry countered. "Now, Bernadette. How does your pain feel?"

Bernadette answered bluntly, "Crushing. Like an elephant sitting on my chest."

Henry's head bobbed in the rearview mirror, the familiar clattering of a 12-lead EKG slipping from its home as Peter pulled onto the highway. The entrance ramp provided panoramic views of the city in a full moon evening, daylight dying in a brilliant sweep of orange and red. Light winked warmly from some homes, others already bathed in exterior floodlights as automatic timers flicked on throughout the city.

Traffic thinned and wrought iron Birchwood trucks were reapers in empty side roads, their thorned *B* stalking the brownstones as Peter picked up speed.

"Refresh my memory. You've had a 12-lead EKG performed before?" Henry asked.

"Of course! Last full moon you did one on me because I was skippin' beats."

"How could I forget?" Henry shuffled around, preparing his leads.

"H, you good back there?" Peter shouted back.

"You're awfully nosy," the patient yelled over her shoulder. "What is your name?"

"I go by P."

"Hmph." Bernadette let the conversation die before continuing through her curated silence. "As a person who cannot keep his nose in his own business, I'm afraid I will have to fire you as my paramedic."

She paused.

"Yes, you're fired."

Peter blinked. Adjusting his hands to ten and two, he kept moderate pace toward the four belfries dotting the skyline.

"Henry, is it possible to pull over and wait for someone else to drive?"

"Of course not, Bernadette."

"Well, that *is* a shame."

The tear of EKG paper preceded a jangle of leads back to their hold. Peter flexed his hands against the steering wheel.

"Clarifying, Bernadette." Henry spoke slowly. "Your chest pain is consistent?"

"Oh, yes."

"And started when?"

"Yesterday afternoon." The woman's crop of purple hair twitched.

"Hmm."

The gentleman's soft footsteps echoed in Peter's right ear, a thin sheet of paper fluttering onto the dashboard.

"Ace, this is a good learning opportunity," Henry said, tracing the EKG pattern with his index finger. "Do you see this?"

"H, I'm on the highway . . ."

Henry traced spiderweb lines on the paper, and Peter did his best to follow the pattern he created, a graveyard of electrical impulses marching out like tombstones across the page.

"How the fuck is she talking?"

"Pick up the pace, lights and sirens. Alert them to call in the cath lab." Henry gave the paper a gentle pat, retreating to the back of the ambulance. "Congratulations, Bernadette! You are actually having a heart attack."

"Of course I am!"

Peter reached for the radio. "Why did you wait so long to call?"

"Again, with the intrusions." Bernadette sniffed. "I didn't go yesterday because they might have sent me home before the full moon finished, and that will not do!"

"Ah, yes," Peter grumbled, clicking on the line to dispatch. "Makes *perfect* sense."

The sudden rustling of sheets preceded a yellow-dressed woman depositing herself in the bucket seat beside him.

"Hey!" Peter leaned away with his eyes on the road. "What is she doing? What are you doing?"

"It makes sense, Peter."

The quiet certainty of Bernadette's words struck Peter in the gut, and his radio needled his palm with static. He matched the woman's unblinking eyes, and they fixed on him as acidic gray air marched between her pores like an anthill.

Henry stood inside the doorway, speaking firmly. "Bernadette, you cannot be up here."

She ignored the gentleman, whispering so only Peter could hear. "It's happening again."

"What do you mean?"

Bernadette's eyes became a depth beyond what Peter could comprehend. He didn't know what they looked like before; he didn't pay attention. Now, however, they were limitless, a creamy yellow that seeped into her sclera.

"Just like before," she choked. "And she'll be in danger. You can feel it already."

The woman's bony hand flew to Peter's shoulder, and gray light jumped from her skin like fleas. The ink beneath his sleeves flashed white-hot as he wrenched himself away.

Bernadette responded sharply, withdrawing to cradle her hand like a sick cat. "That was very rude!"

Fluorescent lights above them flickered once in the ebbing energy, and Henry dove for the steering wheel. "Watch it!"

Peter slammed the brakes, bringing the ambulance to a screeching halt under the light off exit 22, inches from the intersection. Cars stalled before them, uncertain.

Peter hit off the lights and sirens with shaking hands, jaw clenched as the infamous Bernadette shook her head once. The gray mites on her skin blended into the air, staining the wake of her movement.

But they were no longer on the offense.

Peter breathed harshly out his nose, watching Bernadette's hands drop into her lap, fingers tangling in the yellow sundress.

For a deceptive moment in time, she appeared her four-foot height.

The sight deflated the paramedic, speaking quietly as he adjusted himself in his seat.

"Get in the back, please."

Henry reached for her arm, escorting Bernadette to her stretcher.

She'll be in danger. You can feel it already.

Lights and sirens resumed under Peter's thumb, and he edged the ambulance into the intersection with care. The older woman's head was visible just above the stretcher, his mirror giving him a view of her fatigue. Gripping the wheel at ten and two, Peter navigated the back roads of Crowe County with half a mind on his task.

It's happening again.

CHAPTER FOUR

Mother Dahlia's Dock,
Crowe Harbor, 23:07

Peter and Henry looked forward to a peaceful lunch at Mother Dahlia's Dock. Moonlight brightened the sea and patchwork wooden boardwalk before them in full force, allowing a moment of unusual serenity. A distant howl punctuated the night sky in a mournful tone, uncommon in the city, even on a full moon night. Peter exchanged a long look with Henry as the echoes faded into distant screams, and the elder practitioner rolled up his window halfway.

"Not often we hear one of them in the city."

Peter took a pensive bite of his tuna melt. "Hope they keep safe, or Birchwood is gonna have a fucking field day."

It was a thought Peter voiced reflexively, without his usual level of concern. After three medicals and a car crash, all he had mental strength for was his tuna sandwich from Mary's Diner.

He was enjoying his soggy fries and half-crispy tuna melt with pickle-soaked bread.

He was enjoying the silent company of Henry, the late-night static on the local radio buzzing in his ears.

He was enjoying the soft moment by the water.

And he even managed a bite of his sandwich right before a bloody hand slapped against the window behind Henry's head.

A milk-sour face pulled itself into view, streaking crimson across the glass.

Two things were evident at that moment: this man was shot through the jaw, and Peter would not get to finish his tuna melt.

Peter knew both to be true because the owner of said hand pointed to his jaw and yelled, "I bl'een shl'ot!" before attempting to climb into the driver's seat. In turn, Peter's attention was removed from his sandwich.

Henry cranked up his window with vigor, leaving it cracked an inch to be heard.

"Sir, you need to go around to the back of the rig!" he shouted.

"Bu' I been—"

"Shot. We see this," Peter said, placing his tuna melt on the dashboard. "But we can't drive you anywhere with a bloody window!"

"Why not just reheat the sandwich?" one might ask.

"Go to the back," Henry repeated. "We will assist you there."

Mary's tuna melts don't reheat for shit.

It was a universal truth.

Peter watched Henry balance the radio in his hand, both practitioners acknowledging a fact not regarding diner food or interrupted dinners.

The dock was dangerous.

Bare concrete parking lot stretched acres around them in any direction, bathed in the moon's sedate glow.

The ocean blockaded them to the front, its waves lapping beneath the patient's panic. A second howl pierced the night, overwhelming the ragged breath of their frightened charge.

Peter unlocked his door with a careful glance at the stillness of the lot.

"Call dispatch. I'll get him in the back quick."

Once outside, Peter realized how small the man was, at least a head shorter and stocky as a bulldog. These, and the jaw hanging precariously by ligaments alone, were his most defining traits as he slumped against the side of the ambulance, sliding down to sit on the pavement.

"All right, lemme take a look here," Peter mumbled, opening the side of the rig for light and a monitor. "How is your breathing?"

Nose intact, the man inhaled deeply.

Peter flicked a flashlight over the wound, noting the spoils of necrotic decay creeping toward the man's eyes, darkened veins infecting his skin. Dark bruises ran the periphery of those same eyes like glasses, emphasizing rectangular pupils embedded deep in his sclera.

Like a goat.

"Sir, are you a shape-changer of some kind?"

The jawless man twitched, managing a stiff nod. His eyes widened in pain, impatient but unable to act on it.

"You got some areas of gray spoiling and decay. Are you sensitive to silver?"

Peter caught the man's hesitation contained in the silence between them as he placed him on the monitor.

"Sir, I just wanna know so I don't accidentally hurt you with my own safety provisions. Are you silver sensitive?"

The man jerked a pained nod.

"Thank you for letting me know." Peter removed the silver bracelets adorning his wrists, holding them up before shoving them into his pocket. He paused, touching the strap of his vest.

"I heard some howls, so I'm gonna keep my vest on till we're in the ambulance, but its silver plated, so keep wary of it, okay? We'll get you to the hospital quick. One sec."

The nature of the injury kept Peter moving, banging the side of the ambulance once with the palm of his hand. "I'm getting the stretcher. Help me get him in."

Without pausing for response, Peter yanked the stretcher from the back just in time to hear the radio slide back to its home. The driver's side door opened as he rounded the vehicle.

"He's sensitive to silver with exposure. So let's get him loaded up and—"

Piercing pain knocked Peter into the ambulance, words dying abruptly on his tongue as gunfire splintered the air.

The jawless man froze, watching the paramedic frantically take stock as bullets ripped into the side of the ambulance, missing by scant inches. Peter's fingers dug into the holes in his shirt, the surface of his vest harsh and reassuring as he rolled onto the cement under the hail of fire.

Henry roared from behind the driver's door. "Get him in!"

Absent his partner's help, Peter hiked the man by his shirt, tumbling into the ambulance directly on top of the patient. Henry twisted the key thrice, the engine howling to life.

"We're in! Fucking move!" Peter screamed, a human seat belt pinning his patient to the floor as the ambulance tore from its spot.

Metallic thuds sprayed the rig, and the jawless man screeched in pain as Peter's vest pressed into his skin.

"I—hurts! Stah—!"

"I know! I'm sorry!" Peter roared over the back of the rig slamming open again and again in the wind.

The monitor skittered off the bench, missing the man's head by inches as a pothole wrenched the ambulance. A bright string of expletives flew from Peter's mouth.

"Drive better!"

He swore, checking his patient with his heart hammering in his throat. The wind of travel made distance between themselves and the gunfire.

The man was pale, dreary eyes latching onto Peter's face as the paramedic stood to move within the confines of the open ambulance.

"M'nah dwyvin'."

Peter reached for gauze, holding it to the man's head as they barreled through the streets of Crowe. "Well, that's lucky for us."

Crowe County Hospital, Ambulance Bay, 23:53

Henry brought the ambulance to a screeching halt in the Crowe Hospital ambulance bay, illuminating the trauma team in his headlights. The ambulance slammed into park, and practitioners clad in protective white jumpsuits ripped open the back door as wide as it could go. A familiar gray-haired woman was first inside, extracting the patient from beneath the windswept paramedic.

"What the fuck happened to your stretcher?" J demanded.

"Had to leave it," Peter said, hauling the patient onto the hospital's transport.

Henry placed a hand on his shoulder, stopping him from following the trauma team farther.

"Get yourself checked out, Ace."

Then Henry continued his briefing.

"Man of unknown age, GSW from the dock. Exit wound in the cheek. Unknown blood loss. Sensitivity to silver with necrotic infiltration. Maintaining airway on room air with oxygen saturation above—"

The team disappeared through the etched-glass doors, and Peter slumped onto the back step of the ambulance. He recognized pity from J as the elder nurse lingered to observe the carnage of their rig. A wave of pain pulsed from Peter's sternum as he shrugged his silvered vest to the ground, sucking gulps of gasoline-tainted air.

J removed a sterile cap, gray hair plastered to her forehead just the way Peter left her.

"Dispatch said there was an active shooting at the site."

Peter delicately peeled his shirt away, revealing an exceptional peony of a bruise. It overtook swirling runes inked across his chest, and Peter marched his fingers along the site for breaks.

"Dispatch . . . did not lie."

J removed her mask, mouth pressed in a thin line. "Those vests aren't meant to be bullet resistant. You got very lucky."

Peter nodded, resting his elbows on his knees.

"You know . . . that's just how I'd describe myself right now. Lucky."

She scowled, causing Peter to avert his eyes.

"You should get that looked at."

"Nah. The night will just be picking up, and we're already an ambulance short," Peter rebutted, chancing a small smile at the senior nurse. "I could use a spare shirt, though, if you got one."

J's expression was severe, lingering on the ambulance. "We got some new shirts for recruits in the charge office. You can pick one up there."

The etched-glass door slithered open, admitting Henry to the ambulance bay, giving J a wide smile as she approached.

"H."

"J."

The nurse paused in the doorway, observing the pair with calculating eyes. The bunker was empty, save for rig 415, and she let herself use that room to think.

"We have no stretchers for you, by the way. So figure that out."

And she disappeared into the ED.

The distant sounds of Crowe filtered through the night as Henry perched beside Peter. Threats wafted on the air, exchanged between parties at street level as the gentleman closed his eyes.

"That is an impressive welt, Ace."

The paramedic stooped to catch his breath. Hot tears pricked the sides of his eyes as the argument in the distance welcomed another voice.

"Hurts," he grunted, wiping his eyes with his shirt. "Gods damn . . ."

Henry's voice was placid but firm. "We will take a break, get more dinner. Find our stretcher."

Peter's stomach growled as if on cue. "Sounds like a plan, boss."

The gentleman did not move. At the base of Peter's neck was the familiar twinge of something unspoken, and he paused, waiting for his partner to find the words.

"How are you doing tonight?"

Peter squinted at the bruise consuming his sternum. "Been better, Henry. I'm not gonna lie to you."

Henry smiled gently.

"I don't mean to discredit the shooting, as that is an event, but I question the call to see Bernadette. I was going to discuss it over dinner, but we had other priorities. You've been quiet tonight after that."

"Am I not always quiet?"

The light in rig 415 flickered with every syllable of speech. Peter tried his best to ignore it, suddenly consumed by gravel grit embedded in his right palm.

Henry idly observed the fixture brighten to its normal glare with volumes of speech contained in his silence. Peter stood stiffly beside the rig, absorbing the shock of pain that coursed through his sternum in response.

"The Birchwood pagan shit got to me tonight. I . . . I'm unsettled."

"That's unlike you." Henry cut the lie to its knees with one observation. "What Bernadette said unnerved you more than anything."

Peter blinked at the mention, wrestling with a vise clamp on his temples, a sudden stabbing pain that flared from already frayed nerves. The older man looked on, attentive and unreadable, but overwhelmingly kind.

That kindness was a lure.

One that Peter bit.

"My sister . . . is working the anniversary tomorrow night, and Bernadette . . . I think she mentioned it. I'm scared for her."

The older man's expression fell into one Peter recognized implicitly. One of gentle concern, relief.

"That makes sense. It's a dangerous night. You and Miss G are both very close."

Henry's support did not need time to consider his words. It just was.

"You rest, Ace. I'll grab you a new shirt and some coffee, and perhaps we can wrangle something near a Mary's tuna melt. We can talk about your concerns with a little food in your stomach."

Without room for argument, Henry disappeared

beyond the rune-scribed glass, leaving Peter to fold onto the end of the ambulance in the empty bunker.

To have a moment alone.

The moon's dull blue glow filtered among the concrete, illuminating Peter's trembling hands. Orange light licked his fingertips, heating the air as they collided with the lunar company. Closing his eyes, the paramedic planted his feet on the concrete, sighing until there was nothing left in his chest.

Hold.

Hold.

Inhale, moving air deliberately through the cracks and crevices of his pained lungs, expanding his bruised sternum and the runes beneath. He repeated again, and again, siphoning the energy through his limbs, past his throat, to his stomach and knees, until it passed into the earth through the soles of his feet.

Peter opened his eyes, observing his boots with sudden exhaustion as the orange flickered away like feathers on a breeze. Resting his forehead delicately against his palms, the distant fight faded into the night, and he waited for his coffee.

CHAPTER FIVE

Somewhere Lost in Suburbia,
Hamlet of Crowe County, 01:28

The Hamlet of Crowe County was Crowe distilled to a fine suburban aesthetic.

Cul-de-sacs wove a quilt of three-bedroom Capes, which faded into edges of the wooded Sticks. Residents of the Hamlet would navigate this indecipherable maze the respectable ten minutes it took to board the interstate on the way to respectable office jobs in neighboring cities, returning respectably at six for dinner.

These were the only respectable habits of Hamlet suburbia.

The full moon light exposed a smattering of people in light woolen cloaks wandering manicured sidewalks. Some strolled, while others were brisk to disperse through the midnight crowds on their way home. Their shadows sprawled across the pavement, as identical as their houses circling alveolar cul-de-sacs.

Cul-de-sacs named after fruit, mostly.

Glass jars sat on front steps, stuffed with stones or bones or filled with water, accompanying bundles of dried herbs and tools hanging from porch beams, intent on charging for workings in the month to come. As rituals ended for the evening and residents made their way home, some lingered in front of *not their* lawns like the home and garden committee, with silent judgment of their neighbor's ingredients, left to bake in the lunar effervescence.

The Hamlet of Crowe County was a place where neighbors' opinions were a greater concern than theft.

Peter brought the ambulance to a crawl among a cluster of these front porch skeptics, rubbing his eyes at blurring street signs.

"Are we going to Clementine or Orange?"

Henry's arm rested on the open window, the first to notice a slew of silent lights emanating from two streets down. "That's it. Mandarin Ave. Drive carefully, Ace."

Peter slowed for a group of three identical-looking women adorned in pine crowns, returning their thankful wave for safe passage as he brought the ambulance into the chaos of Mandarin Ave.

Blue, red, and sickly yellow lights flickered silently from a smattering of vehicles. Police cars, fire trucks, and ambulances were pulled onto the curb, parked kitty-corner to one another in an attempt to get closest to the scene.

An imposing Colonial at the top of the cul-de-sac claimed the attention of cloaked suburbanites gathering along the crime scene tape. The crowd kept a healthy distance while half a dozen police officers held the perimeter. Each officer came adorned in battle-ready attire, pale green helmets and vests strapped firmly to their person. Silver knives glinted in the moonlight beside familiar shotguns as a deterrent for the curious onlooker, though these were not the officials from which onlookers were keeping distance.

In the July heat, the members of the crowd were doffing their robes, exposing marked skin on the majority. Runes and designs designated their sects and covens, but the bond between them was irrefutable. Their collective worry was drawn to the hulking black carcass of two Birchwood security vehicles, placed closest to the scene.

Peter parked behind the crowd, observing the pale blue house with eggshell shutters.

A dollhouse framed in madness.

Its crimson front door was propped open, emitting absolute darkness from inside, despite the moonlight's persistent glow. A manicured front lawn was pockmarked by personnel boots of a practitioner anthill working the scene.

Of course, this all paled in comparison to the grand reveal—what the crowd was really there for—as five cloaked figures marched from the front door at the hands of police officers and Birchwood forces.

The party filed one after another, disarray snagging their heavy cloaks on their boot heels, fraying their hems on the concrete. Hoods were whipped from their heads as they emerged, leaving underwhelming human faces in place of the mystery, all in varied states of humiliation and rage. Stark white clothing underneath their cloaks was untucked and ripped, with dark liquid drowning the material like a Pollock painting.

The last of the accused struggled against his bonds like a feral cat, the balding man's cloak gilded in bright red embroidery that crowded his hood. A Birchwood agent barely contained him, his struggle evident.

"He will be free!" The gilded man thrashed at his captor's knee. "And his loyal followers will be saved the wrath—"

Birchwood's elbow planted hard in the detainee's throat, and the prisoner's zeal exploded outward like a grenade, warping the air before him. A whirlwind of energy pulled at his cloak, expelling into the sky with a pained gasp. Birchwood ripped the gulping man forward, leaving nothing but static cling in their wake.

In the new silence, the crowd began its hasty retreat to their homes.

Henry's hand found Peter's shoulder, and the paramedic jumped.

"You all right, Ace?"

He nodded, lying.

The musk of ritual wafted from the detainees' cloaks even at this distance, and a familiar sting of decay settled deep in Peter's nostrils as he slouched against the steering wheel. In the flickering yellow light of the black vans, the deep crimson soaked their garments black. The image of Frances's body stained his mind.

Watching the line of men pass, he was able to name each offender from the safe distance as they filed into the back of the truck.

The large city was small, in that regard.

"Hard to watch . . ." Henry squinted at the dissipating crowd. "You grab the supplies. I'm going to see if whoever's running this show might still need our services."

Peter nodded once, the slam of Birchwood's truck colliding with the back of his skull. "Will do, boss."

Shouldering the door open, Peter dragged the stretcher from the ambulance in silence. Nausea rocked his stomach as he retrieved his bags, keeping the black vans with a briar of thorns in his eyeline.

Henry meandered to the front lawn with the pace of someone who never rushed a day in his life. Though, Peter deemed it appropriate to take one's time here.

The scene's chaos was wrapping up as MEs skipped through the premises in their crinkling bunny suits and blue shoe covers. A drape was laid over the uniform front lawn, lined with reliquary from the scene. Peter imagined they were taken for processing, but he never truly knew where the artifacts of old gods ended up after confiscation from their scenes.

A gold scepter caught his eye, placed in the center of skeletal plaques. It boasted a prominent figurine at its tip, a twisted elm emblazoned with gnarled branches writhing from its trunk. Peter stared at the symbol, the significance tickling his memory in the recesses of his Crowe public schooling.

The knife, now this . . .

"Second time tonight, you bastard," he mumbled. "Who do you belong to . . . ?"

"What's going through your head, Ace?"

He greeted Henry's return with a jump, pointing toward the scepter.

"That symbol. It was on the knife at our body extraction this evening."

Henry paused, wringing his hands. "Unfortunately, that makes sense . . . From what I was told, there were human entrail offerings within."

The savagery inflicted on Frances's rib cage shot through Peter's mind like a lightning bolt.

I think he hurt me.

"Seems they revived the offering victims and took them to Crowe. All the detainees are off to Birchwood headquarters for questioning, and none of them were injured in the fray. With the exception of the obvious."

Peter exhaled, picking himself up off the stretcher.

"That's amazing. Do you think we can head back to Crowe so I can get some run forms done before—"

"Medic!"

Peter's upper lip twitched as familiar footsteps approached. " —we get another call?"

A sharp tap on his shoulder deflated his hope.

Peter turned stiffly to a face he'd hoped not to see twice in the same night. Removing his silver bangles, he shoved them in his pocket.

The night managed to destroy Clarence's pristine black uniform since Persephone Tower. The right sleeve was torn and replaced with sloppy bandages looping down his frame. And what Peter initially thought to be heavy bags hung under his eyes were blossoming bruises, with necrotic tendrils that curved across the bridge of his nose.

Peter shoved his hands in his pockets. "Clarence. You look awful."

"Pseudonyms, Pete. Come on . . ." The man flinched at the address, sparing a quick glance at Henry, who seemed not to notice the misnomer.

"Right! Genuinely I forgot. I'm sorry. What can we do for you, Agent?"

Clarence gestured to an adjacent house, warmly lit from every window. It was a small version of the neighbor's place, the yellow paneling inviting as a summer's day, sporting a wraparound porch and gingerbread trim.

"We found a woman in labor in the neighboring house on our post rounds. There are reports of her returning to the house shortly before police forces turned up, and we're concerned for any connection. The human sacrifice, looking like they were summoning something. She's reluctant to accept help from Birchwood. However, she's consented to medical aid given the dangers of childbirth after conjuration within her neighbor's house, seeing as we've yet to identify the entity. If she's hiding something—"

Henry's posture straightened, face brimming with delight. "Someone is having a baby?"

Clarence blinked. "Yes, but possibly connected to—"

"Delightful!" Henry made a break for the home. "A baby. New life! What a wonderful turn of events. George is inside?"

"He is."

A single laugh escaped Peter, watching as Henry's jaunty step carried him up the porch and into the house.

Clarence stood in apparent confusion beside the ambulance.

"I feel like . . . that could have gone better. I could have worded the danger of potential incubus birth after conjuration better," the Birchwood man observed quietly.

"I mean, are incubi really all that common?"

"Pete."

Peter let his smile linger briefly despite the conversational partner. "We don't often get called to full moon 'sacrifices' to help a life into the world. He's willing to take the risk. It has been a night."

The man grunted something close to agreement, running a hand over his brutalized face.

The paramedic hesitated before gesturing to the spiderweb of bruises laced across Clarence's nose. "Someone got you with silver?"

The man grimaced, lowering his hand as they proceeded slowly through the house's white picket fence. He watched the front door close behind Henry, consuming the house's light, before answering.

"My partner did it."

"Fucking what?"

The man sneered abruptly, catching Peter's expression. "Can you fix your face? I'm fine."

"Did he know you were silver sensitive?"

"Yes."

"Did you file a complaint? He can't fucking do that."

"That's not how it works. Birchwood —"

"Doesn't give a shit about you!"

"Gods almighty, Pete," Clarence snapped. "I don't need your opinion, all right?"

Heat burned Peter's temples as he stared belligerently at Clarence. The deep gray spoils carved along Clarence's cheeks, staining his veins like cracks in a vase. The sight brought bile boiling to the crook of Peter's throat, as if he might breathe fire.

"Of course. Keep 'em to myself, *Cowl.*"

Clarence's face was difficult to read, an impassive mixture of embarrassment and fury trained on the cookie-cutter Cape before them. He shoved his hands in his pockets.

"I really am fine."

"Sure you are."

The slam of Birchwood's truck echoed in Peter's right ear, its engine kicking on with a rattle, preceding its crawl from Mandarin Ave.

Peter endured the distraction as the vehicle trundled slowly down the road. The front windows were tinted near black, but even through the scrim, Peter made out two hulking figures seated beyond clear sight.

Clarence stood kitty-corner to Peter, providing partial cover as the behemoth disappeared down the road. Peter adjusted the obstetrics bag over his shoulder, watching the man fidget, playing his signet ring over the last knuckle on his pinky. This close, he caught a peek of old cologne from Clarence's uniform, the scent of spring water and pine, the same scent from his perfectly manicured hair. Not a strand out of place, even in the humidity.

With the truck gone from sight, the Birchwood man gave himself two steps of distance, his boot scuffling rocks on the path as he spoke.

"Your family okay?"

Peter exhaled the cologne, meaning to keep his response short. But when he began talking, the words tumbled into familiar ears almost without his assent. "Yeah, they're okay. My sister started up at Crowe, so that's terrifying. She goes in tomorrow for her first shift off orientation."

Clarence's roaming eyes latched on the side of Peter's face, and the air shifted like needles around his cheek.

"Seriously?" His response was immediate and sincere. "Is she gonna be okay? Is she okay with that?"

"I, um . . . I'm not sure yet." Peter was caught in Clarence's gaze. There was a hint of something there, heavily guarded, while a dusky rose painted the man's ears. "Not gonna lie, I'm scared shitless. You remember the anniversary I worked couple years back?"

Clarence's heavy boot knocked a small stone down the front path, childlike for a moment in time.

"I do."

"I'm fucking *terrified* for her. The thought of what happened that night . . . And I was *outside* the hospital. Were you um — were you this worried?"

The Birchwood guard opened his mouth, unspoken words dying in the space between them as the house welcomed the two with its wraparound porch. Wind chimes sang delicately from gingerbread trim to an audience of dense, pristine shrubs.

No jars laid out. No herbs hung to dry.

There was something strange about it.

Both men paused before the set of steps, giving time for Peter to claim his medication pack and supplies from the stretcher.

Clarence placed his hand out for a bag, watching the chaos of the street fading behind them. The medical examiner's office and Crowe's police were packing up their work, and it was like looking into a snow globe, separated by scene tape. Peter fell into observing the disintegrating scene alongside him, his shoulders relaxed.

"I always worried about you, Pete." Clarence peered up at the moon directly above their heads. "But . . . you were always hard to worry for. You didn't allow it much."

The corners of Peter's mouth twitched. Quietly, he held out the OB bag to Clarence.

"I'm sorry I was."

"Nothing to be sorry for, really." Clarence shrugged. A faint smile pulled at the corners of his mouth, taking the bag. "You got your own way of loving, is all. And I got mine. Being young and not realizing those two things can concede and coexist is hard."

Peter exhaled into the night sky as sweat drenched his collar. "Fucking right on that."

Clarence laughed once, a booming sound that resonated deep from within the man before he turned for the door. "Besides, it sounds like you're getting a bit of your own medicine with G. There's poetry to that."

A grimace found Peter's lips immediately, following in the man's wake.

"My own medicine is very bitter."

Clarence lurched open the front door, stepping aside to admit Peter with a faint smile. "Don't I know it."

A raven-haired woman sat on a plush green couch directly before him, with her hand resting on a watermelon-sized bump under her lace-plagued blouse. The living room air invaded Peter's lungs with stale warmth, rendering the sweater the woman wore, in his opinion, obsolete. Thin fingers curled beneath her sleeves, pressing against her belly as a wave of pain left her delicately maladjusted.

Henry sat beside her on the couch, filling the terse room with quiet words of encouragement.

"Ah, Ace!" he chimed. "Welcome. Please meet May. She is in active labor with a darling baby boy and would like to be transported to the hospital."

"Sounds like something we can provide, H."

Peter reclaimed his bag from Clarence, noticing the room's third occupant.

George leaned on a worn wooden mantel, watching the second hand of a carved clock tick away the minutes. His Birchwood uniform was stark against the pale pink carpet and paisley wallpaper, an eclipsing presence.

Bruises littered the older man's knuckles, and Peter's chest burned white-hot. Through the open door, the moon's radiance pressed into his back like an iron fresh from the fire, aching for release.

He knew there was nothing to be done about it now. That Birchwood were people he could not tangle with.

But that hand better fucking hurt.

"Pagan," George huffed. "How's the night treating you?"

Peter shrugged once. "Got shot. And how about yourself, Agent?"

The elder Birchwood let out a low whistle while Peter did his best to avoid eye contact with Clarence, whose brutalized face was busy morphing into different levels of horrified.

"Busy night you got there." George tapped the cuckoo clock with a grimace. "Cowl over there got himself roughed up a bit as well. Otherwise, we been all right."

Clarence shifted in the doorway.

Peter was cognizant of May watching the conversation like a hawk, so he put on his best showman's smile. "As always, for patient privacy reasons, we're going to have to ask you for time alone with our patient."

George whistled sharply for Clarence, covering the space in three strides. "We'll be outside. Make it quick."

Clarence was on his partner's heels out the door, pulling it shut behind them.

And the entire room exhaled.

"Congratulations on your soon to be," Henry said, beaming. "Tell us, how long have the contractions been?"

"It's been a couple hours," May said, her expression softening at the gentleman. "It's my first baby. And I really don't want to risk being left here on my own after my . . . my neighbors. Not with Birchwood running around."

A cuckoo clock nestled on the living room wall chimed in desynchrony with the one on the mantel, its cluttered design blending seamlessly into the room as a whole.

Pinks and blues popped from the furniture, the puce shag crunching as Henry knelt before the couch, his hairline dripping in sweat. Damning time and place, Peter shoved his sleeves to his elbows, wiping his upper lip while inspecting the doilies under an impressive porcelain figurine collection.

Little cherubs, disturbingly.

"Do you feel comfortable accompanying us to the hospital?" Henry mopped his hairline with a handkerchief. "And walking to the ambulance, perhaps?"

May threw the practitioners a *look*.

"I . . ." Her eyes floated to Peter's uncovered arms and back to Henry as she pushed herself from the couch. "Yes, I'll come along."

Exiting the house, the moonlight illuminated the woman's pointed features, which did everything they could to avoid the shadows of George and Clarence standing on the porch. Peter slowed to walk beside her, the stretcher clattering over the uneven walk like a puppy at his heel. Henry's quiet conversation with the men wafted their direction in the form of incomprehensible whispers.

The harsh light from the back of the rig deepened creases in the woman's forehead, highlighting freckles and graying hair at her temples, as Peter lifted the stretcher into the back.

"Would you like to call anyone to meet you at the hospital? The rig has a phone."

The woman leaned against the ambulance, breathing

slowly. "No. I don't have any family in the area. It's just me and little man here."

A smile tugged its way onto Peter's face as he aided the woman up the step, and she settled on the stretcher. "Do you have a name picked out?"

"No, I want him to tell me what it is." Her hands resumed their perch on her belly. "It sounds silly, but I think he'll show me who he wants to be once he's out."

Henry appeared in the bay doors, a frown twisting his cheerful demeanor. "Ace."

"Yeah?"

The older man stepped up and closed the doors behind him. "As the scene has not been fully cleansed, Birchwood Services will be following us to the hospital."

Peter's hands stalled, untangling the heart monitor as the information marinated. Fully aware of May's eyes on him, he was careful with what he gave.

Birchwood following meant they were not certain the patient would reach the hospital, and caution was imminent. It was as much a warning to the paramedics as it was a daunting shadow on their journey.

"Well, that is their prerogative." Peter forced a smile. "Let's get moving. Radio Crowe and tell them we're coming."

"Certainly. And Ace?"

"Yu-huh?"

"That Cowl fella said he got his medicine in their truck, in case you were concerned. The bitter stuff."

Clarence was worried.

Henry squirmed through the door to the driver's compartment, starting off at a speed meant to be easier to follow in a hulking armored truck.

Lights and no sirens.

May consented to the monitor, her heartbeat coming to life in the small cabin. It was slow, steady as heart rates go. And her eye contact could not be understated.

"The other two men are the ones from Birchwood?"

Peter's answer was brief as the blood pressure cuff deflated, *123/65.*

"Yes."

"You're afraid of them."

Peter sat on the bench beside the stretcher, documenting vital signs on his run form. "I'm wary."

"That's a relief!" May sighed, tugging both hands through her hair. "Honestly, the only reason I'm going with you is to avoid having to remain in my house with them skulking around. I saw your tattoos back at the house and thought you might be the better option."

Copper bands studded with turquoise and clear purple gems clanked on her wrists, catching her sweater sleeves to reveal intricate designs blasted against her skin. Their unfaded ink was indicative of fresh symbolism. New art.

She hid them in the house.

Peter watched the markings disappear. "I can see why you might think that. Those are new?"

May extended her arms with a smile. "A little of both! The lower ones are newer. I grew up in a supernaturally inclined family, mostly Christian witchcraft, and recently fell back into a different sect. How about yours?"

Peter wondered if he could evade the question, but the woman's expectant expression motivated him to prop his forearms forward. "My upbringing was in a legacy witch family as a hearth witch, secular. I didn't have extraordinary gifts but enough intuition to get me into the craft as a whole. I can energy sense, mostly. Felt the need for protection in this line of business, so they're my family's protective sigils . . ."

May traced his art with her eyes, and Peter watched her shoulders relax into the stretcher. In a way, it was nice to see someone make contact with the equipment, after Frances's golden haze earlier that night.

"That's nice to hear. I love the stories of people who grew up in a family of followers. They're always so worn with love."

"I suppose, yeah."

Her gentle laugh filled the back of the ambulance at Peter's response, and his stomach knotted. The rumbling of Birchwood's van outside shook the back of his skull, and he tried to keep the hesitation around his patient from becoming evident.

Slowly, he released his breath.

"Everyone I speak with automatically assumes I'm a violent cult member who sleeps with demons." May laughed. "I'm sure my neighbors have done nothing to assuage those fears."

"*Rosemary's Baby* wasn't exactly setting anyone up for success either." Peter removed his arms, settling on the bench.

May's smile became intensely earnest, displaying a gap-toothed grin that whistled when she spoke. "Do you ever find it difficult, belonging to a craft and working in medicine?"

Peter paused to consider the question as the yowl of Birchwood's truck sputtered behind the ambulance doors. Nausea bit the back of his throat, as he deeply dreaded that question.

"I mean . . ." He faltered. "Yeah, obviously it comes with its challenges, but, um . . . I think we've gotten to a point where almost all medical practitioners have some connection to the preternatural world. So it's, um . . . I mean, I think it comes in waves a bit. Court of public opinion can be harsh. But we've come a decent way from the witch trials, if that's what you're talking about."

The woman was expectant. Affirming. "It boggles my mind how quick the judgments come."

The expectation left little room for silence, and Peter

found himself rambling through the Birchwood truck roaring into another gear.

"I suppose I understand a little . . . because some horrible things have happened. I mean, when faith becomes organized — and I'm not just talking religious faith but faith in any type of ideal — there is high likelihood of inherent corruption since organizations are always made by humans. With flaws. And flaws are nature's way, but when the organization is corrupt, the faith of those supporting it becomes so as well."

Peter sucked in a breath, vomiting the response into the air in defiance of the rumbling gaining at their bumper. "I fully believe a faith-filled person may have beliefs so far as they are critical of men playing God, or else we blindly deify flawed and dangerous people. And that's truly the real danger in any belief. Birchwood, paganism, religion. The real dangers are corporeal beings who long for power and deification and exploit the needs of others to achieve it."

He trailed off, absorbing the shock of how much he spoke. A distant sigh echoed back from the driver's seat.

May's smile widened. "I enjoy hearing your opinions. And I even agree with most of them."

Peter blinked, uncertain how to respond.

Silence settled between the two. Amicable in many ways.

"Do you mind if I . . ." Peter cleared his throat, feeling himself tread on quicksand the moment his question was asked. "Do you follow multiple deities or just one? Or none?"

"I can . . . respond just, hold on. Pause for talent."

May took a beat, counting her breath with her fingers pressed into her belly.

Henry whistled as he drove, filling the silence born of contraction.

As the moment passed, she carefully shrugged her cardigan over her shoulders. The ink read in sharp contrast against her white lace top.

"I just received a tattoo of their signet not long ago."

A bloody sigil oozed under cling wrap on her right bicep. Hours old, if that, the jagged elm tree wrapped around her arm, its tendrils overtaking the other designs.

Henry's cheerful song hit Peter's ears with the weight of one thousand church organs. The image of a scepter seared Peter's vision. The memory of a knife.

His heart stuttered, palms tingling with warmth as he spared a glance at the hatch to the driver's seat. Gray curls were visible through the opening as Henry cruised through the endless suburbia.

He needs to know.

Conducted by an invariably cruel fate, May's fingertips dug into her stomach, a whimper dragging Peter from his panic.

"I think I just peed myself."

Henry needs to know.

Reaching for gloves, Peter swallowed against an immovable lump in his throat. His patient's gaze was potent and probing, the intensity of someone who knew they'd played their hand and were waiting for their opponent to fold.

He spoke slowly. "Is it okay if I perform an exam?"

The woman nodded, pained delight creasing her face. "Of course. We have tattoo talk to get back to."

Lifting the woman's dress, Peter visualized the burst water. That he was prepared for.

"I think you'll be interested to learn about my deity."

What Peter wasn't prepared for was a curd-covered crop of brown hair sandwiched between his patient's legs. He met May's eyes as she leaned forward, too close for comfort in this performance they were both putting on.

He recoiled inches from her proximity. "The baby's coming."

"Perfect!"

The ticking of the heart monitor swelled, and hostile glee broke along the fault lines of May's expression. In the time it took Peter to catch Henry's attention in the rearview, the charade was cracked.

"She was part of the ritual!" Peter shouted. "Radio Clar—"

The paramedic's feet flew from the floor, and he was confronted by the freckles dusting May's nose as she held his collar tight in her grasp. "You're not going to do any of that!"

Peter choked, grasping the woman's hands as the ambulance slammed to a halt. "Lemme—"

May's pupils expanded, consuming the sclera until the entirety of her eye was dripping black. Her knuckles stripped white as she twisted Peter's shirt collar. "Don't stop! Keep driving, or I swear I'll kill him and everyone who steps foot in this goddamned rig!"

The strip of fluorescent light seared overhead, shattering to punctuate her threat. Gulping against her hold, Peter met Henry's eyes. It wasn't the first time they'd been held captive in their own ambulance, but it was never a fun experience.

His partner retreated to his seat, shifting the ambulance into drive. Peter gasped as May leveraged his windpipe, the reek of metallic blood and delicate rose perfume soiling the air between them.

Tears streamed down the woman's freckled face, inches from his own, as another contraction caused the ambulance to shudder and shake. The metallic ceiling perspired, and her heart rate ticked higher.

And higher.

160s, 170s, 190s, and down.

160s, 190s, 210s, and down.

The radio flickered between channels. Fluid bags melted like M.C. Escher clocks. And Peter knelt before the stretcher; his throat compressed painfully under her grip. Blood pounded in his ears, and gray scattered across his vision as his fingers pried for purchase on her own.

"We can't let them have this baby," May hissed. "We can't."

Peter spluttered, eyes wide and unable to respond as a final contraction swept over May with a scream that ricocheted off the ambulance walls. Peter crumpled to the floor, abruptly released by the woman consumed in pain.

Fluid bags pooled underfoot, sloshing against the wheels of the stretcher. They melted into the bottom of the rig, clinging to Peter's new shirt. The humidity was as stifling as it had been in the little gingerbread house on Mandarin Ave.

Suffocating.

Staggering to his feet, Peter fumbled for the stability of the back doors, throwing himself on the handle. The door clicked once, twice, locked as the rumble of Birchwood's van remained barely audible through the chaos.

"Careful!" Henry hollered from the front, slamming the rig to a complete stop.

Peter screamed in return, thrown at the foot of the stretcher by the brakes. "It's fucking locked!"

"He's here!" May's tears spilled from the ceiling in a dense mist of rain, hissing into the pool of plastic below. "Help me! Please help me!"

Peter steadied himself, giving a futile kick to the doors before shoving his sleeves to his elbows. He knelt at the end of the stretcher, suffocating in humidity as he wrestled gloves over damp hands.

A head was present, thick fluid matting the baby's curls to a molded scalp. Peter blinked the saline rain from his eyes, bringing his mind to focus as the child slid into his arms with a final push.

Autopilot consumed the paramedic, doused in fluid and dizzy from stagnant air. A charred towel slithered from the warmer to dry and dry the infant's blue limbs as they flopped in his arms. The distant click of doors unlocking and locking echoed around him, but he didn't stop.

Ten seconds passed. May's screams turned from pain to something else entirely. Something feral from deep in her chest.

But he didn't stop.

Come on, kid.

Twenty seconds.

Peter flipped the blanket, reaching for a bulb suction. A slurp of fluid filled the hazy ambulance as he dried and suctioned. Suctioned and dried. Cradling the infant in dry blanket after dry blanket.

Thirty seconds.

The child coughed and inhaled.

IV fluid froze underfoot.

Condensation turned to a chasm of delicate icicles above.

Air abandoned Peter's lungs.

All as the infant in his arms began to cry.

The ambulance doors flung open in time for Henry, flanked by George and Clarence, to experience the infant's wail slice the air in a melody of steel wire dragging violin strings across shards of glass.

A note that tilted the world.

Peter's arms became lead as the child's eyes sank directly into his. Flecked with orange cream starbursts, they consumed him, invading his mind with ugly brute force. His knees locked, and Peter met the metal of the ambulance with a shock that stunned his thoughts.

A petite shadow stole the child from his arms, the infant's luminous eyes wide as his wails constructed madness throughout suburbia. Car alarms assaulted Peter's senses, below streetlamps that bowed like gentlemen, bringing their lights shattering against the blacktop.

Delicately, a whisper slithered amongst his thoughts.

Peter . . .

A barrage of images seared Peter's eyelids. Chaos of purple scrubs and white coats, a crowd pleading from iron bars. The screeching of red light that hissed from cracks within whitewashed walls, through pale blue tile.

There was a light, white-hot pain that splintered every limb.

Peter's insides coiled, slumping off the ambulance to the concrete below as darkness overtook him. Shallow breaths stuttered through his lungs, and the voice seeped from the back of his skull into the pavement below.

Peter . . .

Time stretched the way time does when you're alone.

"Peter!"

Ow . . .

Or he wasn't alone, but wishing he was.

"Peter!"

Ow, ow . . .

"Ow! Stop . . ." Peter mumbled into the concrete.

Grit from the pavement ground into his head, forcing his eyes open to the top of a streetlamp touching the blacktop inches from his face. He turned tenderly into the darkened sky. The full moon lingered directly above, its face staring down at him.

Mocking, he was sure.

To its left was Henry.

"Why . . . why y'gotta hit me?"

"Barely a tap, Ace."

Peter explored the plagued neighborhood around him. Surrounding houses had their doors open, lighting their front walks as infinite eyes watched the ambulance pulled against the curb in front of an empty Birchwood truck. No one approached Henry as he knelt beside Peter, preferring to stare, instead, at the steaming ambulance. The centerpiece to the destruction the infant wrought.

Peter planted his hands against the ground, gazing into the emptiness of their rig. Clamps were missing from the side table.

Gone with the woman and the infant's world-rending eyes.

The thought bucked his stomach, splattering coffee and ibuprofen across the road in a Picasso display. Hardly a welcomed sight in the Hamlet Wonderland distorted around them.

Henry was steadfast through the fallout, flicking vomit from his shoe with a frown. "That was quite exciting."

Peter dragged an arm across his mouth as he stood, rubbing his eyes. "Was it?"

"It's not every day you stare into the eyes of an incubus and live, Ace." Henry held out a blanket from the rig. "If that Clarence fellow hadn't been so intent on getting in, the mother might have let you be its first claim."

Peter shivered, the slithering whisper lingering in his mind.

"I saw her sigil. It was the same as the one at the site. And in Frances's apartment. I think . . . I want to say it is . . . I think I know it. I have to go home and check some texts, but *whatever it was* spoke to me, H. In my fucking head just now."

Henry watched the corner of their rig, interacting with the information deliberately, with careful precision Peter was certain he would never acquire.

The ability to process thoughts privately before speaking.

"The medical examiner's office is convinced the entity they were worshipping is one called Alagor, which is becoming a more prevalent sect within the city. And I believe Birchwood is now intent on killing that entity's son."

The name struck a chord in Peter's chest, and he struggled to place it through the discomfort. "Do you know it?"

"No." His partner's shoe scraped the pavement. "And I don't want to, if tonight is any indication."

Peter steadied himself against the rig, wrestling with the information. The footprint of whispers drifted among his thoughts, and his hands shook with the urge to remove his skull. To scrub his mind clean.

Alagor . . .

"Do you think they'll catch her?"

Henry closed the back of the ambulance, intent on watching the moon, which sat serenely above the chaos and the cause of it all.

The consummate professional, he didn't answer.

CHAPTER SIX

<pre>
The Sticks,
Crowe County, 04:43
</pre>

On the outskirts of Crowe County was a rural neighborhood desired for an unpolluted lake where residents kayaked in the summer and occasionally drowned in the winter skating months. Serviced by Crowe County Ambulance Company, the Sticks was dreaded for a host of reasons, not least of which was the refuge they provided lycanthropes on full moons. Isolated and safe, it took a while for the long arm of Birchwood to reach the Sticks in a pinch, and this was a benefit.

Unfortunately, the same applied to other services for werewolf transformations gone wrong. Lycanphylactic episodes, so they were known.

Henry closed the bay doors as Peter secured the jump kit atop the stretcher. The house before them was modest and a mile from any main road. Boxwood topiaries lined the front path, swept and clean, a grandiose entrance to the Cape, whose upper windows flickered with a dusky orange glow.

The whistle of someone's breath raking over a tightened airway was joined by a distant howl ringing from the woods in the waning night. While from different sources, the torment of the sounds was eerily similar.

Peter sped down the walkway toward the former.

A twentysomething man met them at the bottom of the front steps, desperation carved into his round face and clutching a small figure. The sunken eyes of what dispatch informed them was a ten-year-old boy reflected in the dim porch lights, staring through Peter as they closed the distance.

"Please help him," the man said, rushing to meet them. "I gave him his epinephrine shot, but he's getting worse."

Henry stepped forward, his placidity stern. "We will. If you can place him on the stretcher while we ask some questions. What is your name?"

"Eric. I'm Eric."

The man moved stiffly to the stretcher to deposit the small boy, who was decked in oversized plaid pajamas that matched fluffy moose slippers. His hands gripped a well-loved knit blanket held together by the force of will and synthetic yarn.

Peter cracked his kit as Henry placed a stethoscope against the child's shirt.

"What's his name?"

The man stepped back from the stretcher, crossing his arms. "Phillippe."

"And how old is Phillippe?"

Eric did not have time to answer, interrupted by Phillippe's hands holding up ten fingers.

Peter swallowed, forcing a quick grin. "Ten. Okay. I'm going to look at one of your arms, Phillippe."

The boy's arms flopped to the stretcher without protest, his breath coming quick and short.

Henry slung his stethoscope around his shoulders,

a dim cloud of the twentysomething's cologne hanging between them like Hitchcockian fog.

"Are you his father?" Henry asked. Silence persisted, followed by, "Eric, what is your relation to Phillippe?"

"He's my little brother. We live here with my grandmother, but she's . . . she's out of town." Eric grasped Phillippe's hand. "Can we go? The emergency line said they'd be sending Birchwood . . ."

Peter tightened a tourniquet around the child's thin arm, and Phillippe's hand clenched in preparation. The small boy bore his lycanthropy in the shape of a pink scar shredding his arm from shoulder to wrist. The old bite marks formed trenches in his skin. But the antecubital was still there.

Big pinch, sorry.

Henry's hands flitted around Peter, placing the child on a monitor, which dwarfed him, at a speed Peter rarely saw. "It's a long ride. We are going to get an IV in and give him some more epinephrine before we leave. Hopefully it will help his breathing. You gave him one shot?"

Peter's hand steadied, aspirating blood into his IV with a rueful grin. He gave the line a flush, and Phillippe's fist extended a weak thumbs-up.

His wheeze cut the air between them, but as the young boy met Peter's eyes, he gave a timid smile.

"He usually only needs one, and . . . they're expensive now. We can't afford to keep more than one in the house . . ."

Peter handled the epinephrine with reverence, the practitioner ballet in Crowe's ED springing to his mind.

In the meantime, Henry mined for information. "How long has Phillippe had lycanthropy?"

"Oh, I don't think . . . I don't think he has that," Eric said with his eyes on Peter as the medication pushed through the line.

"When was he bitten by the werewolf?" Henry simplified.

"Oh, right. Um . . ." He trailed off, fixated on his brother. "Is it working?"

Peter wondered that himself, listening to the child's heart rate increase. Phillippe's thumbs-up fell apart as the oxygen monitor's tone trailed slowly downward, and Peter hastened to unlock the stretcher.

"We will bring Phillippe to the hospital for further treatment," Henry said. "You may ride in the back if you wish."

The twentysomething didn't respond, fumbling for his brother's hand as the stretcher trucked down the path. Distant wails of a low thrumming alarm fractured the tree line; the flickering of pale yellow lights danced among the dense forest.

Peter loaded the stretcher in the back of the ambulance, securing their charge and ushering Eric in quickly. He landed among them with a leap, closing the door with a definitive snap.

"Those are Birchwood alarms," Eric stammered, guided to the bench by Peter as the ambulance leapt forward.

Peter nodded curtly, navigating the space.

"Dispatch sends Birchwood for all lycanthrope-related calls," he rushed to explain, tending to Phillippe as the ugly truth became another passenger on their ride.

Birchwood was Crowe's contingency to prevent public health outbreaks, and Phillippe was a public health risk.

Henry's pace through the Sticks bordered on inappropriate, the ambulance bucking over packed dirt roads. Eric steadied himself, clutching his brother's hand fiercely.

Peter slipped a hissing mask over the child's face, cranking the dial on the wall.

"A treatment to help his lungs and a bit of oxygen," he explained concisely, tapping the bubbles from another dose of epinephrine. "When was he bitten?"

Eric answered this time, pained. "Last year. We moved to the Sticks to help him adjust away from people. We were getting threats in the city, and . . . it wasn't fair to him."

Peter placed the epi to the side, drawing a different syringe as the wheezing curdled his blood, high-pitched and tight.

Any optimism was performative.

"This is something to help with the inflammation. It will make him sleepy."

"Like the Benadryl?" Eric asked, eyes latched on the IV. "The doctor said we should give him a Benadryl before every full moon so we don't have to use the epinephrine as much . . ."

"He always needs his epi?" Peter asked, checking his watch before giving another dose.

Two doses should be more than you need to get to the hospital. Bullshit.

Eric shook his head. "The last couple months. We're trying to get him into those, um . . . those immuno . . . immunosup . . . the, um, the immune system tests and stuff, so he can be less reactive. But they upped the price of the epinephrine, and he needs it a lot, so we can't . . . can't do the trials."

Heat rose behind Peter's ears, anger hot at his back like at May's house. Pinpricks of energy tickled his palms, but there was no room to breathe here, nowhere to root himself as he placed his stethoscope against the child's chest.

"No one should ever worry about paying for treatments," he spoke curtly. "I'm sorry you're going through that."

Phillipe's lungs were in a vise clamp, twisted so only

the upper portions exchanged air, and Peter moved to the head of the bed, snatching intubation supplies from his drawers.

Well stocked where it matters.

"Has Phillippe ever needed a breathing tube before?"

Whatever color remained in Eric's face vanished. He squeezed his brother's hand as Peter lowered the head of the stretcher. "Yes. He needs one?"

"Yes, it will help him breathe better. What you can do is hold his hand, let him know everything is going to be okay. Henry! Please pull over."

Eric held Phillippe's limp hand as Peter threaded a stylet through the plastic tube. He attached a syringe to the side, bending it before clicking a metal device in place that looked like it should be anywhere but a child's throat.

For a moment, his hand hovered over a thinner tube, snatching it up for the same preparation.

Fuck.

"Tell the ED we're going to need respiratory and a vent set up," Peter told Henry, tilting the child's head back as the ambulance slowed to a halt.

The music of the monitor alerted his partner. "You need assistance?"

"Yes, please. I need meds pulled up. We need an airway."

Henry's weight shifted into the back of the ambulance, and he cracked the medication box.

A quick flush, a paralytic, a sedative. Not in that order.

Concentrating on the monitor's tone, Peter held his expression carefully as he slid the scope against Phillippe's inner jaw, pulling delicately upward. Peter reached reluctantly for the thinner tube, giving himself a beat. The monitor's oxygen tone slid downhill as he visualized what he required. Barely.

Vocal cords.

Pulling the stylet, a purple bag that fit in his hand unlike anything else hooked to the tube jutting from Phillippe's teeth. Squeezing gently, Peter noted chest rise on both sides while struggling his stethoscope into his ears. Air flowed freely, disrupted by the low thrumming alarm of a familiar black truck gaining traction outside the ambulance.

Got it.

Peter allowed himself ten seconds for breaths, the oxygen monitor recovering with each squeeze, before ripping tape strips from his pant leg and wrapping the tube into place.

He glanced at Henry, nodding once. "We have an airway. I can maintain it, but we need to get going."

"Birchwood is outside," Henry noted, deft fingers siphoning medication from vials, laying them prepared before jumping back to the driver's seat.

Peter spared a glance at Eric, whose cheeks were spoiled-porridge gray as he held Phillippe's hand. The image was brutal.

Keeping with his ventilation, Peter spared a civil phrase.

"Radio Birchwood we will not be needing their services. We have Phillippe well in hand."

Driving Like Mad,
Crowe County, 05:37

Back to the bag. Administer epinephrine. Sedation now.

Peter rinsed and repeated, steadying himself as Henry flew down the freeway to keep pace ahead of the low alarm that did not take kindly to being unneeded.

"Two minutes out!" Henry called back.

Peter took the information in stride, compressing the bag at a rate he knew by heart to keep the monitor in acceptable parameters. Eric gripped Phillippe's hand, incapable of doing anything else, unable to elicit a response from the boy.

"We are almost at the hospital," Peter repeated, dredging Eric from his thoughts. "When we get there, your moniker will be E, and Phillippe's will be his patient identification number until he's out of the Emergency Department, okay?"

"Sure, sure," he said. "Will he be okay?"

Peter set his face, concentrating on his tube placement and the child's chest rise. "We will do everything we can for Phillippe to get him through this. Crowe is well equipped."

Eric rested his forehead against his brother's fingers, exhaling once. "Thank you."

Peter fell into silence, depressing the bag rhythmically as he watched the pair. His stomach roiled, indiscernible through his dormant expression as he reached for the last dose of epinephrine, attempting to keep all worry from the brother.

Attempting to keep worry from the brother in the way he might want it, despite the knowledge their fifth dose of epinephrine was barely holding the child steady.

"About a minute out," Henry said into the back.

Trenches dug into the creases of Eric's face, and Peter saw himself in them. He knew the worry, knew the fear.

He cleared his throat, screwing on the epinephrine between breaths. "The hospital . . . will hopefully be able to give you some resources, especially if he's been hospitalized before."

"They, um . . . they won't take him away?"

Peter opened his mouth to respond, the standard lies stalling on his tongue. He had no words of safety for the guardian until they were within hospital walls. Until then—

Shhrack.

Phillipe jolted from the stretcher.

Peter's blood siphoned through his heart like a mountain river dumping into a lake. The boy's chest caved inward.

Shhrack!

Then, out like a barrel, his collarbone halved with a snap.

Phillipe's eyes shot open, a creamy glaze covering his sclera. Silent screams tore from his mouth, gagging to make noise past the tube.

Peter plunged the epinephrine through the IV.

"Tell them to have a containment team at the door!" he ordered Henry, the splintering of bones reverberating through the ambulance.

Peter untangled the breathing tube from Phillipe's flailing hands, helpless as he watched what he'd only ever seen in training video animation. Each of Phillipe's bones cracked, bending to their will. The hue of dark blood flowed under his skin, over the fibrous mesh of new distorted limbs. In moments, the child occupied the stretcher's length, skin ripping and stitching together in a rush of blood and viscera.

The video's voice-over was there in Peter's head.

Lycanthropy is a disease with a mortality rate of 92.3 percent. Those who survive to transformation are few. Those who survive first transformations are fewer. Proper supportive measures are —

Peter grappled the breathing tube to siphon more sedation into his syringe. Phillippe's blood soaked his shirt in a crimson crawl as the paramedic fought to get medication through the IV. Eric fumbled to quell the bleeding with his hands as a familiar bump into the ambulance bay hit the underside of the rig. The stretcher was moving before the doors opened, a white-clad trauma team present but trapped behind an intense complication.

Peter's feet met concrete. He continued to bag as they

skidded to a halt in front of Birchwood's finest: Clarence and George.

Clarence bore a deep gouge patched haphazardly on the left side of his face, balancing the black eye that had crept toward his hairline since Mandarin Ave. George was intact, pristine as always despite living the same night as his partner, and Peter was ominously aware of the shotgun slung across his back.

Stepping in front of the boy, Peter continued his ventilation efforts, addressing J at the helm of the team beyond.

"Ten-year-old exposed to lycanthropy nine months ago with a history of increased epinephrine need during full moon lycanphylactic episodes."

George matched his step. "You weren't playing nice in the sandbox, medic. Protocol states Birchwood Services is to risk assess lycanthropic occupants of Crowe County before entrance to the hospital."

Peter darted a glance at Clarence, who stood silent behind his partner, watching the other Birchwood man. His features flickered in yellow lights that neared from outside the ambulance bay, their backup close and waiting.

"Patient received five doses epinephrine, one push Benadryl, succs, etomidate, and 20 mcg propofol. Tube is four point five, ten at the gum with color change and bilateral chest rise."

"We could have you arrested for this, but instead—"

"Heart rate has been consistently tachycardic to the 180s, SpO2 100 percent since prophylactic intubation—"

"We will simply conduct our assessment now before allowing—"

"BP has been low, received 500 cc normal saline bolus," Peter continued, feeling Henry at his side, taking the bag from him to continue the breaths.

"Before allowing you to endanger the population of this city!"

"He's *ten*, and he will die if you don't let us treat him!" Peter pushed up his sleeves, covering ground quickly toward George. The movement was enough for the Birchwood man, who flipped the butt of his rifle. The cold metal fell to rest on Peter's chin.

"You were already shot once tonight, pagan."

Peter froze in his spot, fingertips on fire as his feet rooted to the cement in front of the stretcher.

"You have no right." Peter backed away a step, out of the rifle's reach. The lights swelled beneath his words, and Peter's teeth clenched as he reached back to the stretcher. "To deny him his care."

George sneered, looking to the trauma team, who remained tensely silent beside the exchange. He swung his rifle to train the barrel on the boy.

"Seems I got enough."

Shhrack!

And chaos erupted as it usually does.

Shhrack!

Violently.

And all at once.

Phillippe's long-limbed mess of viscera launched from the stretcher in a single bound, consuming the space behind Peter. Though only ten, his pointed ears scraped the bunker's cement ceiling as he stood full height on the stretcher, his leathered skin stretched thin against jutting bones.

In a horrific turn of events, the oversized pajamas fit perfectly on his blood-soaked frame.

Peter stumbled backward into George's rifle as Phillippe's bony fingers, the length of fly swatters, enveloped his carefully placed tube. The boy dragged it slowly from his throat with a trail of saliva that coated the floor.

Free from the gag, Phillippe arched his back with a long pained howl that reverberated against the cement walls. Delicate clicks of a shotgun pricked Peter's ears, and without a single thought, he lunged at the wolf. Phillippe moved a scant foot under Peter's weight. A single shot missed the pair by inches.

"Henry!" Peter shrieked, toppling off the stretcher to the cement floor.

Henry snatched a sheet from the stretcher, scrambling around the wolf as Peter's arms flew over his face.

Phillippe's claws wailed on his forearms, tearing into his skin. The pain was immense, and Peter dodged frantic snapping jaws as a flash of practitioners collided with the chaos. The containment team rushed forward in full force.

If the prior code was a ballet, this was a mosh pit. Indelicate, imprecise, and effective.

Phillipe slammed into the ambulance under the force of the onslaught, and Peter huddled on pavement, scrambling to miss being stomped by the boy's hooked feet. The ambulance exterior absorbed the attack, pinning the ten-year-old for just enough time to be wrestled away with the stretcher blanket. Phillippe thrashed, his elongated jaw solidifying in a wash of new tendons and hair, snarling and snapping against the linen restraint.

Cradling mincemeat arms, Peter scrambled from the ground, stooping beneath the werewolf's jaws to heave the stretcher toward the Emergency Department. Without a word, Clarence was at his side, shoving the stretcher forward beside him. Two shotguns clattered on his back as the team passed George, kneeling to the side. The elder Birchwood cradled the side of his face, leaning into his radio with venom as they disappeared into the Emergency Department.

The few remaining occupants of EMS hall clocked the group with bleary-eyed curiosity.

Peter rasped the remainder of his report.

"An 18-gauge IV placed in right AC . . . How 'bout that, still patent. About two minutes ago, the patient began to physically change, which you saw the completion of. Assumed blunt trauma to the chest, right elbow, and bilateral lower extremities. But you know all this."

The trauma bay welcomed them in a flood of static, and Clarence disappeared forcefully at the door as J caught him by the chest. The wolf thrashed violently as they moved him from the stretcher to the trauma table, his crimson mess shocking the carefully laid drapes, bringing vibrant color to the whitewashed room.

Peter moved with his stretcher, keeping away from practitioners beginning their work. Phillippe's reassuring thumbs-up was long gone, and Peter's voice echoed on deaf ears.

"Additional sixth dose of epi seemed to stop the course prior to Birchwood interference. He came with a guardian, a brother. Wait, where's his brother?"

He blinked, looking around the trauma bay for Eric amidst the chaos. J flitted around the room, grabbing supplies and genuine restraints. Henry was aiding the team, searching for more IV access, rattling information of new trauma, securing monitors. Bones popped in Phillippe's feet like Rice Krispies, and Peter flinched, his limbs numb as an anonymous chaplain guided him to the door.

"Brother is in the waiting room," was the only response he received.

Peter dragged his stretcher out of the trauma room, forcing his final words. "But he wants to be with him."

And Phillippe disappeared from view in a slam of the door.

The paramedic faced the wooden slab, unable to hear the assumed turmoil beyond as the way-line below his feet flickered black, the color of indiscriminate lockdown.

Bright crimson claw tracks on his arms dripped steadily onto the tile floor sizzling as they hit the light, and Peter suddenly remembered he was in pain.

Sharp. Hot.

The wounds left a slug trail as he shuffled to a sink across the hall, stretcher in tow.

Warm water hissed from the faucet, and Peter cupped his hands underneath, watching them overflow. For thirty seconds. A minute.

He brought the water over his arms, scrubbing cheap orange soap into every crevice until they stung, the wounds pulsing with every slow heartbeat. He brought the water across his face, dragging his hands over the plateaus of his temples, the crevices of his eyes, staining the porcelain sink with grit and grime. Exhaustion left his eyes swollen, observing blood and dirt swirling into the drain below.

Crepe paper towels slithered from their hold on the wall, bunching in his fists as he patted his wounds and turned the faucet off, though it continued to drip.

"All right, Winsted."

With a loose hold on the stretcher, he shuffled past the once-empty security booth, where a body sat, crumpled in defeat. Eric, head in his hands.

A black-clad individual occupied the opposite chair, and where Peter assumed there would be a chaplain was Clarence, a bruise fresh on the bridge of his nose. Stripped of his weaponry and standard Birchwood accoutrement, the man seemed intensely bare and familiar as he sat in silence with the brother.

The clattering stretcher drew Eric's attention, looking up in time to catch Peter's eye. The expectation of his gaze weighted the air between them.

Parking his stretcher on the side of the hall, Peter shouldered his way into the security booth. Heavy Velcro disturbed the silence as he shed his vest, letting it fall to the ground with a wince before sitting silently next to Clarence. The Birchwood man acknowledged his presence with a look, with silent understanding of their purpose in this room, sitting among the carnage the full moon wrought.

Peter sighed, cradling his arms across his chest to remove the silver bangles, placing them away from Clarence. When he spoke, his lips were numb.

"I'm sorry, Eric."

The brother did not appear to hear him. His sight never left the eviscerated stretcher in the hall, the blood-stained vest left for dead on the floor.

Clarence leaned gently against Peter in response, shoulder to shoulder for an instant.

"I'm getting a doctor . . . You need to get looked at."

Peter could not bring himself to look up from his dull shaking hands. But he didn't protest.

A placid voice crackled overhead.

"Pediatric Trauma Alert, Trauma Room 5. Pediatric Trauma Alert, Trauma Room 5."

Wonder what that could be.

CHAPTER SEVEN

Downtown,
Crowe County Arts District, 06:59

Respectfully, Walter, I've had a shit night. Either get in the fucking ambulance or sign the declination papers."

A set of powerful whiskers twitched indignantly. Reedy arms folded staunchly across a barrel chest, smearing blood on his wrinkled linen suit as the man's eyes crossed on Peter.

Double vision does not an accurate identification make, but the mustache was certain of the paramedic's ill intentions.

"N'ah geddin' in no ambulance wif an occultist and 'is f'ggin' b-b-b—"

In the style of nauseous Jackson Pollock, the rest of his words splattered onto the pavement.

Peter shoved his shoulder off the lamppost, his voice terse. "Enough."

An armpit of the man's stench stung Peter's eyes as he hauled Walter to a tenuous standing position, careful to avoid touching the filth with his newly bandaged arms. "You can insult me when you're sober, bud. Meantime, let's get that head stitched up."

"M'not your bud!" the man rebutted, landing hard against the stretcher in the back of the ambulance. "An' I wouldn't le'you stitch me up f'n'you were the last occultists on Earth!"

"Then bleed!" Peter snapped, muting the string of indignation with a slam of the ambulance doors.

The moon matched the sun on the horizon as Peter strode beside the bullet-ridden rig, hoisting himself swiftly into the passenger seat. With the dignity of a man who had lived this day multiple times before, Henry watched the rearview mirror as Walter sluggishly squirreled under the thin stretcher sheet.

A breeze from the air conditioner left Peter colder than usual, and it was then he realized the windows were shut.

"Your windows are up," he grunted, rubbing a speck of vomit from his sleeve.

Henry smiled in his way, finding the crank to roll down the windows entirely, just as he liked them.

Peter clicked his seat belt with a defensive snap.

"What's the smile for?"

The older man shrugged, reaching carefully to adjust the rearview mirror a quarter inch, leaning the ambulance slowly from neutral to drive.

"You have a way with people, Ace."

PART 2

MONDAY NIGHT WITH GIGI

CHAPTER EIGHT

Good evening. My name is Daniel Fjord, and I am press secretary of the Birchwood Agency for Preternatural and Supernatural Reform. I am conducting this brief on the investigation into events that happened at Crowe County Hospital yesterday, July 7, 1982, at 4:49 p.m.

"Birchwood Services received a call requesting aid to Crowe County Hospital's North Belfry, where an entity of unknown origin took root. Our team responded at 5:20 p.m. to the facility, where they promptly assessed and took action. Crowe Hospital's North Belfry was immediately quarantined and cleansed with methods reserved for unrecoverable areas of high paranormal activity. This was accomplished by 6:17 p.m."

Gigi Winsted lingered by the open door of West Belfry 10's ancient staff refrigerator, basking in the dull glow of a dense twelve-inch television seated across the break room. The man on the screen adjusted his orange bow tie, distracting the young nurse as she crammed her brown lunch bag between a stale sheet cake and two liters of flat cola.

It had been three months since Gigi began working at Crowe County Hospital, and she could not remember the break room with the television on.

Tonight was different.

"It is the duty of Birchwood to restore Crowe County Hospital and Crowe itself to a standard of security. As our world continues to age and hospitals turn centuries old, it is imperative we keep ahead of weakening infra-structure, preventing these tragedies before they occur."

He cleared his throat, shuffling papers on his podium.

"Our intelligence shows the destabilizing entity within North Belfry has been removed, and the commu-nity of Crowe can be assured the hospital has returned to acceptable levels of activity."

"Acceptable levels of activity" struck Gigi's memory, from a floral family room, curled on a plush couch beside Nana, a woman with hair starting its journey from blond to white.

A rough-hewn man with a thinning pompadour watched from the kitchen doorway, holding the ner-vous energy of the room taut in his overworked limbs. Gigi's brother took up space in the window seat, look-ing out at the cityscape toward the belfries of Crowe Hospital.

That night, the newscast was different. Daniel Fjord was different than he would be the morning after.

Minutes before the tragedy, he was ambitious.

"Heartless" was the accusation many would make.

Daniel didn't wear a bow tie the night of North Bel-fry's cleanse. Instead, his full form was decked in Birch-wood Service's black slacks, his hair slicked to the side, immovable.

"We advise community members to evacuate within a city block of the hospital," he commanded. "Birchwood Services will cleanse imminently."

"What about evacuation!"

"Incomplete. We cannot afford to wait. Any further questions can be forwarded to—"

A sharp pop sent Gigi springing from her Nana's floral cushions. The television snapped to black, and the house followed suit, darkness all consuming.

The lights of Crowe County were visible in a brief sweeping glance from the living room window before neighborhoods were swallowed by blackouts that overwhelmed the city. Emergency lights flashed in desynchrony with their sirens, the only sign of life, speeding toward lean towers jutting against the gray horizon: the four belfries of Crowe County Hospital.

Gigi met her brother's eyes as he turned from the window.

She saw his fear.

"We wish to inform community members that the number of deceased will continue to rise as authorities begin recovery efforts. Please direct efforts at locating loved ones to the resources provided. Avoid utilizing local mediums and cultists for the location of the missing or deceased. This is a tragic time, and we should exercise caution with the doors we leave open, now more than ever."

Hindsight roiled Gigi's stomach as her memory remained in the darkened living room.

Unable to understand its implications as a child, the meaning of Daniel Fjord's warning became clear as Crowe grew in North Belfry's shadow.

There were doors about to be opened. That was an unfortunate certainty.

"Hospital leadership urges vigilance be kept by community members seeking care in the hospital, especially those with high-ranking psychic ability. Silver and iron will be used in excess during recovery. Werewolves, shape-shifting entities, and others with sensitivities should consult primary care providers and urgent care centers before entering the hospital, with exception for dire emergency.

"Crowe County Hospital now ranks as America's only Level 5 facility, and we encourage this to be handled with appropriate caution as security programs are unrolled. The world is intensely diverse, and hospitals remain beacons of neutrality to serve the diversifying communities within. I will do my best to answer any—"

Gigi's attention flew to the break room door as the TV cut to dark.

The culprit slouched against the doorframe. A familiar figure whose keen features appeared mischievous when backlit from the hallway. The mousy woman blinked slowly behind wire-rimmed glasses, her blackened abyssal eyes scanning the shoebox of a break room before replacing the television remote next to the door.

M was never one for pleasantries but made an exception for her recent preceptee.

"Daydreaming?"

Gigi managed to close the refrigerator door as Daniel Fjord's face faded from the television screen, enveloped by sizzling blackness.

"Sort of."

"There's no need to watch that nonsense. Hardly the truth anyway."

A careful smile tugged the corners of Gigi's mouth. "My parents were working here in South Belfry when it happened."

"That was fortunate for them. I was in North." M removed herself from the doorway, setting her bag on the dump-salvaged table. Fluorescent lights whined above their heads as she navigated around Gigi to the fridge. "How old did that make you? Seven? Eight?"

"Six. I was at my Nana's . . ." Gigi trailed off, watching her mentor wrestle with her own lunch. "There's room above the sheet cake."

"Thanks." Finding success, M slammed the refrigerator door and delicately cleaned her glasses with the hem of her plum-purple scrub top. "This is your witch nana? Works here. Gave you the little watch thing."

Gigi adjusted a tiny copper watch pinned beside her badge, received at her nurse pinning ceremony months prior. The watch defied nursing tradition, which dictated your first piece of protection for work came from your school. It was meant to identify your institution in whatever facility you worked.

Nana found that foolish, taking the honor upon herself.

Fear nothing tickled Gigi's fingertips in gently engraved script while its second hand marched steadily against her palm.

A familiar creature's heartbeat.

"She was the one most scared for me to come here, wanted me to have something of substance," Gigi said.

M snorted, tucking a pencil behind her ear. "Not your brother?"

"He was a close second. Doesn't want me here tonight, that's for certain."

"The anniversary is a scary time."

Gigi made a show of rolling her eyes but couldn't stop them landing on her badge.

To double-check.

Triple-check.

G2 met her gaze in gray typeface above *Registered Nurse*.

G2.

Two Gs.

Gigi.

"Security didn't change your badge."

Heat stung Gigi's cheeks, the accusation landing square on her shoulders.

Gigi grew up on the tales, the rumors. She listened to her nana, read the books, and took the classes. In the centuries it took for the supernatural to embed itself in the everyday existence of humans, they'd all said the same thing: regardless of your practice or your beliefs, names are important. They were homing beacons to your being, and a strong sense of self was integral to protection. Something could take your vulnerable moment and invade if it knew so much as your name. Demons, untitled entities, and other practitioners all took advantage of the hospitals, the funeral homes, the places where people were most vulnerable, and it had become standard to shield names in places like these.

Standard to respect others enough to shield their names once you knew.

"I was gonna try and get it replaced again. But I woke up too late to do it before shift. And then my brother insisted on driving me in, and I couldn't really say no."

M's sigh followed Gigi around the break room as she slung her stethoscope around her neck. "You're killing me, kid. There's nasty shit here that will know your identity from that badge, and I might not be there to help when they do. Go fix it during shift if there's time, okay?"

The break room door slammed open against the back wall.

The assailant crossed the room in two strides, forcefully depositing her bag into an empty chair. Permanently scrutinous eyes observed the world between jagged ears that wrestled their way into view behind a headband woven with rose thorns and thistle sprigs. A thin mask of a smile barely concealed a career's worth of disdain, a pugilist with gloves poised at the slightest provocation.

This was L. And L was a famously unpleasant person.

"First admit spot again!"

Two others followed in her wake.

O sported delicate gold filigree woven hem to hem on her plum scrubs. Similar markings littered her visible skin, shouting across ash-hued fingers, curling inside her ears.

She hung her bag delicately on a hook, nursing an iced coffee not long for this world.

L2 entered the room on a cloud, serene and unbothered. Copper wiring was worked through her tumbling brown curls, the youthful bounce betrayed by creases at the sides of her wizened eyes.

O took up the mantle of breaking the tension.

"You could talk to management?"

"They don't listen." L ripped the refrigerator door open, staring.

It seemed as if the whole room held its breath as Gigi watched the thin wire that was L's remaining patience snap.

"Why is there no room in this fucking fridge?" the woman ripped the sheet cake from the shelf and shoved her lunch bag in its place. "Why is there a two-week-old cake experiencing evolution in here? How hard is it for day shift to throw out their fucking trash?"

M stood beside Gigi, expressionless. "You're in a ripe mood."

With a huff, L tipped the cake into the bin. "Birchwood stopped me on my way in."

The room fell silent, except for the tinny buzz of the fluorescent light fixture overhead.

L2 cradled her coffee, her soft voice filling the room. "Which was very scary for her, as it would be for any of us."

L flinched at the phrasing but didn't deny it. Without a word, she retrieved a stethoscope from her bag.

"What did they think you did?" M asked.

"They were questioning me about some random shit with an incubus death last night." She spread her arms wide. "Do I look like a person who would birth an incubus?"

L2 answered immediately, with her patented smile. "Yes, and you would make a lovely incubus parent."

M snorted, which L2 waved off.

"No, no! I'm genuine. She would be so lovely and understanding. But firm when she needed to be! She would give them structure, which they need."

L seemed lost, the tips of her ears blushing pink as M and O devolved into laughter, the small room brightened by it.

"Fuck you all." L sneered, betrayed by the faintest twitch at the corners of her mouth at L2. "But thanks for the vote of confidence."

Gigi leaned against a bargain-basement chair, which groaned in protest.

"My brother was at that," she interjected. "The incubus birth. I guess they got the infant, but the mom . . . got away."

She did not expect the news to rob laughter from the room. But it did.

Tough crowd.

O chewed the straw in her coffee. "Was it a known entity?"

"I don't think they knew, but I, um . . . Oh wait, no I—it was Ala, something," Gigi fumbled.

The four nurses took a moment to collectively stare. Unimpressed.

"I can ask him in the morning."

L's gaze, in particular, was potent. "It's your attention to detail that makes you a spectacular nurse."

M flicked the time clock, moving to a thin shelf of time cards on the wall.

"Don't start. It's her first night alone."

A chill coursed through Gigi, toenail to fingertip.

Alone.

"She knows I'm just fucking with her." L smiled, the expression working against her face's natural function. "Right?"

Gigi did not, in fact, know this, but had enough sense of self-preservation to nod.

The group clocked in, gathering around the table one at a time. The process was foreign to Gigi, the pre-shift ritual barred from her during training. Everyone had their place in the circle, and Gigi found herself a small opening between L2 and O.

The group's well-worn plum scrubs contrasted against her freshly purchased pair, with pendants of protection adorning their tops. Gems and metals and fresh plant sprigs were scattered among the scraggly night crew.

And she felt bare, in every way.

M's abyssal eyes raked the group.

"G's first eulogy. Anyone care to explain?"

O sipped her coffee, raising a hand. "Pre-shift ritual for staff. Someone new goes every shift, and we give a little prayer, word of encouragement. Whatever gets you going, with whatever your beliefs are. Called the eulogy because we're hilarious and this shit's dangerous."

Gigi laughed through the pressure crushing her chest, mistakenly catching L's eye across the circle.

Staring down the barrel.

"New grad," L said.

Gigi's face fell.

"You're up."

"Oh—sure."

Gigi exhaled forcefully through her nose, toes pressing through the soles of her sneakers into the concrete below as her coworkers let their eyes close.

She followed suit, back in her nana's darkened living room on the same night, fifteen years prior.

"May the gods bless us this evening," she began. "Keep us safe through this anniversary night. Keep us well supported by the hospital and each other. And if they don't, give us strength to raise hell on the way out."

Gigi opened her eyes.

"Um — Amen. Or . . . break, I guess."

The group took their time, eyes opening as the wall clock struck 19:00.

M shoved her hands in her pockets.

"All right, you heard the nurse. Everyone, have a good shift, and we will see you on the other side."

Gigi flipped her badge to the blank side with a terse nod, entering West Belfry's medical step-down unit at the back of the pack.

She learned of many hospital idiosyncrasies on her first day at Crowe County. The most important lesson was regarding time and energy within its walls. They wore at the medical floors in strange ways, until they were nothing more than hovels of paranormal energy requiring repair.

Some could be fixed.

Others, like the quarantined shell of Crowe's North Belfry, ceased to exist.

West Belfry 10, she considered, was on its way out.

The unit's seventeen rooms wrapped around three nursing stations, which lined up its center. Each nursing station was small, with a counter shielding the desks. They crowded on islands of tile amidst the carpeted hallway, with mismatched chairs and old food littered about, giving the unit a scent of stale broccoli and sharp varnish.

A glow of stagnant light filtered from the threshold of every nurses' station and patient room, way-lines flickering beneath fluorescence overhead.

Following the night crew, Gigi's sneakers snagged on vast sections of carpet that were worn to their foundation where inscriptions littered the uncovered cement. These were remnants of security improvements after North Belfry's siege, and O reminded staff at least once a shift that half of the sygils were wrong.

Gigi was not surprised by this fact.

Neglect aside, the worst part of West Belfry 10 was the inconsistency.

On certain shifts, the building's foundation shifted and twisted the mind's eye, creating impossible-to-navigate loops. Go for a syringe in supply room 2 and you could exit accidentally into the front nursing pod. Or one might end up in the second-floor cafeteria freezer, where D from medical intensive care was discovered a month before, frozen among the beef shanks.

Wednesday, mostly.

Wednesdays rarely behaved.

There were rumors this phenomenon occurred because the North Belfry fell on a Wednesday, and all the excess spirits unable to be cleansed or purged returned to grasp the hospital with vengeance. But Gigi knew the bigger truth of it all.

Wednesdays weren't special, and every night shift at Crowe County Hospital had the potential to be plucked from a Carpenter film. It was why they made significant shift differential over day shift and had the option for superior life insurance policies.

A symphony of alarms assaulted Gigi, blaring from a central monitor behind the first nurses' station. The screen glitched, its cascade of sound twitching with static. Why they had monitors with the interference in hospitals was beyond Gigi, but she had to admit they were a reassurance when they worked.

Just beyond the malfunctioning equipment was the front nursing station of West Belfry 10. It was the largest of the three stations, stacked high with paper charts sheathed in brown folders.

Gigi placed herself among the night staff with dental floss nerves, falling into the prison lineup of shift huddle.

Charge Nurse, Head Nurse, Captain of their Sinking Ship observed all from behind the desk. Copper beads trimmed her neckline like soldiers, and a single pendant of black tourmaline was strapped to her clipboard with brutal efficiency.

Sometimes she was B and not Charge Nurse. But that was a rare occurrence.

"Evening, everyone. Let's get started. Census is fifteen, but it won't stay that way for long. We have two potential admissions in the ED, and awaiting one late OR case for recovery. For safety concerns, the middle nursing station's way-line is on the fritz. Environmental Services should be up to repair it within the hour, but in the meantime, use station one as your point of egress in case we have unexpected Downtime."

Charge paused, giving staff time for rebuttal before continuing.

"Hospital security asks us to remind staff that exiting the hospital tonight would be inadvisable with anniversary activity throughout the city. Questions?"

M piped up from the back of the group. "What about smoke breaks?"

As if on cue, Charge let loose a cough that purred inside her chest.

"Important question. Security opened the roof tonight for the nicotine addicted. First night I ever seen anything like that, so it must be bad out there. Use your judgment. No Mary's delivery."

A smattering of laughter came from the night crew.

"All right." Charge cleared her throat. "Assignments. O, you will take rooms 1, 2, and 3. I'll have rooms 16, 17 and 18."

O slouched against the counter with scant acknowledgment of Charge as she sipped her sweating iced coffee. "Sure."

Gigi released her watch pendant, wiping her hands on her scrub top.

"L and L2," Charge continued. "Second nurses' station tonight, rooms 4 through 6, with 7 through 11 to divide among yourselves. And 8 is the first admit spot."

L2 leaned toward L. "I can take it—?"

"No." L grimaced. "It's fine, I got it."

L2 patted her friend twice on the shoulder, like the flutter of a butterfly's wing.

"Now the back pod." Charge Nurse looked over her clipboard, directly at Gigi.

Dread built itself a home at the bottom of the young nurse's stomach.

Room 9 tugged at the corner of her eye from directly down the hall, and it appeared like all others—a sterile white doorframe lined in a strip of dim yellow light.

But everyone knew better than to underestimate room 9.

It was the room of tragic codes and profound patient violence. It was home to the spirit of Julie Winter, who'd jumped from the now barred window ten floors to her death, and the room where a pack of shadows tore the flesh from a respiratory therapist like scarabs when the hospital's defenses were down.

It knew violence and death.

It knows fear.

"I know it's your first day off orientation, but the patient was stable all day. Should be appropriate." With a death warrant flourish, Charge Nurse finished writing 9 beside *G2* on the assignment board, trusting the script to speak for itself. "M will be your resource."

Gigi caught M's eye across the crowd, receiving a dry wink.

And that was that.

CHAPTER NINE

Crowe County Hospital,
West Belfry 10, 19:13

igi slumped cautiously after M toward the back nursing station and room 9, where the room sat—when it felt inclined—at the curve of the horseshoe-shaped unit in sight of their desk.

The patient is a fifty-six-year-old gentleman admitted for chronic heart failure. Began to withdraw while he got fixed up, so he's on the ETOH protocol. Discharge set for tomorrow.

Gigi looked into the depths of room 9, where the end of the bed was visible from the doorway. A rustle of bedsheets filtered to the hall as she fired questions at the reporting nurse.

"Have you been medicating?"

"He didn't meet the requirements. Family was at bedside all day, kept him pretty calm."

"Nothing scheduled?"

"Didn't think to ask. Sorry."

Gigi shook her head, prompting Day Nurse to break for the front of the unit. They left Gigi with nothing more than a halfhearted, "I'm back tomorrow."

A lightbulb shattered above Gigi's head.

She jumped, scrambling toward the nurses' station while a wheeze of a laugh raked across the air from room 9. Delicately, she shook a shower of glass from her hair.

"Whatever likes to pop that lightbulb really has it out for maintenance," the young nurse joked meekly to M, who observed from behind the desk. "Third time this week."

"It's your first withdrawal off orientation."

Gigi practiced indifference with a shrug. "Yeah."

Silence wedged into the conversation, the alarm of a distant monitor travelling to their pod.

"Medicate him for everything he needs," M advised. "They're susceptible to increased activity when undermedicated."

"I remember that one during orientation—"

"He doesn't count." M jabbed her pencil toward room 9. "I don't like what I feel in there."

She paused, allowing Gigi to fret.

"Some real fiendish shit can occupy a person when they're going through alcohol withdrawal. Remember? It's—"

"The withdrawal with the highest rate of entity occupation," Gigi answered impatiently. "Yeah, I remember."

M's pencil met the desk with a dull click, the woman pressing her fingertips together in a gesture Gigi recognized well.

She was practicing patience.

Flicking loose carpet with her toe, Gigi backpedaled.

"I'm sorry. It's just . . . I'm nervous. I think I'll be playing catch-up. Day Nurse said he was perfectly fine with family, so he didn't give him any sedation . . ."

The older nurse ruminated on Gigi's worry as the lightbulb filament above room 9 seared white-hot, a firefly against the ceiling tiles. With no glass to destroy and no further fanfare, its filament faded to a tame glow, leaving Gigi to wonder if the entity responsible was disappointed in its lack of destruction.

"Well . . ." M sighed, rubbing the bridge of her nose. "Check your other patients first. Do your best, and let me know when you need help."

Let her know when you need help.

Gigi adjusted her badge.

Twice.

Three times.

Or you could allow yourself to be completely overwhelmed all on your own until help is the only way out of the mess you manage to create.

As certain as a nonclairvoyant could be about a course of future events, Gigi removed herself from the nurses' station and stepped across the way-line of room 9.

My name is G2, and I'll be your nurse tonight.

The patient's slick ponytail trailed along his protruding spine while he perched on his hospital bed like a gargoyle.

My name is G2, and I'll be your nurse tonight.

An unknowable expression pulled to his earlobes, mouth wide and eyes drilled into the ground as a hospital gown clung to his shoulders like an animal hide of faded teal checkerboard.

My name is G2.

Rhythmic ticks of Nana's copper timepiece filled the silence of the room, settling the uncertainty prickling Gigi's skin.

I'll be your nurse tonight.

She cleared her throat. "Hello. My name is G2, and I'll be your nurse tonight."

Success.

The words hung between them, an unpleasant smell on a windless day.

Gigi's smile fixed itself as she addressed the bird of prey white-knuckling his footboard. "What is your moniker?"

"Gregory."

Something in her shriveled. "You're really not supposed to use your full name."

"Gregory."

His stale sclera was visible from where Gigi stood at the door, the whites of his eyes sickly yellow as they probed a floor-to-ceiling window in the back corner. Musky sunset clashed with the sterility, wrestling the room's white fluorescent light into a distorted yellow glow. The heavy cream monitor bolted to the wall above his head put up a fight with its own blue tinge, adding to the artificial veneer bathing the furniture.

An antiquated porcelain sink sat under a mirror to the right of the door, its clouded glass scattering the light into its depths. The man's gaze fixed on this light show, staring into the reflective surface without reprieve.

Gigi's smile wavered, her sneakers squeaking against broken tile as she crossed to the sink. Pinching a black scrim bunched at the top of the mirror, she flicked it deftly to cover the glass.

"Both of our names start with G, Gregory. How funny."

Gregory's toes dug into the mattress, his brow stretching skyward as the cloth fell over the mirror before he diverted his attention to the nurse.

She mined for civil discussion. "Your family visited today?"

"Yes."

"Did you enjoy their visit?"

Gregory responded with a distant appraisal. "My family is nervous in hospitals."

Same.

Gigi scuffed her sneaker against the floor as a mumbled message passed through overhead speakers in the hall.

"It is now the end of visiting hours. Visitors, for your safety and the safety of our patients, please exit the building in an orderly fashion. Exemptions may retrieve their extended visitor's pass with signed waivers in the West Belfry security office. Thank you."

Static. Then silence.

Gregory's thick hands flexed, fingertips pressing one by one into his thumb. He extended his wrist, bringing a metal band clamped where a watch might go inches from his eyes. The identification number seared into the jewelry was distinct, a patented Crowe design for patient protection, echoing the color of the way-line.

"Gregory?"

He lowered his arm with a growl.

"What?"

Gigi retracted her shoulders, taking a step away from the bed. The man stared, a blank expression fixed on hers.

Everything about his look shook the nurse to her core.

"Why don't you lie back? It's safer for you."

Gregory's attention persisted as he crawled to the head of the bed, tangling himself further in his monitor wires. Relief siphoned through Gigi's spine like a sieve, watching the patient settle against his pillows.

"Wonderful. Thank you. That's . . . that's safer, I think."

Gregory resumed his distant inspection of the sink. Without a word.

"Well, it's nice to meet you. I'll be back soon. Just . . . ring if you need anything?"

M sat at the nurses' station, scribbling an assessment on charts stacked high on pod 3's desk. The pencil wavered as gigi stepped over the way-line, the older nurse scrutinizing her charge.

"What's wrong?"

Gigi clutched her watch to feel its thready march.

"I don't know. He seems off, but . . . I don't know if he's strange or if he's exhibiting symptoms."

M's lips pursed into a thin line. "Do an assessment. If he fits the criteria, give him some medication. He's got access?"

"Yeah, he does. I just don't know if . . ." Gigi trailed off as mumbled conversation drifted from the depths of Gregory's room.

M set the pencil down, her eyes raking over the way-line, which breathed itself to life in a wildfire of vibrant orange. Gigi recognized the distance in her mentor's gaze from afternoons in her grandparents' living room, from breakfasts at a small kitchen nook. Memories of Nana's fantastical "conversations" with household energies filled her head as M removed her spectacles, squinting at the door.

There was a comfort to the display, despite Gregory's indecipherable mutterings from within room 9, while M read something in the air. Something not quite here and not quite there.

Gregory's one-sided conversation subsided.

Thirty-seven.

The young nurse exhaled for the first time in thirty-seven seconds, apprehension built like a house of cards between them.

"Notice anything useful?"

Donning her spectacles, M abandoned the fading way-line for her paperwork.

"It's not right in there, G. Be careful."

The house of cards crumpled, and Gigi took that as her cue to leave.

Crowe County Hospital,
West Belfry 10, 20:19

"Gregory?"

The man stood at the sink, lost in the uncovered mirror. Monitor wires trailed behind him like tentacles, while parchment skin made him into a living corpse, a wax figure come to life. His gaze was glued to the glass, and Gigi could only imagine what appeared to a corpse in a hospital mirror—staring into it as if he could see God, his back bathed in the empty glow of the monitor.

"Do you know"—stretched the low lilt of his voice—"how good I am to my wife?"

Though not a choice, Gigi's silence was present. And it was deafening.

He spoke again. "That waif was beaten and broken. I picked her up. I'm *good* to that bitch."

Heels firmly on the way-line, Gigi leaned forward inches to match Gregory's stare in the looking glass, his gaunt eyes pinning hers like a butterfly to cork.

". . . I'm sure you are, Gregory."

"Don't sound so righteous."

Doing my best, you terrifying piece of shit.

"I think you should get back to bed."

The man's neck bent, his body rooted in place.

"Is that what you *think*?"

Spittle flew from the corners of his mouth as Gregory's eyes wandered to the vial of amber liquid pinched between Gigi's fingers. A hunter's expression followed her shaking hands as they siphoned the syrup from its container, but the nurse was busy remembering her staples of medication administration.

We have a patient.

There he is. Gregory, drooling on his gown, which I inevitably have to clean.

Giving it at the correct time.

It's 19:35. Only eleven more hours 'til I can clock out.

It's the correct amount.

A stupidly small amount of sedation for too large a man, coming right up.

I can put it where I need it to go.

Coming at you, forearm IV.

Gigi approached Gregory like she would a snapping turtle, anticipating a spring-loaded neck poised to pierce her skin. But he complied, his waxen features unmoving. He raised his arm, allowing her access to the IV.

She threaded a syringe of saline to the extension tubing with clumsy imprecision, depressing the flush with her thumb.

A clear saline pool gathered where the catheter hub met Gregory's skin, dripping sluggishly from his forearm. In suspended time, it hit the floor, wetting a sliver of jagged linoleum beside Gigi's shoe.

It was blown.

Fucking fuck, god dammit to hell, motherfucker.

The young nurse found Gregory's eyes, inches from her own.

Shit.

His hand was around her wrist faster than she could react, the flush swinging like a hanged man from the dead IV.

"Let go!"

Distance closed between them as his hand clamped down.

"Your wrist, it's so small."

"Gregory—"

"I could break it," he muttered.

Gigi freed herself in a single wrench, stumbling from the sink.

"Stop."

A cackle cut the air, Gregory gleefully matching her step for step as Gigi scrambled backward. "Stop it!"

Gregory's breath was a foul haze that seeped into the back of her neck. Disarming. Gigi froze at the way-line, overcome by the wet wood-rot stench pouring from his skin.

The world tilted gently, and she reached to clutch the doorframe, growing warmer under her hand.

What —

Gigi was pulled through the doorway, stumbling into the hallway inches from a familiar face.

Kind.

Concerned.

M did not wait for Gigi to recover, removing her firmly from the threshold.

"Pod 2 is calling security. Are you okay?"

A shout from room 9 left the question to die.

"Let the little one come back and play!"

The IV catheter hurtled from the room, grazing Gigi's ear. She swiped at her face, whirling on Gregory, his bleeding arm on full display. Scowling in the way-line's glow.

Sweat raced down the young nurse's spine, gathering at her waistband as the man took a long drag from the hallway air, savoring it like a cigarette. The way-line flared to life in response, its orange tinge forcing him back into room 9.

The line stymied him. For now.

"I, um . . . yeah, I'll be okay," Gigi lied. "But I think we need a new IV . . ."

M frowned, the pressure of her hands guiding Gigi to the nurses' station. "Okay, new IV. Simple enough."

The intercom crackled overhead.

"Attention please. Code Gray, Security Assist, West 10. Code Gray, Security Assist, West 10."

Gigi clenched the empty vial of medication in her pocket, anticipation seated in her marrow. Room 9's contested way-line flushed the hallway, its light brushing her skin a deep red.

M walked. Gigi was on her heel.

"What now?"

"We get the meds you have ordered, and we prepare." M moved to the medication dispensary within nursing station 3.

"Security will get him down, and then it is our job to get access and treat him. Grab his chart so we can verify the meds."

Gigi reached for the brown folder on the desk, the thin file a quick read.

"We have lorazepam and midazolam if needed."

"Great, so we will grab them both," M continued, a steady tone crawling into the preceptor roll she recently shed. "We worry about his airway with the sedation, so Charge is calling the ICU in case intubation is needed. Since you're cross-trained, you'd most likely follow him if he ended up needing that level of care."

Gigi's hand travelled to her watch, feeling the second hand against her palm, half the rate of her heart.

"I'll grab the code cart?"

The medication in M's pockets clattered as she turned to Gigi. There was a beat of consideration, where Gigi could hardly maintain eye contact with the blackened sclera of her mentor.

"Yes," M said finally. "That would be best."

Without a word, Gigi hurried to station 2.

L and L2 stood at the edge of their tile island, watching her soundlessly heave the code cart from its home beside their pod.

"Are we expecting a medical emergency?" L asked.

Gigi tugged a hand through her hair, pausing to knot it on the top of her head.

"Potentially . . . I'm not really sure how this will play out. I don't think M is either."

L2 shook her head, brown curls bobbing perfectly with the motion. "That's a scary thought, but you could not be in more capable hands."

Gigi allowed a small smile, erased by the sudden chorus of voices from the front of the unit. Her eyes darted down the hall, managing a step before her arm was caught in a firm grip.

The soles of her sneakers scuttled across the exposed cement as L dragged her to the nurses' station.

"Is that them?"

"Oh, yes." L crossed her arms carefully, a hunter's gaze tracking two people moving their way swiftly down the hall. "New players on the board."

The elder sported a well-kept buzz cut flecked with salt and pepper. Distinguished. Proud appearing. He walked with a steady soundless gait, steel-toed boots striding across exposed cement with purpose. A pale scar shouted across his jaw, disappearing beneath the wolf-gray collar signatory of Crowe Hospital's security personnel.

Benign at first glance, closer examination exposed his button-up and slacks were punctuated with chest loops and holsters, where chittering glass vials and two knives hung in defensive array. The figure's presence grew with each step, holding himself with the stature of a man who knew his job and knew it well, though crow's feet around his eyes bent to the ground, ladened with time and exhaustion.

Gigi did not need to read his badge to know there was an *S* in aged typeface. He was a guard most children in Crowe County knew by name.

Stew Michelin.

The second guard was a handful of years Gigi's senior and possessed a lighter step. He held himself confidently in the wolf-gray slacks, with a broad silhouette that consumed the hall. While his uniform did not hold the same wear as his partner, the weaponized accessories were the same. Coarse auburn hair clung thickly to his head and jaw in dense curls, masking an easy grin.

His badge read *N*, partially covered by the tip of his beard.

Not-Stew, perhaps.

Watching them pass from her position at the center station, Gigi noted the nurses around her observe the duo's entrance through the length of the hallway. The night crew was frozen in place, carefully observing the pair.

O chewed on the straw from her coffee like a cigar, exchanging inaudible words with Charge that made the older woman frown. Standing so close, Gigi could feel the kinetic force between the Ls as they each stepped a fraction of an inch in front of her.

The guards seemed to do their best to not notice the fear they wrought.

There was a mutual understanding that safety in numbers existed on both sides, and the guards stayed in step as they passed.

"Good evening." Stew passed with a tired smile and a careful greeting.

Gigi's reply stalled on her tongue as the man's face flashed in her memory. He appeared beside Daniel Fjord in his orange bow tie, standing at the man's shoulder. Younger then. But grossly familiar.

He lived in infamy within Crowe County.

A lump clogged Gigi's throat, but she slipped between the Ls, quietly falling in step behind the guards. Or as quietly as one could while dragging a code cart that wanted to go any direction but straight.

Not-Stew turned to the source of the ruckus, quirking an eyebrow before falling back a step to help steer the belligerent cart.

The corners of his eyes crinkled, and she could almost make out a smile beneath the beard.

"Thanks."

"Of course."

He paused, a single thought wrestling across his face in the span of an instant. The way he grappled with the information he was processing, she assumed this thought was life or death. Of the utmost importance.

The man sucked in a breath, tossing a glance to Stew Michelin before saying, "They don't train these things very well, do they?"

Stew groaned.

"That was *funny*, S. I promise you, it was."

"What was funny?" M stepped from the third nursing station with the same clatter to her pockets.

The elder guard shared her stoic demeanor, his posture unfaltering. "A low-quality joke."

M levelled her gaze on Gigi. Disappointed, maybe?

Stew noticed, waving a hand dismissively. "No, no. From mine. His humor isn't great."

Gigi choked on a laugh, placing the code cart against the wall. The young guard gave a valiant effort at being shamed, but the pride in his eye was unmistakable.

Stew exchanged a tepid greeting with M. "What is the situation here?"

"G has a withdrawal patient that she believes has been taken over," M said. "He is in need of new venous access and sedation. Also becoming combative."

Not-Stew's brow furrowed. Warmth stained Gigi's cheeks as he leaned against the other side of the desk to listen.

"Combative how? Could this be benign agitation?"

"He grabbed me," Gigi interrupted, her flush

deepening at the speculation. "Threw an IV from the way-line 'cause it prevented him from crossing."

The information marinated between the guards before Stew picked up the questioning.

"Any prior history?"

"Not that I know of."

"Will a chaplain be needed?"

The mention was a nine volt to the brain.

A chaplain.

Gigi stepped over a knot of carpet into the nurses' station to place the desk between herself and Stew in a maneuver she did not attempt to mask.

The mention of a chaplain wasn't a threat. But it was close enough.

"I don't know."

Stew responded tersely.

"You didn't 'sense' anything when you were in there with him? Anything that might give you that indication?"

Gigi whipped an uncertain look at M, who sat stiffly at the desk.

"I . . ." Gigi said. "No, I don't have any . . . psychically I can't . . . I mean, um."

She gestured to herself, head to toe.

"This dog don't hunt."

If she were a curated museum exhibit, Gigi imagined the guards would've looked at her the same way they did in that moment.

Like an eel with three heads.

"Well." Stew spoke carefully. "I am certain medicine will be a very prolific career choice for you, even without abilities."

"Moot point," M sniped from her chair. "Let's get on with this, S. A plan, please, before I die of old age."

Stew admitted the younger guard in his place, positioning his hands behind his back, his mood an amalgam of distance and intrigue.

Not-Stew leaned into the nurses' station, near enough that Gigi could smell peppermint gum masking the faint scent of cigarettes on his breath. The younger man's hands wrung over the counter, picking at his thumbnail.

"With potential entity occupation," he began, "I would like to take a nonaggressive approach to see if we can deescalate. If that's unhelpful, we will restrain and get access for the medication cascade. S?"

"Reasonable."

Not-Stew addressed Gigi with a twitch of his auburn beard. "You ever done one of these before?"

"Not like this, no."

"Sounds like we're gonna have a good time, then." He smiled, and Gigi's shoulders relaxed incrementally from her ears. "Do y'all's code carts have the cleansing drawers like the Emergency Department's?"

Gigi gratefully removed her attention from the terse elders, moving for the equipment.

"Yeah, they should. Lemme see."

A forceful tug popped the code cart lock through the air, its top drawer illuminated by the way-line. Jars of dried herbs were lined in the upper aspect, above bags with sloppy notes tacked to their front labelled *blessed water*. Syringes beneath them marched like soldiers, each brightly colored with indicators for different oils, their colors a rainbow of familiarity.

The burst of musky perfume from the drawer hit Gigi's nose, and she breathed in slowly.

Like home.

Vials strapped to the young guard's vest clattered in her left ear as he disturbed the dense drawer, piling supplies on top of the cart.

"Blessed normal saline flushes," he narrated, with the lilt of a child on Christmas. "Used to cleanse from the inside if we have access. We can also start a drip, but that can be dangerous depending on their other issues. A lot of strain on the body."

Gigi nodded along, eyes tracking each instrument as they moved through his hands.

"They got all sorts of engraved syringes and whatnot in here too, but I don't know how to work those medically, so that's all you." He chuckled, the laugh filling him from stem to stern. "We use a lot of topicals. Infused lotions for recovery. Oils for burning or application on the affected person if the water ain't cutting it."

He put his hands on his hips, observing his collection atop the cart. "You got any ques—"

"—What about the four-corner incense?"

"Four corner . . .?"

The guard's question travelled over Gigi, where Stew stood removed from the nurses' station. And M, by design.

"Incense used in some craft. For containment and cleansing," he said. "Calling in the four directions or the elements to aid in the cause. Chaplain will bring that, 'cause it's usually a practice preference of theirs."

Not-Stew processed the information like a dial-up computer, returning the conversation to the nurse, delighted. "Seems we're both destined to learn something tonight."

A small knock punctured the air like a nail, deflating any comfort gleaned from the lesson.

Gregory was framed in room 9's doorway, quietly observing the cluster of practitioners. His knuckle rapped once on the wooden frame, before replacing the hand on his bleeding arm.

A change overtook his visage, performative gentleness under a searing red way-line.

"Can I trouble one of you for a Band-Aid?" he rasped.

Both guards straightened themselves, and Gigi

watched the genial eyes of Not-Stew harden with the flick of a switch.

Stew spoke first, his voice steady.

"Good evening, sir. We can certainly arrange that for you."

Gregory turned his attention on Stew, emotion flitting across his face that was almost too delicate to place.

But it was there, and Gigi claimed the emotion as her own.

Recognition.

The guards approached the room, Stew continuing to face their operation.

"We're going to join you for a chat, sir. Would you rather it be here or on your bed?"

Gregory's eyes were feverishly bright as he removed himself from the doorway.

"The room will be fine. Nurse said I have to sit on my bed anyways. Take it easy, you know?"

"Of course."

The three retreated to the confines of room 9, its inky mire swallowing them into its depths.

M was moving before the final person disappeared from sight.

"S and I have worked together a long time, through the fall of North Belfry," she said, heaving the code cart outside room 9. "Apparently he forgot his own shortcomings as a new hire, or he would not be so severe."

"Shortcomings?"

M's hands sifted through supplies, exchanging blessed saline syringes with her response.

"Let's just say that most of your history books are true, in that regard. You go in. I'll be right out here if you need me, okay?"

Nope.

"Okay."

CHAPTER TEN

Crowe County Hospital,
West Belfry 10, 21:05

S ir, will you sit on the bed?"

Gigi stood just inside room 9, uneasily toeing the sway-line.

Gregory sat gingerly on the edge of his mattress. In just the short time they were apart, his body had decompensated, with hollow eyes sunk into his face and pale chapped lips.

His façade of normalcy was thin as he addressed the guards.

"How can I help you?"

Stew pulled a chair from the wall, sitting a stone's throw from the patient. Not-Stew took up space beside him. The younger guard's hands were steady, held before himself in an easy way.

"Sir, my name is S, and this is N," Stew continued in his diplomat's tone. "As you can probably tell by our uniforms, we are here from hospital security."

No response.

"Do you understand why?"

Gregory's porcelain face cracked a grin, and the way-line quivered beneath Gigi's shoe with each syllable he spoke. "It has to be some form of misunderstanding."

"From what I was told, you accosted one of the nurses. Misunderstanding or not, you can see why it has to be investigated."

"Oh my, yes, I'm sorry. That was unfortunate of me."

"And why was that?"

"The mirror. I was standing in front of the mirror, and she took me by surprise. Even lost my IV in the process."

Gigi leaned forward into the room, noting the black scrim lying like a wounded bird on the floor, leaving the mirror exposed. Her stomach roiled, recounting his hand in a vise grip on her wrist.

The smell.

Stew placed his hands delicately on his lap with a twitch of his lip.

"We're going to replace your access to place another IV. There is suspicion you're withdrawing, and as is common knowledge, this leaves you open for entity occupation. Our goal is to prevent that."

Gregory's stale smile fell a fraction.

"It would be ideal," Stew continued, "if you would cooperate by allowing your nurse to replace your IV so we can deliver proper treatment. If you don't, we will have to restrain you for the safety of yourself and your practitioners. Can you work within those expectations?"

A moment suspended between the two, like children engaged in a staring contest, blowing in the other's eye to make them blink.

Gregory didn't.

"Of course."

Stew gestured at the door for Gigi, though he remained in his staring contest with the patient.

Gigi stepped into the room, the atmosphere around her shoulders thickened to the consistency of soup. Dense and humid. Beads of sweat dripped from her hairline, the nape of her neck, and all the supplies she laid out beside Gregory were damp in her hands.

She tightened the tourniquet around his arm, looking for a site with Not-Stew by her side.

"This is going to be a big pinch."

Gigi's finger prepped the catheter like a dart, bracing for Gregory's jack-in-the-box self as she plunged the needle into his arm. Blood return flashed back with satisfaction. With it, a whisper, snaking between Gigi's thoughts.

"Excuse me?"

Not-Stew started at the sudden address. "What?"

"You didn't say something?"

"No."

The whispers grew, a cacophony of screams, the storm of pleas screeching across Gigi's thoughts.

She jumped, hurrying to wrap the IV under her thumb before chancing a glance at Gregory. His attention was unrelenting, and words that were not her own floated through her mind.

Free us.

Gigi swallowed, quietly swapping a syringe of blessed saline onto his IV tubing. Sweat pooled in her shoes, the screaming escalating in volume as the entity inside Gregory reached out to communicate, battering her thoughts.

Free us.

"No thanks."

Her thumb depressed the syringe, flooding his arm with the saline.

Gregory's shriek shattered the thousands of screams in her head to dust.

The patient's heavy hands gripped her scrub top, and Gigi lost her purchase on the ground before being launched into the doorway. She fell to the floor, a sharp pain coursing through her hip.

It happened in a heartbeat.

Wind gushed from within the shoebox room. It whipped from hairline cracks in the plaster, while the searing way-line clashed with gray steam unfolding from beneath the bed. From within Gregory's mouth, his eyes.

The man twitched like a marionette, his limbs plucked by imaginary strings. From the doorway, Gigi watched Gregory's body writhe, a single twitch flinging him into the ceiling.

M was beside Gigi in the doorway, heaving her to her feet.

"Are you okay?"

Absolutely not.

"Yeah!" Gigi rubbed her chin as it throbbed. "He hits like my grandmother."

Hard.

Gregory dragged himself fist over fist to the lighting fixture above the bed. Laminate showered the practitioners as his knuckles splintered the fluorescent's covering, gutting it with a single stroke.

"Restraints!" Stew demanded.

Gregory heaved bile into the wind, creating acidic rain that stung Gigi's cheeks.

"Got 'em!"

M shoved four slithering ropes into Gigi's hands. They snaked around her ankles as she dragged them into the room. They were silvered and branded, their script ancient. State-issued and intricately engraved, they slithered along the broken tile. The nurse skirted the room, handing off the supplies without time for thanks before retreating.

Stew collided with the footboard, silver chains clenched in his readied fists.

Not-Stew circled the bed, uncorking a vial of pungent oil from his vest. He flicked the thick liquid toward the ceiling, and the stench of charcoal permeated the small room from the soles of Gregory's feet.

The patient screeched, crawling fist over fist across the ceiling. Meaty hands gripped the wall monitor, ripping through its cinder block mount as he threw his body backward over and over.

"You're on left! I'm on right!" Stew commanded, leaping onto the bed with two straps in hand and taking full advantage of the patient ripping at his monitor to wrestle an ankle into a restraint.

"Right secure!"

Gregory snarled, whirling on Stew. The distraction left Not-Stew able to deftly contain the left.

But there was a game here, and Gregory knew it.

The young guard pulled taut on the chain without Stew picking up slack on his side. Gregory followed the momentum of the restraint, his foot slamming into the side of Not-Stew's head with a crack that split the air.

The young guard's body seized, crumpling off the bed, out of sight.

Gregory lunged after him in feral fixation, only held away by Stew falling on his own chain, keeping the leash taut.

NO.

Gigi's feet found traction with strength firmly rooted in fear. She covered the room in three bounds, over Not-Stew's crumpled form, to throw her weight on his abandoned restraint. Gregory's bloodied forearms sprang inches from her shoulder, stopped by Stew heaving backward again like a fisherman.

Gregory's face stalled inches from her own, screeching spittle from his acrid mouth.

But the marionette was acquiring strings.

She turned her face from the assault. "What do I fucking do? Tell me what to fucking do!"

Stew wrapped his chain once, twice around his forearms. "Get him to the bed!"

Nursing school drills were in the forefront of Gigi's mind as she pulled hand over fist on Gregory's restraints. They spoke through these protocols in class, mimicking deescalating techniques her antiquated instructors swore would work at bedside.

She'd stood at the back of a group of nursing students while the "psychiatric patient" from the acting school paced and raved, and her classmates succeeded in their clumsy attempt at reason.

Nothing prepared her for the silver chains digging trenches into her palms, how they seared Gregory's leg as she pinned it to the mattress and lashed him to the bed rail.

"Left leg's down!"

Okay, that should be fine. This is fine. We're fine.

"Right is too!" Stew's response was buffeted by the winds, but he grappled for purchase on Gregory's arms as the man lunged for Gigi.

The tips of her patient's jagged nails sent her heels over head into Not-Stew, hitting the linoleum for the second time.

A trickle of blood dripped from his hairline as the dazed guard blinked slowly at her from the ground, struggling to his knees. Gigi grabbed the second restraint beside him, throwing herself onto the bed. She wrestled Gregory's arm into the slithering chain like an elaborate handshake, his charred skin flaking into the air as the ancient effigy seared his wrists.

Gigi rolled from the mattress, falling on the restraint to secure it to the bed rail with a *click.*

A screech of pain drowned her senses as Gregory craned his neck toward her. "Bitch!"

Gigi's shaking hands fumbled for the watch on her lapel, the chains sliding against the bed as Gregory lashed out again and again. "I'm going to blow your tits off and shove your head through the fucking wall!"

He's tied down. You're okay . . . I'm okay . . . I'm . . .

Stew mirrored her success as Gigi scuttled directly into Not-Stew, huddled on the tile.

Are you okay?

Gigi blinked, focusing on Not-Stew with renewed determination. She reached for his head automatically, careful to avoid his bleeding temple.

"Are you okay?"

Not-Stew grimaced, bracing himself as she helped him to his feet. "I'm fine. I'll be fine. Are you?"

Gregory thrashed. His wild eyes trained on the practitioners as violent insults came in a ceaseless barrage. Gigi nodded a fraction of an inch, losing the conversation in racing thoughts as the wind died around them.

Are you?

Stew met the two where they stood, examining his partner.

"What happened?"

"Good knock to the head." Not-Stew groaned. "I'll be okay."

Stew turned to Gigi, giving her a swift pat on the shoulder. "That was strong work. We are going to see if we can uncouple this entity from his host, if you would be so kind to get us supplies."

Gigi's eyes stung as the adrenaline fled her limbs. "Thank you. I'll, um . . . I'll have M help us get ready."

She ducked around the guards, bile nipping at Gigi's throat as she hurried for the way-line.

I have no idea what I'm doing.

As she peered into the clarity of the hallway from room 9, Gigi saw a gathering by the third nurses' station.

O perched on the counter, her scarred filigree prominent from the short distance. A comforting familiarity. L's sharp features were scrutinizing and concerned, the semblance of tender emotion intensifying as L2 murmured to the group, causing any intact lights to flicker a sickly beige above them.

Observing her chaos.

Why am I here?

Seasoned nurses sat before her, all too skeptical of the devolving situation to be of any help. They allowed M to approach the doorway, sitting as specters in the background.

That was the mentor's job, after all. To handle this kind of danger.

To be a friend.

The older nurse gripped Gigi's shoulder as she stepped across the cracked way-line.

"Can I help?"

Gigi nodded, tears racing to her collarbone.

The weight of M's distant gaze sat square on her person as she closed ranks. Vials clinked gently in her hand, amber syrup sloshing along their glass walls as she maneuvered syringes with dexterous precision, siphoning her doses.

"You're okay. We're going to get through this." M pivoted to root herself between Gigi and the bed. "Take a minute. I'll step in."

Without hesitation, Gigi retreated to the corner, bracing her hands against the sink. Nausea bubbled in the crook of her throat as her hands clutched the rim, the electricity of the room prickling up her bent spine. Gigi sucked the thinning air, ozone filling her lungs, twisting the mirror's scrim in her fingers like a death shawl tangled around the faucet. Its rough crinoline needled her palms.

Breath came through stiff ribs. Short. Labored. Sucking in the humidity around her like pond water sitting in her lungs. Noise from the chaos at her back punctured the air like gunfire, fading to a dull roar that pounded against her ears.

Something pulled at the tips of her eyelashes.

Her grip on the sink intensified, crumpling the useless scrim in her fists, the pull on her eyes more pronounced. Magnetic.

Something was directing her.

Something wanted her.

Every follicle of hair on her head lifted as a tidal wave of goose bumps flooded her scalp. And, Gigi allowed her gaze to travel to the uncovered mirror.

To stare into its dusky abyss.

Through unremarkable giftless eyes, she latched onto a blotchy reflection.

Hers. Frightened and disappointed and fearful.

The reflection wasted no time, giving in to despair as it leaned over the sink, heaving sobs from somewhere deep in its chest. They robbed Gigi of her own breath, falling in line with the reflection as it hitched, gulped for air.

Gigi observed quietly as the porcelain carried her doppelganger's tears into the rusted drain, swirling. The reflection retched into the sewers. Loose curls tumbled into the tears, and Gigi reached for her own, fingertips brushing a knot of hair secured atop her head.

This isn't me . . .

A whisper tickled Gigi's right ear.

"She will be . . ."

The reflection abruptly slumped over the sink. Limp.

A tide of deep crimson seeped from the dense curls, filling the stained porcelain sink in a blink.

"Gigi . . ."

The whisper ground thought and sense to dust, a misplaced voice calling out as the reflection disappeared in a thick tide of blood overflowing onto the floor. Gigi recoiled, dragging her eyes from the sink's reflection to another pair in the glass. A ravenous gaze.

Gaunt.

Skeletal.

Gregory sniffed, exhaling into her ear as a lightbulb sighed to death above the sink.

Stale words seeped onto her cheek as the glow of his eyes cut through the dark.

"Protect your name."

A Cheshire grin stretched Gregory's parchment skin.

"Gigi."

No.

The nurse stumbled from the mirror into nothing but air, surfacing from the reflection with remnants of Gregory's taunts gripping her senses.

Gigi's shaking hand gripped the watch pinned by her badge, its ticking silenced by whispers ricocheting in her skull. The harsh concrete barely resonated beneath her sneaker's thin sole as she stomped to try to feel anything. Anything real.

M hunched over Gregory's arm, placing an IV as Stew and Not-Stew righted a bedside table, laying oils across its pocked surface with intention and focus. No one but Gigi paid attention to Gregory, who remained still as a corpse, lost in the mirror and all that lay within it.

Gigi double-checked her badge.

Triple-checked.

He knows . . .

G2.

Two Gs.

Fuck.

Fear overtaking her, overwhelming her, she tensed to run, fast and far. But there was nowhere to run, nowhere to escape. Once it was done with Gregory, it would move on.

It would find her.

Words spewed from Gigi's mouth, thick with fear.

"He knows my name."

M spared a glance from her new IV. "What?"

Every thought in Gigi's head ground to a halt but one.

"H-he . . . he knows my name!"

Silence.

The Stews turned sour-milk gray as a gentle breeze rustled the younger's auburn beard. Teasing, a whisper began in the back of Gigi's mind. Faint, but growing in volume, it dug into her temples, seeped through her skull.

Gigi . . .

Gregory began to laugh. Cackle. The glee broke from somewhere deep within his chest, splintering the headboard in two with a deafening crack.

"He knows my name! He knows my—"

M sprang across the way-line, and the overhead speaker came to life in the moments it took the Stews to respond.

"Code Gray, Chaplain Assist. West 10."

Everything was still.

And then, it wasn't.

Carefully laid oils shattered as a sharp gust of wind slammed into the room. The Stews abandoned words in a desperate scramble to resecure their bonds, barely containing Gregory's limbs as he renewed his thrashing with otherworldly strength. His crepe paper skin seared at the effort, burnt flesh assaulting Gigi's nostrils.

The whisper grew in volume, digging into the top of her spine as the room blurred.

Gigi.

"Stop!"

She stumbled into Not-Stew as her heels skirted the doorway. The way-line's violent glow illuminated his thick hand grasping her wrist, holding her in place while his branded palms scraped her skin like daggers. Mere moments aged him years as he shifted to block Gregory from her sight, of Stew planting himself on the man's chest. Violent banishment cascaded from Stew Michelin's mouth, torturous words that made a frantic folly in her mind as the entity dug in.

"Into the ether we commit thee!"

"He's in your head!" Not-Stew roared, violent wind consuming his words. "You can't leave until you're cleansed or we deal with this!"

Gigi searched within the young man's warning, beyond the unwelcomed company's thoughts pressing into recesses of her mind. Screams swelled over her thoughts, a typhoon of pain shattering her will. In that moment, Gigi knew where these screams originated.

Ripping her arm from Not-Stew's grasp, the way-line nipped at her spine like a molten dog. The heat seared her scrubs, stinging her back.

"I don't want to be cleansed!"

Not-Stew held his hands open before her, palms out. A five-pointed star rose from his flesh, brandings illuminated in the light from the doorway of room 9.

Leave.

Metallic blood ran down the back of Gigi's throat. She forced a swallow, tears flowing freely down her cheeks like trails of acid.

I'll keep you safe.

"But . . . it'll burn me!" Gigi sobbed, the way-line's heat melting the heels of her shoes.

The screams renewed in response, swelling to life like a radio, crackling through her consciousness.

Not-Stew fought the room's chaos with a round of reason. "You don't have to leave! You don't have to hurt yourself! We can help you. The chaplain can help!"

Throttled screams were brought to a crescendo at once in a flash of white. Gigi's fingers flew to her scalp, digging into her roots as fire burned behind her eyes.

Not-Stew was nothing but a gray blur before her as the whisper continued its battery, echoing in the void of her thoughts.

Run, Gigi.

"I can't . . ."

Free me.

Not-Stew's voice was an echo at best. "Hey! No, come back! Fuck. She's . . . she's down!"

Gregory's presence snaked among the crevices and cracks of her mind like smoke unfurling from an extinguished candle. The world came into view in a blur, through eyes that weren't hers.

She watched Gregory's limbs screaming against heavy chains, and those limbs were her own, sweat pooling on her chest as she thrashed against sopping wet sheets. The metal bed frame crashed into her back over and over, searing pain swelling in her chest worsened by Stew's knees crushing into her sternum.

In her new sight, she saw the auburn-haired guard, stooped by a way-line that roared across his features, contorted in fear.

In his arms was a slight figure, dressed in plum scrubs that twitched as her vacant eyes fixed on the ceiling.

Anger swelled in Gigi's borrowed chest.

Useless piece of shit! Get up!

A shadow appeared, its presence filling the doorway like a stone, applying gentle pressure as it assessed the space.

Gregory's torment paused for an instant as the chaplain stepped into the room.

Tight black curls clutched the stranger's scalp, bright almond eyes meeting Gigi's with ease. Stretched earlobes bore the weight of copper spangles tinkling painfully through the wind, with tattooed symbols barely darker than the hands they marked.

Gigi was struck with a fear that was not hers, hearing the chaplain's firm voice collide with the whisper in her head.

"You don't belong here."

With immense effort, Gigi unlatched a hand from her hair in a reflexive grasp, the world reeling as she was flung back to her own eyes, looking up at the chaplain who stood beside her in stark contrast to the turbulent room. Her eyes fixed on Gigi, as if the woman was able to make out every fish and plant existing below the surface of an ocean.

A forever gaze.

Without a word, the chaplain strolled into the fray.

M broke through the way-line on the chaplain's heels, and Gigi met her mentor's attention with a tepid smile, blinking M into focus through tear-stained eyes.

She managed a croak. "I'm scared, M."

The nurse gripped Gigi's shoulders, every muscle taut as her faraway eyes raked her charge. "No reason to be, G. You are going to be okay. Your brother's been called, and he's . . . he's gonna come up when the unit gets off lockdown, okay?"

Gigi longed for the familiar face. "Thank you . . ."

"No thanks needed. It's protocol. Now, I have to go help. You . . . You're just gonna sit this one out." M paused, throwing Not-Stew a warning glance as she stood. "You. Keep her safe."

Not-Stew did not respond but aided Gigi to sit against the doorframe as M joined the fray.

Gigi managed to breathe once.

Twice.

Stew dug his knees into Gregory's chest, slinging an exorcism as the chaplain and M crammed clumps of greenery in the four corners of the room, lighting them ablaze. The scented smoke snaked through the air as the chaplain drew symbols on each wall with her palms, pink salt splashing onto the concrete with intention in each granule.

Gigi recognized the steps, the protection, remembering a jar of similar salt in her grandma's yellow kitchen, how safe it felt lining the doors. The gentle tick of her watch settled in the air around her, pinned to Nana's white dress on a hanger in her mind's eye, white hosiery soaking beneath gray water in the bathroom sink.

Incremental peace settled in Gigi's bones as she looked to the young guard, finding him through the memory.

"Tell me the truth," she croaked, watching Not-Stew's face twitch at the request. "Have you seen people . . . survive possession scares?"

The guard blinked once, suddenly very interested in his fingers.

His expressions underwent rapid change, and the corners of his mouth softened. "It depends. I . . . um . . . I don't see why you wouldn't."

Liar.

The whisper tested the waters, crawling from the base of Gigi's neck, chasing away the gentle anticipation of her brother's arrival. Her stomach roiled.

She rested her head against the doorframe, a trembling hand finding her pin. The chaos behind Not-Stew faded to din as she focused on the heartbeat of her strange little watch.

"I can hear it in my head again."

Not-Stew blanched. "The chaplain here is the best. I don't know of many things she can't clear. But how can I help?"

Gigi took a moment to think, working twice as hard

as the cloud seeped around her thoughts, muddling her words.

"What are those?"

Not-Stew looked down at the vials on his lapel. "Blessed oil."

"I'll take some of that."

He removed one without thought, handing it over uncorked. With shaking hands, Gigi tilted the bottle onto each of her wrists, rubbing them together like an exclusive perfume. The acidic sting of lemon hit her nostrils, clearing her mind for the briefest moment.

"Lemongrass . . . is my favorite."

The guard slotted the oil with a smile.

She continued. "You make it?"

"I'm sad to admit I bought it, actually."

Gigi pulled a face, shaking her head a fraction of an inch. "Missy's on Elm?"

The man blinked, surprised. "How'd you know?"

Words left her breathless, but she persevered for the sake of slamming Missy's business model. "Smells like her stuff . . . It's good, I'll give ya that. But . . . she gouges her prices."

He smiled, settling on his knees beside her. "Oh?"

"Tell ya what. When we're done here, I have a great batch at home. I'll show you how to make your own—"

Gigi.

Not-Stew's face performed contortionist acts, his souring expression the last Gigi saw as her eyes rolled to the back of her skull. The whisper courted her, its voice smooth and deep, pricking her ears with every full consonant, every alluring vowel.

So much better.

Warmth pressed against her side as her body slumped like a rag doll. Not-Stew's voice blurred into the background of chaos. "What do you want me to do?"

So close . . .

"Keep her contained!"

Keep it contained.

The howling wind, the screaming of practitioners, and the whispers fell silent save for in her mind. Sensations of the fight between her and Gregory pierced her, over and over.

Nothing they do will work.

Somewhere, she imagined M pulling up a vial, Stew Michelin clamping a broad hand across Gregory's eyes as a brief discussion took place with the chaplain. Should they cleanse the room? Would the banishment be enough? A syringe made its way between the chaplain's tattooed hands before M received it and depressed the liquid into Gregory's IV.

We can do great things together.

Pressure gripped the nape of Gigi's neck like a firm hand, causing the world to buck.

Electric agony shot through every bone as Gigi's muscles tore at their insertions. A scream ripped from her throat, the slams of Gregory thrashing into the bed rails pummeling her head. Hit after hit.

Solid warmth pressed against her side, and somewhere in the recesses of her mind, Gigi wondered if she was bleeding.

Translucent tendrils crept through her memory, a cancerous form taking root everywhere it could. Tears burned Gigi's cheeks as the pressure gained traction, her memories splintering like the plastic cover of Gregory's fluorescent light.

His gaunt face followed, leering behind her older brother making a wish on sixteen birthday candles in a yellow kitchen. Stone-faced in the corner of her bedroom as she cuddled her dog on a quiet Sunday morning. He waited at the bottom of her grandparents' basement stairs, where Papa's familiar whistle wafted to the kitchen.

Gigi's mind fell like the rolling blackouts of Crowe

Hospital, swallowed by Gregory's influence until it was nothing but that sickly pale face, born of courtship and invasion, brutish and ugly.

Desperation clawed her throat as an avenue to speak opened through the siege. A moment meant for her to respond. To accept.

I . . .

The warmth shifted around her, enveloping her. It was floating in an ocean on a summer's day, comfortable and safe. Gigi sank into the sensation until only it remained, consumed by it. She opened her mouth to speak, only to find her jaw inches from unhinging as tendrils slithered inside her skull, but the warmth held her still.

I need . . .

A shock of auburn filled the air above her, sudden color on the tar-black landscape of soiled memories.

I need to stop.

Exhaustion settled in her limbs like lead, but Gigi felt her hand drag along her starched scrubs to a trinket beating a miniscule rhythm against her chest. Its etchings tickled her fingertips, solid and reassuring.

Fear nothing. Love, Nana.

The words nudged her spirit like the cold nose of a childhood pet as the second hand of the pocket watch ticked away. Gentle at first, the reminder sank deeply into her bones like runic script.

Gigi breathed deeply.

Once.

Twice.

Burnt pine wafted from the corners of the room, the scent of a frigid winter day piercing her nose.

A memory snapped into focus. One of burying her hands in a fresh snowbank in front of a pale yellow Victorian house. The wraparound porch bore the weight of pristine snowfall, undisturbed except for a path carved from a wide front door. Pine needles littered the front lawn, stark against the pale landscape. Gigi knew she would be tasked with collecting them for smoke cleansing after playtime was over, but now, as the cold filled Gigi's lungs, she moved swiftly with the intent of sculpting the most pristine snowball to ever exist.

She scraped and shaped a sphere, focusing on her craft as snow touched delicately around her boots. A gloved hand smoothed and molded the medium until it sat in her palm, almost glassy in its lack of defects.

Satisfaction swelled in Gigi's chest before she noticed it. A figure over her pristine creation.

It stood in the corner of her mind, under the pine tree whose rotted lower branches left a perfect archway for the specter. The shadowed form stretched a pale green smile across its features.

Fear raced through her limbs like lightning, disappearing into the ground. The creature tilted its head as the setting trembled around them, inspecting it at its leisure.

"What are you?" Gigi whispered across the snow. The message skipped across falling flakes toward the shadow stepping from beneath the tree.

Its face was indistinct, melted, with the edifice of Gregory seeping from its bones, weeping from its skin like rot. A throttled voice echoed from its core, causing the pine tree above to shed its needles, cascading to the ground.

"The End."

A crack of thunder shook her core as the sky above began to shift from light gray to red.

Crimson crashed around them as thunder swelled from below. An alarm which brought a mire of fog that plagued her boots, staining the snow.

And Gigi heard screams, clashing like bells against concrete.

She should have run.

Should have been afraid.

But the house was still visible, and in it, two figures standing at the front window.

Shadows themselves, tucked within the warm confines of the home. Gigi sucked in a lungful of cold, holding the snowball to her chest.

Fear nothing.

Focusing on the ice pressing against her palms, Gigi concentrated through the red mire, through the screams, on the creature before her, the wet shadow whose features melted and dripped off borrowed bones. She met those pale green eyes through the dense fog. Through Gregory's fog.

"Get out . . . of my head."

The mire entangled her ankles, her legs, whirling tighter and faster as they pulled against her shoulders like a scarf. Fog and snow spun together, pressing into her skin as the creature approached, step after step.

Gigi clenched her teeth in a grin, breaking the mire's hold to match the movement of The End. With every step, she dragged red from the snow. The viscous sludge crawled up her limbs, siphoning onto the snowball. Pulling tighter and tighter around the small sphere as it disappeared from the landscape.

The creature paused, watching the memory slipping from its grasp.

Screams faded, flying to the snowball on the back of the red fog and thunder, the threat growing smaller and smaller until it skirted the surface of the snowball like a sandstorm encompassing the earth, violently visible from the heavens.

Gigi stood steps from The End, shivering as she clutched the sphere in her hand. Like a god creating a planet, she stole everything from the creature before her. She made it in her own liking.

The pale green eyes were creased with malice and

something Gigi could not decipher, but she met them in defiance, showcasing the ball of ilk in her grasp as gentle snowfall resumed around them under a crisp gray sky.

He was stagnant in the palm of her hand, and her lip twitched to a manic grin, exhaling elation into the thin winter air.

"Get out of my fucking head."

Gigi's fingers pierced the snowball, though it no longer felt like ice. Rending it piece by piece, she dug her nails into the flesh of the creature before her, ripping its form apart in an ear-splintering shriek.

Until nothing was left but clumps of crimson sinking into the snow around her feet.

The elation of a childhood memory faded as the memory returned. The yellow house, the pine tree, the gray sky. Gigi basked in the image of its warm lit interior, the dollhouse that built her. The shadows in the window were gone, but the nurse took time to wave with her gloved hand like a child, a gesture that was too big and somehow not big enough.

A moment hung suspended between her and the house.

Wake up!

The towering Victorian was gone, and Gigi pried her eyes open.

Not-Stew's auburn beard flickered into view above her as she slumped into his wolf-gray uniform, his arms holding her firmly in place. The chaplain's coat bleached her gaze next, illuminated by the way-line as Gregory's desperate form lay splayed on the bed before her.

Stew and M took cover beneath the sink as the chaplain's bespangled arms stretched over the patient, their clashing spangles deafening against the wind that had whipped to tornado frenzy in Gigi's absence. Breathless words exhaled from the chaplain's age-worn lips as filaments crackled and seared above Gregory's head, aflame with new life. White light engulfed the room.

The watch ticked against Gigi's palm, and she clenched her fist with what remained of her might. Warmth and will grounded her like roots that shattered the concrete below, sinking and sinking until they pierced the earth and held her to it.

Broken tile cut into her free hand like shale as Gigi channeled a gorgon's might to freeze Gregory in stone.

In his last desperate moments, a flicker illuminated Gregory's gaunt body, the shadowed figure embossed over his person for a fraction of a moment. The entity's upper lip curled in its disembodied form. Eight shadowed claws dug deeply into the mattress, agonizing eyes staring from its throat.

Gigi.

The chaplain's symphony built to a crescendo as Gigi met the sickly eyes embedded in her patient's neck. Fear frayed the shadow at its edges, splintering into the air around him.

It was desperation.

The chaplain's words latched onto the being's presence like nettles, tearing its grasp on her mind with finality.

Left in its stead was stillness.

Blissful emptiness.

The static shadow stepped from within Gregory, flickering against the molded wall. It swirled like the storm, rocked by thunder and the flickering of bright white light bathing room 9 that singed the ends of Gigi's eyelashes. The room broached the precipice of unbearable heat, bright as the sun. But Gigi stared down the being's fading form.

She took back her voice.

Get fucked, Gregory.

The shadow was eviscerated in a flash-bang of light, leaving stars in Gigi's gaze.

Leaving the room silent and empty.

Gigi's scrubs clung to her frame in a sickly damp, preying delicately on each nerve peeking through her skin, fraying and exposed. Her breath caught full and quick, expanding the space in her lungs previously held by Gregory's grip. There was room between her ears for thoughts to flow, crashing back to her.

Gigi pressed her palms to her ears, feeling the silence of solitude like the pain of half-swallowed soda. Her sight reeled as it came into its own. Without thought, she sank against the solid warmth behind her, taking a long moment to adjust.

Not-Stew's silhouette was stark in the way-line's sedate glow, its pale yellow hue the only light to see by. He adjusted himself to keep her upright.

"Take your time . . . You all right?"

Gigi steadied her limbs, flexing slowly as she tested her mobility within the guard's support. "No, probably not."

The young man had grace enough to look sheepish, offering a steady arm as Gigi sat apart from him, quaking from her core. She took it.

"Careful."

A beat of uncertainty stretched between them as Not-Stew kept his hands on her shoulders as if afraid of her vanishing.

"You held on for longer than I—" He swallowed hard. "I lied. I've never seen anyone survive that bad a possession."

Gigi pulled a face, arms crossing over her chest as her body quaked under his hands. "Well, thanks for lying? It helped, I think."

The young man's beard twitched, the corners of his

eyes creasing with a smile, which chased the cold from Gigi's cheeks.

Reality sped up.

Meager daylight illuminated the room.

M strode over the way-line without a second thought after an offhand comment about getting new linen. Stew stooped over the marionette man, confirming that the crucified Gregory, peaceful among his own bile and waste, was unconscious and not dead. Without the entity's distortion, his soiled gown was stretched too snug over his full frame, the real Gregory's face round with expressive lines digging trenches beside his mouth.

Almost pleasant.

His chest rose and fell in his sleep, but the victory of it was halted by the tap of the chaplain's cane on the broken tile floor. The woman beckoned Gigi forward.

"Let me see your badge, Nurse."

Not-Stew's new and familiar warmth helped Gigi find her feet. Persistent chills coursed through her as she separated from him, stepping forward with the grace of a new foal to hold out her badge for examination.

The chaplain scrutinized the plastic from behind warped glasses that balanced on the bridge of her nose. When she spoke, her authority was certain.

"This is unacceptable."

Gigi opened her mouth to speak, silenced by the chaplain's hand.

"I'm sure you were told the moniker was appropriate, but anything this close to the truth should be reported immediately. Understand?"

The faraway gaze shifted from Gigi, falling on Stew. "S, you will get this young woman an appropriate badge and file an incident report. Whoever was responsible for this misnomer will be sent to the chapel for review."

Stew bowed his head, departing under the scrutiny.

Gigi caught Not-Stew's eyes, exchanging a small thanks before he followed on the heel of his partner.

The chaplain's bracelets brought her back to the conversation as the woman hobbled toward the door.

"This could have been a very bad night for you. Possession here is not uncommon and is usually a career-ending occurrence. There will be follow-up with the chapel and with your management."

Gigi's pallor deepened at the mention. "Thank you, again, for your assistance."

The chaplain tilted her head, mischief tweaking her left eyebrow. "Many of these situations can be avoided if our protocols are followed. I do not enjoy this facet of my job, so please ask for help sooner. Also . . ."

She tilted her head toward the uncovered mirror, a wry smile crossing her features.

"I know your Nana taught you better than to look into one of those at night."

Before Gigi could formulate a response, she was alone.

CHAPTER ELEVEN

Gigi heaved unconscious Gregory onto his side, new sheets bunched underneath as M drenched the man in warm soapy water. Conversation filtered from the hallway, the normalcy of daytime at stark odds with the destroyed room as they quietly cleaned the patient of his excrement.

"Hey, M?" Gigi asked, holding Gregory to the side with fading strength.

The woman peered over her glasses.

"Thank you for tonight. I appreciate everything."

M nodded solemnly, drying Gregory's back before changing his soiled gown.

"Hey, M?"

The woman gave no response, though Gigi noted a flicker of a smile as M rolled Gregory just enough to get the new sheets through.

"Thanks for not letting the demon take over my brain."

The elder nurse tossed the dirty linen to the floor, pausing with her hands on her hips as Gigi continued.

"Oh, hey. Hey, M?"

The woman met Gigi's eyes as they boosted Gregory in bed, her button nose sniffing in anticipation. "What?"

Gigi pulled the sheets over her patient, tucking the man in before leaning against the side rail. "I think we should both call out tonight."

M braced herself against the bed with a sigh, exhaling into a laugh that began in the depths of her diaphragm until the two nurses were unraveling. Clutched over in hysterics, their bathwater crashed to the floor, adding another layer to clean, sending the two into another fit as they mopped the broken tile.

"Everything okay in here?"

Gigi looked up from mopping bathwater with subpar paper towels. L stood framed in the doorway, her usual scowl gentler, if that was possible.

"Oh yeah. Just slaphappy."

M tucked Gregory into bed as the young nurse deposited the linen in the hamper. His belly poked from the bed, sleeping deeply after the eventful night.

"What can I do for you?"

The woman gestured for the young nurse, waiting for Gigi to close proximity before holding up a clear biohazard bag.

Gigi's eyes widened.

"You're really going to make me walk down your labs? After tonight, are you kidding?"

"They're not labs." L scowled, shoving the bag into her hands. "Just open it."

Gigi took the bag carefully, struggling to open the seal with fingers that still didn't know how to work. Prying it open, she stared into the plastic for a long moment, uncertain of the contents.

"It's from us," L clarified.

Instantly, she understood.

Copper beads littered the bottom from Charge. A scrap of embroidered cloth from O's scrubs rested loosely among thorns from L's headband and a tourmaline bangle from L2.

And sitting at the top was a tiny snowdrop pin.

M's snowdrop pin.

Tears welled in Gigi's eyes, and she closed the bag with reverence.

M dried the bath bucket, resting it to the side as Gigi struggled for words.

"Thank you . . ."

L shrank to the doorway as she spoke. "Don't go getting emotional about it, all right? But strong work tonight. You did good, kid."

She was gone without a word, leaving Gigi to look for M.

"Thank you."

Her mentor's abyssal eyes were here and elsewhere, all at once.

"We're proud of you, G. That can't be understated."

The words hit like a truck to the chest.

"You coming to huddle?"

"You go . . . I'm gonna take a sec before report if that's all right."

M nodded once, disappearing over the way-line, into the hall.

Gigi cradled the bag, uncertain.

Quietly, she righted in the visitor's chair beside Gregory's bed and sat beside him. The light of day filled his room, emphasizing the carnage but also the success.

Resting her head on the back of the chair, Gigi savored the silence of room 9.

Security Office,
West Belfry 10, 07:45

Security, the misfits of Crowe County Hospital, was hidden away behind the elevator mechanics room in two locations: one in West Belfry and one in South. Gigi entered the former with her badge in hand, greeted by a blank room that held a singular desk and too many secondary doors to count.

Not-Stew waved to Gigi with a sheepish yawn, removing his feet from the desk long enough to be of service.

"You got something for me?" Gigi asked, settling into the visitor's chair.

The man threw half a shrug her way. "Depends on what you're after, I suppose."

Unceremoniously, her badge landed in his lap, the same heat building behind her ears. "Ring any bells?"

"Ah, yes." He feigned remembrance with a frown. "The cause of all my grief these past twelve hours. How could I forget?"

Gigi relaxed into the chair as Not-Stew rifled through the top desk drawer, allowing herself a moment as the exhaustion of the night hit, sudden and complete. The same yellow Victorian with a wraparound porch still existed, imprinted on the backs of her eyelids amongst snow and pine needles. Blurred against the great white expanse. A piece of her chest ached at the thought as two silhouettes in the window faded into a comfortable haze.

A familiar warmth of a bearded redhead was beside her as Gigi opened her eyes. One of his hands rested on the back of her chair with a slim piece of plastic held in the other. Not-Stew's eyes were framed in delicate lines and darkened circles, but observed her keenly.

"You okay?" He relinquished the badge, helping her stand.

Gigi nodded, the ID weighing down her arm. "Yeah, I'm fine. I was just thinking. Will the guard who made my other badge get in shit with the chaplain?"

Not-Stew paused on his way around the desk, a cautious tone persisting. "Hopefully not, but he's on tomorrow morning. So we will see then, I suppose."

Gigi turned for the door, furrowing her brow as the young guard slumped into the chair, replacing his boots on the desk. The concept of someone hired through Crowe security returning to a home where they slept and had a break from work was cerebral. In the imagination of the children of Crowe County, these agents belonged to dry hovels where they curled up on piles of silvered weapons for vague periods of hibernation before returning for violence.

Those were the creatures Gigi grew up imagining.

Blinking once, she cleared her throat. "Well . . . thanks for this anyway."

"Of course. You going to get some sleep?"

Gigi threw a shrug his way. "Manager actually gave me the night off tonight to get my, um . . . head on straight. So I'm going to garden."

"Right! Lemongrass?"

The intrigue on her companion's face was unexpected, the man's expression lightening.

"Always wanted to try gardening. Have a bit of a black thumb though."

Gigi's delighted laugh devolved into a snort. "Well, you'll have to give a shout soon. I'm more than willing to help someone who aided me during an exorcism grow a pansy."

"Really?"

Gigi paused, examining the man not three strides from her. Cigarette smoke clung to his clothing, that wolf-gray uniform she regarded with trepidation, but his expression was excited. Earnest.

So, she nodded. "Or a sunflower, or a tomato. I guess there are a lot of options."

He brightened, tumbling into his words. "That's great! Then I'll hunt you down when—Poor choice of . . . We'll make a date . . ."

He stopped, scratching the back of his neck, and Gigi could feel his thoughts recalibrating from across the room. "I'll catch you at work soon, and we can figure out a time. Sleep well in the meantime. Whenever you sleep."

"You too. Whenever you, uh . . ." She stalled, hand on the door. "Do you sleep? I've heard—actually, don't answer. Nah, I'm sure you do. Don't answer that. Good night."

Gigi exited the whitewashed room into Crowe County Hospital's familiar West Belfry foyer. The main hospital's foot traffic jostled her tired form on her way to the Emergency Department in East Belfry to meet her brother and rid herself of this night.

Well, most of this night.

On her way, she took time to double-check her new badge.

Triple-check.

G3 met her eyes in bold gray typeface.

Great.

PART 3

D'ARCY AND ALEX'S TUESDAY ADVENTURE

CHAPTER TWELVE

West Belfry 6,
Alex's Room, Nighttime

I do not know what the humans are saying. This is typical.

Only the chaplains speak my language, and what they know is minimal and necessary. We live by very simple rules: Do not harm the children. Do not venture into the human realm.

And that is it. I pay attention to those rules and little else the humans say.

Nothing is happening I need to know about, so I lie by my pit and soak up its warmth. Nothing can compare to the warmth of my home, and I bask in its beams.

In a sense, I am working. On the clock. So, in this way, my home is my office.

I enjoy my job. It is preferred for species like me who have outgrown the challenge of closets and do not appreciate the frigidity of lagoons. Or basements.

I am picky, and I do not like the cold.

Some say I have impossible standards.

I cannot disagree.

Two pairs of feet move to the door, their coverings squeaking on the floor. On tile, so it is called. I do not like tile, and my office has a thin layer of cushion so I do not have to lie on it, which was contingent on my settling under this particular bed.

As the two pairs of feet exit my room, a perimeter light flickers and dims, a crystalline array of colors fracturing energy in the air, which I know, from my own research, the humans cannot see. To them, it is the color the child chose.

Pink.

Which is very boring when you have more rods and cones in your eyes than four humans combined.

Alex likes it, however. It makes the child happy, which is an emotion humans experience when they smile a lot.

In my culture, smiling is an aggressive act, and it took me a long time to separate the two in my mind. Human children do not like it when you threaten them back because this is not what it means to be "happy."

Happy is, to my understanding, similar to my feeling when I lie by my hole and bask in its warmth.

So, I adjust my frame of understanding.

When two new feet touch the floor next to my office, they are also clad in foot coverings—large decapitated duck heads, except plush.

Words I cannot understand announce the child's presence, and a small hand lifts the blanket obscuring my view. A luminescent pair of eyes meets my own.

Alex bares their teeth.

I bare mine in return, but friendly, remembering my human sensitivity training.

My toes stretch across the linoleum toward Alex, scratching thin lines into the soft stone. The child settles on their knees before me, reaching to clasp one of my toes in their comparatively miniscule fist.

I tolerate this. Briefly.

"Walk?" the child asks quietly.

In the time I've known Alex, they've taken care to learn small words of my language to express what they need. I believe the hospital provides a pamphlet, but no child has attempted prior.

And make no mistake, the pronunciation is horrible.

But I appreciate the effort.

With a yawn, I stretch and slink from my home, my back arching to scrape along the bed frame I dwarf as I clear its underbelly. The impaled ducks scramble back in anticipation, squeaking as the child stands to an insignificant height, their patterned robe sweeping the ground.

The room is brighter than I like, overhead lights blaring ugly fluorescence on sparse hospital accommodations. Thankfully, Alex put their time to good use, muting the white paint with confusing dark-colored scribbles. I click along at the child's heels, catching sight of a sloppy painting done with care, a quadrupedal tan-and-black creature with a graying saddleback, fur plucked away in patches.

It is me.

If Alex did not get my ears correct in all their pointed glory, I would be offended. But there they stand, wisps of fur giving them even more glorious height in the child's rendition.

Not many of my kind make it to my age with them intact, and it ranks as my great vanity they were not mutilated by my littermates in my youth.

My glorious ears twitch in the open room, the child's movement meeting them in a flurry of noise, spectacular jewelry clanking on their person. Macaroni charms are hollow and dull against tinny aluminum chains along the child's arms, high-pitched and unpleasant.

Some creatures in the hospital would call them unbearable.

To me, they are not unbearable but unpleasant.

Springing to the light-line in all their spangled glory, Alex places one foot across. They look at me expectantly, and I remove my eyes from the curling wall art, treading behind. Crossing the way-line does not faze me like it does others. They are not designed to keep me confined.

It is always a fun game to see a shadow dart stupidly from its corner. They become zapped in the best of ways and sometimes explode, which is great fun to watch.

Others are not so fun. They stalk the halls, pacing the light-line to scare the children. I wish they would explode in the same way. If creatures of those types show up, I really have to work, though they never leave without help from the gray slayers or the Black Coats.

The breeze of energy ruffles my fur patches, and I am allowed into the darkened hall.

Human children have their own wards, I learned, decorated to make merry infirmaries. In the long hallway, I glimpse a locomotive wisping feathered energy as it runs along the ceiling. Copper piping provides an efficient track, guarding the upper wall perimeter as light cascades downward to the edge of the tile floor. Frivolous paintings glow dimly in my sight every few steps, their frames dusky and dim compared to the brightness of their surroundings.

Alex skips ahead, beckoning me forward as I creep at a sluggish pace to keep in step with the child, giving me time to study the artwork.

It is brighter than Alex's personal fare.

In the first, a landscape sprawls before a gray-stoned castle, and I am reminded of a home I had in my younger years, beneath civility within a court. I was able to cause mischief then, and my youth was far from wasted.

The next sports a field of roughly hewn flowers, bright colors stippled against canvas, disturbingly fake. Then again, I have not seen a broad variety of human foliage and life.

For instance, I never saw a clown until the day I left my home to tour my new job. And I never wish to see one again. I duck my head as I pass the portrait of a black-and-white figure. It holds a flower with a billowing sleeve and diamond pattern.

Smiling.

I get the sense clowns do intend harm when they bare their teeth.

Fur on my flank becomes clenched in a little fist, and Alex walks alongside me, tense.

I breathe in the sweet scent hanging on their shoulders like a deep green cape. I breathe it out.

There is a well-known symbiosis to this relationship. Children and my kind have coincided for centuries because they feel this sweet-scented pond scum, and we feed off it.

We devour it, turn it into something lesser. This is not my intent, to protect a child from harm, but I suppose it is nice to know there is a side effect of the sweet treat.

This is part of my payment for my job. Safe lodging. All the violence I can hope for against hospital entities meant to do harm against my designated child. And the endless green.

Sweet, sweet green.

Alex's hand relaxes in response, and they smile as the clown becomes a faint memory of discomfort.

The hallway runs in a straight line, rooms on both sides guarded by their light-lines. In the center, there is a point where three nurses sit at their stations on either side of the hall. The bottlenecked path continues through this home of nurses, leading us to our destination.

One nurse bares their teeth at the child, voice low. I do not know what they say, but I do my best to translate.

"Greetings, child," the nurse says. "What are you doing away from your quarters?"

"I wished to roam the halls with no purpose!" Alex shouts.

"Oh, well, that appears to be a good way to spend endless hours in a hospital," another nurse responds.

"I think so too!" the child replies. "I would like a treat from the cold box."

The first nurse contemplates, reluctantly stating, "Wander safely, small child. Retrieve your treat and be back in your room promptly."

Alex gives a hearty wave, continuing on their journey.

I wander past the nurses' station in the child's wake, unseen by staff despite my bumping against a sitting implement. They likely blame a minor entity, which are sensational patsies should one ever find themselves in a bind.

The unit entrance lies just beyond this nurses' station, a significant double door locked from inside and out. It is rampant with light and tart oils, inundating my senses in a nauseating way.

I never want to wander farther into the human world. But if I did, the door would deter me, smelling the way it does.

A tug on my side reveals the child pointing down the expanse of hall.

I turn to see where they are pointing, toward a blurred form pacing wall to wall. It has foot coverings too, so I'm assuming another human. One of the past.

I know them to be images, nothing less or more, but I understand Alex's hesitation.

Not all humans are missing half their skull.

At least, not to my limited knowledge.

Another tug on my side precedes the sweet smell of deep green unfurling in my nostrils. I breathe in, slowly, then out.

Alex releases my side, creeping toward the figure as it paces its loop. Pausing briefly, the child continues to stare, and I can smell it beginning again, faintly this time, leaving a scent wafting half-baked in the air before me. The child bares their teeth at the specter, memorizing its pattern before darting across the path, unseen and unnoticed.

I follow at my own pace, not bothering with timing. A rush of cold air hits me, and my hair stands on end. Otherwise, I find no need to rush.

Whatever it is does not notice us.

Alex leads the way to the end of the hall where a glass-enclosed playroom sits, a bubble popping from the flat wall. The perimeter train ceases to run where the reinforced glass sits, steel bars supporting the structure like tent poles, crashing to the ground. The clear casing is made opalescent by etched symbols so old even I cannot read them, if I could read. Pulsating energy teases the tips of my fingernails, digging into the pads of my paws like dull electric shocks.

The child does not feel this, the room providing them with unparalleled safety as they dart through the door, pilfering bin to bin, chest to chest, overturning brightly colored toys that clatter and skitter along the ground. Alex takes advantage of this moment near the bubble, rifling in the chaos until they return to my side, brandishing a wooden sword and shield. Their teeth bare in earnest.

I recognize these weapons from my youth; they were once used to hunt my kin before humans became efficient.

However, these do not glint the way sharp metal does.

Play toys, but the child does not appear to know this.

Hoisting the weapon with a flourish, Alex proceeds toward a small room to the side of this play space.

The most coveted room on the entire floor.

The kitchenette.

I only know this room from the Black Coats, who assured me I could take food as I pleased so long as it was appropriate amounts.

Human food is garbage, and I believe the Black Coats knew this prior to offering the liberty.

Hopping another light-line like a jumping rope, Alex plunges forward into the small room, barely wide enough to accommodate me alongside. A small counter holds boxes of saltines and jellies, a smell so potent it leaves a trail in the air. Most nurses who work overnight do not realize the rank scent of fake grape clinging to their clothing, but it leaves me wondering how any of them have romantic mates.

Thankfully this is not what the child wants.

I lend a nudge with my nose as they heave a chair toward the cold box, scrambling onto its wobbly frame to pull the upper door open.

This cold box, stuffed with slim white packages, is the true treasure trove of the ward.

Alex tears one package from its companions, raising it in their small fist. The child's color is pale now, and it takes a moment for them to descend from the chair, breathless but elated.

"Pop-sicle!" The child speaks slowly for me to hear the pronunciation.

I assume this is a human declaration of achievement, and I keep it stored away in case I require a colloquialism one day.

Alex's sword drags on the tile. Their face is fractured into dimensions of illness as the paper crinkles and tears from the cold treat. I believe this is the reason they do not notice the difference to the unit as we traverse the kitchenette's light-line.

In the time we were gone, the halls' perimeter colors faded, leaving gaps for darkness to form where the floor meets the walls. Chills send clumps of fur between my shoulders bristling. I attempt to quicken the pace of the child, but they are enjoying whatever treat they acquired from the cold box, red dye smeared across their mouth as their breathing increases in effort.

We skirt around the same pacing entity, this time with the joy of a game as Alex brandishes the sword, running through the specter.

It does not notice.

The empty nurses' station greets us opposite the main doorway, that sticky-sweet smell in my nostrils once more. Jellies are open and abandoned across the counter, a trail of swampy green light hanging behind the nurses who fled to check their rooms.

They sense a change too.

Alex remains blissfully unaware of danger, smacking at their treat with the zeal of a person who knows their snack is not long for this state.

No matter, as we are almost to the room, passing the paintings on the wall.

One after another.

After another.

A discontent clown.

After another.

We pause simultaneously, so consumed averting our eyes from our least favorite painting we almost do not realize its occupant is no longer smiling.

Alex and I turn to see the once jolly clown fixed in exaggerated woe.

It is still . . . for a moment.

One lanky arm flops over the frame.

Another arm drops directly next to it, diamond sleeves billowing as they jingle at the wrists.

The patterned horror hoists itself past the frame, tumbling onto the floor in a heap. It blends with the foundation below, and shadows from the hallway corners flee.

They know its terror.

For a moment, the clown has forgotten how to move. The gentle tinkling of bells on its wrists twitch with its body before it stands. In one illustrious movement.

A gloved hand flexes by its face. Its fingers wiggle as the painted smile returns, blackness slipping from its mouth.

Alex stands beside me with a pensive nature, tilting their head as if assessing the foe. The clown dances under the scrutiny, leaping from one foot to the other, gaining ground a tile at a time. The child bares their teeth, this time in the method I am most familiar with.

Two small hands grip the hilt of their sword.

The clown's eyes narrow.

Alex lunges forward.

The wooden sword plunges through the clown's abdomen, and misty tendrils pour to the tile like a waterfall from its gaping stomach. Whatever the clown is does not see their demise until it is too late. It flails and grasps for purchase on the sword, its hands pitifully incorporeal.

Alex holds up their treat and gives it a lick with a boisterous "Ha!"

Red confection drips from their lips like blood. They yank the sword from the clown and watch as the jester scrambles back to its frame.

Alex is triumphant, turning to me in a moment where I feel kinship with them.

For this reason, I am distressed when, where the clown stood, a mist wavers in the air. It stretches floor to ceiling in an oppressive wall of black.

I do not know of many entities that can cause this to happen.

For a moment, I smell the green coming from myself. The emptiness this residue brings is frightening.

I wonder how I can try to stop it, if it tries to hurt Alex.

I sense there will be little I can do.

I step in front of the child and bare my teeth.

And then it disappears with a crash of cold into the tile, scattering itself across the unit until it is spread so thin, I can no longer see it.

I resolve to pay it no more mind at this time and return Alex to their room.

The child and I pass a nurse, standing in the hall with their mouth agape. I am unaware they have seen what occurred. Until slayers visit the ward.

I am made to speak to a chaplain that night, in the broken words they know, and they translate for the slayers. I tell them of the cold and of the mist. They cannot see me well and do not look me in the eye when I speak. This is preferred. When I am stared in the eye, it sets me on edge.

I slink to my home office late, scratching my spine against the underside of the bed before I curl up in front of my hole. Warmth bristles my fur, comforting me from tip to tail after the chill of the hospital hall. Above me, I feel Alex settle into the bedsprings.

The delicate *tick* of an object meeting linoleum greets my ears, and I crack my eyes ever so slightly. A red-stained stick lies on the floor, goopy and unfortunate.

Taking the offer, I extend a clawed paw, scraping the stick under the bed and into my mouth.

Tangy and sweet.

Maybe I will use the kitchenette with more frequency, so long as Alex is there to eat the bad part of the treat.

Their light-line flickers obstinately, followed by the tinkle of bells somewhere in the hall. And I sleep very well that evening despite the many whispers from my hole, the warnings from my kind who see shoe coverings of gray slayers patrolling our hall.

We know something is not right.

PART 4

WEDNESDAYS RARELY BEHAVE...
FOR STEW

CHAPTER THIRTEEN

North-West 7 Bridge,
Fifteen Years Ago

tew Michelin ran for his life. There was no time to think. No time to do anything but get to the bridge between North Belfry and West.

His only way out.

Desperate screams assaulted his ears as the tide of patients and practitioners followed his thought, trampling their way to abandon North Belfry as quickly as possible.

The building rocked under the force of an alarm that bellowed harshly beneath his feet, vibrating through steel-toed boots to his knees. Stew tried to ignore the sensation, arms flying overhead as the sound brought drywall crumbling from the ceiling. Red light seared his retinas, bringing with it flashes of a person in gray he'd abandoned behind him.

F shuffled forward, ignoring the hazards of patients and shadows springing from the walls around him. In frantic backward glances, Stew only saw red staining his partner's skin, drenching his uniform, highlighting his featureless face.

Sweat pooled, pinning Stew's sopping hair to his forehead as he skidded around the corner from North 7 to a narrow tunnel of light streaming ahead. A glass-domed bridge stretched before him, terminating in West 7. His eyes began to water as relief hit him center mass, continuing his breakneck pace away from the chaos.

His ring of keys in hand.

**North-West 7 Bridge,
West Belfry Side, 06:43**

Iron bars slammed into the concrete floor during Wednesday's early morning hours, waking the patients on West Belfry 7. Nurses and doctors alike scrambled for the hall. They lined the periphery of their unit to report to their confused patients that security provisions now separated them from the West 7 bridge that led to the northern side of the hospital.

This was a favorite bridge, with just the right view of Crowe, and many patients would wander between their treatments, taking nightly strolls to this separation between the belfries. They would watch illegal fireworks scattered throughout the city in the month of July, or try to glimpse anything nefarious behind identical iron defenses permanently secured into the concrete before North Belfry. Ever curious about the abandoned vestige and looking to bring stories home from their time in Crowe County.

It was the only bridge open since the fall of North Belfry, and Stew was aware of its appeal.

He also knew—according to Wrought Iron LLC, who'd outfitted the hospital with new equipment last December—these bars were an "impenetrable system." They made it "impossible" for anything to escape a newly discovered hole in North Belfry's gate and access the rest of the hospital.

Improbable, more likely.

That morning, West 7's crew watched from the boundaries of their unit, with concern trained on him and three accompanying practitioners as day shift filed off the nearby elevators.

Stew did his best to ignore them.

There were reasons he typically worked nights.

"So, you are convinced it's weathering?"

A grizzled woman squinted beyond the iron slats through Coke-bottle glasses. A foot shorter than Stew, the woman bobbed along the barrier with the air of someone who knew her skill set and knew it well.

This was Cora, and she hadn't changed since Stew first met her fifteen years prior.

"Oh yeah. Bet my life," the woman grunted, peach lipstick staining her teeth as she pulled her mouth back for a grin. "O'course, if I'm wrong, that's what I would be bettin' with!"

Stew failed to see the humor, observing the gate in front of the North Belfry, constructed of permanent heavy iron in three layers, which blurred visibility beyond their panels. His eyes wandered to the hole in its bottom left corner just as a smoker's laugh rattled from Cora's chest.

"You believe Cora here." She dug in her pocket for a packet of cigarettes, tapping one out into her hand. "We'll get that plugged up in a jiff."

A woman in a black lab coat with a blue pansy pin glinting from her lapel stared onto the bridge as Cora flicked a plastic lighter with a petrified thumb. The chaplain pressed her tattooed hands firmly against the iron security gate, and when she spoke, her voice rang with certain authority.

"You cannot smoke in the hospital, C."

The maintenance worker paid the woman no mind, her shoulders squared off to the pair. "Afraid of names, afraid of smoking. Chap, you got a real rod up your ass, don't you know it?"

Holding back a wince, Stew watched Cora turn abruptly on her heel and trudge toward a heavy maintenance bag with a trail of smoke behind her. There was a running joke over the years that Cora had walked straight out of the hospital walls, a construct of some cultist force, and it was only now Stew realized the shirt under her overalls perfectly camouflaged into the peeling wallpaper. Stew flexed his arm with a scant smile, watching her wander to the fourth player in their travelling band of misfits.

N stood unfortunately close to Cora's maintenance bag, slouching against the door to an antechamber jutting from the wall in front of the bars, waiting. Outfitted with enough munitions to raze any entity to the ground, the young man tolerated Cora flinging excess tools inches from his boot-clad feet with surprising grace.

"Too bad, Cora. Names cannot be used here anymore. We will call you C now." The maintenance worker grumbled, cigarette ash flying over her bag with every syllable. "But wait, Cora, there are two people with C, and you were hired second, so you are C2 now. Oh, hold on, Cora! No more smoking. It is bad for lungs, and the oxygen tank room could explode. Hold this!"

N took the offered smoke between two fingers, uncertain.

Cora's eyes sprang to the young guard, sizing him up. "You can have one drag, young man. But just 'cause you look jumpier than a flea circus."

Stew observed the warmth of the guard's smile as he took a careful drag, complying with Cora's parameters with a muttered thanks.

The chaplain's sigh brought Stew back to the conversation at hand, and he looked out to the bridge with a frown. "You want me to have her put it out?"

The woman's eyes stared ahead as if appraising the value of an antique. "No. Seems she's doing well for your guard there. Everything about him . . ."

"It's off, right?" Stew scrutinized N as a quiet conversation picked up between the guard and the maintenance woman. "He did the possession with us a few nights back . . . I'm starting him on days again for a bit. Trying to keep an eye on him."

The chaplain's expression remained inflexible, severe. "He had some trouble with it?"

A beat passed between them, companionable and brief.

"Yes . . ." Stew responded quietly. "On top of everything, he was on the lougarou in the pediatric ward last month. And that fucker *ate* another guard."

"I recall."

"*Ingested.*"

"I understand . . ."

Stew reached into his pocket, removing a worn purple rabbit's foot before resting his arms against the iron slats. Absently, he pressed his thumb into the dull claws poking from the fur as the chaplain planted her cane on the tile.

"He passed his eval? He's fit to work?"

Stew refused to respond, the presence of the guard expecting to be proof enough of his fitness.

"A lot of practitioners haven't seen it this bad in a while." She adjusted her lab coat. "S'gonna be a shock to a lot of the new ones if things get as bad as they were before North. I'm concerned."

The statement took Stew by surprise, the older guard wrestling his expression quickly past fear to something placid. "Why would it get bad?"

The chaplain spared a sigh. "Pattern wise, a lot of things are happening the same way. Even the exorcism the other night . . . entity referred to itself as The End.

Obviously, unfounded. But federal chaplains have been placed on alert . . . You should warn your guards to keep a weathered eye."

"Why wasn't I informed of this during security rounds?"

"Hospital leadership would like to avoid panic."

Stew's knees popped as he adjusted his stance. Standing in one spot, the uneven concrete sent shocks through his heels, arthritic nonsense bridging the gap in time as Chaplain spoke. He remembered very little from the lead-up to North Belfry's fall, the week scrubbed into a haze at the back of his mind. But the sensation of concrete, the structure of this bridge, he remembered those.

Too well.

He stowed the rabbit's foot. "You know what also helps avoid panic? Careful preparedness and disseminated, consumable information."

Silence.

Certainly, because he was being ignored.

With a sigh, he tried again.

"How's it looking inside?"

"A handful of vague entities." The chaplain resumed without acknowledging the comment. "Otherwise, it appears clear."

"So, Cora's chances of aggravating anything are scant."

The whisper of a grin echoed across the chaplain's age-worn face, Cora's rustling tools reaching their ears. Decisive and indiscriminate. "Minimal, I would say. Of course, I could cleanse before you go in . . ."

Stew's lip twitched once as the chaplain skewed a glance in his direction.

Her hand flexed against the iron, then dropped to her side with a sigh. "That look won't be necessary. There's

a good chance another entity would crawl through anyway during the cooldown, so I won't bother you with
precautions."

Stew scratched absently at the scar digging a trench
into his neck as the pansy-wearing woman brushed
down her lab coat.

"Don't got time for that nonsense. I want to get this
shit plugged up as quickly as possible. Nothing escapes."

The sudden rustling for tools ceased with a horren-
dous clang as Cora's voice interrupted.

"Got all our stuff set!" the woman rasped with wide
eyes. She seemed to open her peripheral vision with
the act, suddenly noticing N smoking the cigarette to a
nub. Plopping a thick welder's helmet atop her head,
Cora squinted at the young man with a manic grin. "Ah,
sneaky! And what's your name, dear?"

"N."

"Oh. They allow ya to have just one letter?"

The guard frowned as Stew approached, pushing off
the wall into straight-backed professionalism. A set of
keys rattled in his hand as he passed them to his senior.

"If I'm being honest, Cora, the last N was recently
eaten so . . . it's not the greatest circumstance."

The maintenance woman let loose a low whistle,
gathering her supplies from the ground.

"Well, that is unfortunate!" the woman praised,
watching Stew's movement with scrutiny. "Personally I
say, call me by my name or call me nothin'. Too old for all
this policy change nonsense."

Stew flicked deftly through the key ring, pulling a set
of two into his palm. The door before him was thirty feet
from the nearest elevator bank, leading into a room that
jutted from the wall like a phone booth.

Iron wires laced through a large pane of etched
glass on this door, giving the window into the sterile

antechamber a checkerboard appearance. Another door rested in their eyesight across this small room. Their entrance to the bridge.

The sterile safety chamber was taken from the CPC by Wrought Iron LLC, a containment booth meant to deter unwanted followers during times of needed repair on North Belfry.

Stew's eyes fell on a copper placard directly by the dual lock, losing sight of the words *To those lost on July 7, 1982*, as pressure hissed from inside and the door swung open.

North-West 7 Bridge,
Fifteen Years Ago

"Hurry!"

Stew Michelin's hand planted against the wall outside West 7's bridge, key jammed tenuously into a small box that read, For Emergency Use Only. *His voice stripped hoarse, he barked orders into chaos as patients and practitioners trampled one another, screaming for safety as the hospital pulsed in a bath of crimson light. He stared across the bridge into the void of the North Belfry, unwilling to break this post.*

"Base to units, be advised cleanse will happen in T minus one minute! Evacuate!"

Stew squeezed his eyes shut and opened them again, fireworks from the city of Crowe punctuating the darkness in horrific staccato as a plum-scrubbed nurse was lifted midway across the bridge and slammed into the ceiling. The stampede of people below her continued to move as she was released, her unmoving form consumed by the riotous trampling below.

Stew's arms were taut, his hand gripping the key locked into the wall as he was jostled by the crowd, his shoulder thrown by the surge of panic while keeping his eyes trained on the opposite side of the bridge.

It appeared.

*F stood in a gray uniform of Crowe Security. In the bright-
ness of the bridge, he had a long white beard and eyes dangling
from membranes in their sockets, plucked incompletely from
his head. The gentleman without eyes limped forward with
purpose, carried by the direction of the crowd.*

*Stew seized, his fingers twitching once on the key. Another
wave of people burst from North Belfry, the building itself
wracking in its foundation.*

*"Hurry please!" Stew screamed, but the eyeless F was
faster than those on the bridge huddling from falling debris.
Without regard for his own safety, the man broke into a
sprint.*

*Stew's hand twisted the key before his mind could com-
prehend the action, and iron slats slammed into the concrete
between West Belfry and the bridge.*

North-West 7 Bridge,
Antechamber, 07:23

Personal protective equipment was stuffed sparingly
into a mounted wall holder within the antechamber, and
N took the liberty of distribution.

Stew received the familiar gear with a wan smile,
detaching his rifle before he stepped into a full bodysuit
of dense plastic. Matte gray particles flecked across the
material, giving the costume unexpected weight.

N was a fraction of a second ahead in his own gown-
ing, adjusting shoe coverings that complained as they
stretched across his dense work boots. He outfitted his
hood next, lowering it carefully overhead until it clicked
in place at the shoulders. A bulky tube ran from the
hood to a belt strapped over his suit, humming with air
filtration. Dense black gloves completed the ensemble.
The young guard tapped against the glass with faint
annoyance.

"The etchings on the hood make it impossible to see."

Stew clicked his own in place. The etchings along the panel clouded his vision, but there were worse things.

"Better to be mildly inconvenienced than facially maimed."

"Ah, yes!" Cora exclaimed, sitting on her maintenance bag beside the pile of protective equipment abandoned at her feet. "Your moneymaker, eh, S?"

The elder guard gathered his weaponry with a snort, a buck knife and vials of discolored liquid attached clumsily to his new belt. "You should really wear it to protect your own."

A fit of coughing followed another boisterous series of laughs from within her rattling chest, a request so apparently unthinkable it did not merit a response. The woman's knobby hands grasped a bulky red machine, hauling her supplies into the room.

N slung a bag over his own shoulder, juxtaposing the miniscule maintenance woman as they faced the door to the bridge.

Stew took the keys from the other guard, speaking to his radio through the helmet as he locked the door leading to the West Belfry. "We're secured."

The chaplain's voice responded brusquely. "Copy that. Commencing five-minute wellness checks. Good luck."

Stew surveyed the area with a sigh, and his hand twitched to his belt. Three knives stood arranged like soldiers, digging into his thigh as he unlocked the second door with a hiss and proceeded onto the bridge.

Cora bounced ahead with unprecedented speed, a one-sided conversation persisting with jovial intent. "Hellfire, I don't think I've been on this bridge for fifteen years or so! The seventh floor always held up so well after securement."

The windows of the bridge opened on either side, bathing the practitioners in bright morning sunlight creeping from the Crowe Bay. The city stretched like a carpet below, terminating at the wharf in the distance where the sea glinted in waves of roiling diamonds. The view from West 7 allowed for direct eyeline at the level of the ocean as it curved with the earth with Persephone Tower positioned to the left, allowing an unobstructed view.

It really was spectacular.

As Stew lingered at the window, Cora moved with purpose, shoving the plug of her machine into the bridge's center outlet and clamping her cord onto the opposite iron gate.

North Belfry mirrored West 7's layout. A hallway continued past the barrier out of sight—tomb-like and silent. Sitting in stark contrast to Stew's distant memory, it appeared benign, though a twin containment chamber jutting from its gate begged to differ.

An echo chamber of the past.

Unlike the booth they passed through, this structure was clumsy and haphazard. Barely a reputable design. Even from the distance he kept, Stew recognized the brass placards adhered to its door, rectangles marching like soldiers off to war. Though he could not read them from his place at the window, he knew all the names by heart.

Those taken by the last cleanse.

Stew surveyed the bridge from West Belfry to North, taking in the carpeted and empty expanse. He positioned himself against North Belfry's gate as Cora danced around him. A gentle breeze fluttered from the rusted hole the size of a volleyball in its lower left corner, hitting the back of Stew's knees as the petite mechanic tugged on a leather jacket and pulled heavy gloves over her hands with satisfied grunts.

"Remember reinforcing these gates after the North Belfry cleanse, S? What a treat that was."

Stew grimaced. "We had different jobs at that time, C."

N removed small bowls of beaten copper from his bag, a credit to his ability to multitask given how easily he eavesdropped. The guard moved bowl to bowl, balancing rosemary sprigs on pine fragranced oil before lighting each, the small pyres burning in a sleepy way, certain to last their maintenance run.

Stew noted his attention and waited until he was finished with his task to elaborate. "I was on the recovery team."

N removed silvered knives from a sling at his side with a grunt of acknowledgment. "I didn't realize they let you recover after everything . . . after the trial and all . . ."

The comment punched Stew in the sternum, and he caught the young guard's eye with a warning shot. "They didn't have much choice. There was a lot to get done. And not many of us survived."

Cora's preparation continued through the silence, and N tugged once on his beard.

"I'm sorry."

Stew reached for his own knives, giving the scar on his neck a scratch through his gown. "You shouldn't be."

"It was out of line."

"It was." Stew paused. "But it wasn't wrong."

The young guard's attention abandoned the conversation for North Belfry's containment booth, shifting his feet in a way Stew had never noted before.

Nervous.

Quietly, Stew unhooked the purple rabbit's paw from his belt, holding it out over the burning copper pots.

"Take this."

N reached for it, confusion speckling his face.

"Just for now. Then I need it back." Stew strained to do it, but he managed a smile. "That things got all sorts of powers."

Cora hit the top of Stew's shoe, gesturing for him to

move from the hole. "All right, begone with your conversation. I got work to do."

Stew readily obliged, stepping sideways to his spot at one corner of the semicircle, strapping in for the long haul with the stillness of North Belfry breathing down on his neck.

North-West 7 Bridge, North Belfry Cleanse Imminent, Fifteen Years Ago

The thirty-seven seconds between the iron gate coming down and the beginning of Crowe County Hospital's first federal cleanse was lifetimes for Stew Michelin. Humans hit the gate with tsunami force, limbs flailing through the slats, grasping the safe air of West Belfry as a deep hum began beneath their feet.

"What the fuck are you doing?"

"Raise the gate!"

A stone-faced man stood among them, his gray uniform as prominent among the crowd of civilians as a crocus emerging from a late winter frost. F's gaze was unmoving, fixed on Stew. Deep red liquid oozed from the entity's eyes into its mouth as it opened with a shriek, swallowed by the alarm.

"Raise the fucking gate!"

"S! Please, please, I have kids. I have kids!"

F threw himself headfirst into the slats.

Again and again, the man pummeled his head onto the iron bars within the growing crowd, slamming until his head began to crack.

Stew felt a slight tug on his belt, preceding a sharp burst of pain from ear to throat. His hand left the key, grasping for his neck as blood poured over his clothing. Desperate breaths confirmed nothing was in dire need of attention.

He whirled on the assailant, a nurse disheveled and panicked with dark abyssal eyes widened beyond reason. She gripped a silvered knife in her hands.

His knife.

She poised it at his throat, screaming. "What the fuck are you doing! Open the gate!"

Stew couldn't speak, the tang of blood hitting his nose as he tightened the grip on his neck, eyes fixated on F as the man worked his way through the crowd.

The nurse followed his eyeline, the knife tumbling from her grasp. Viscera splattered across the barrier as the man threw his head into the bars again, and again. Beating his own skull to a vicious pulp.

Those around him began to realize the corpse among them, and panicked screams redirected, running a rip current through the crowd as they tried to push away from the eyeless man whose neck cracked and bent backward with the force of his escape.

Stew gripped a small rabbit's paw in his hand, shaking as he threw his remaining weight on the emergency key, snapping it in its hold.

**North-West 7 Bridge,
Interior, 12:32**

Midday pink illuminated Cora's work, a sheet of iron welded neatly over the breach. The weathered woman continued welding along her line, nearing completion as the chaplain's voice cut through the static.

"S, please be advised; I note a shift in the northeast corner of the hall."

Stew positioned himself opposite N at separate ends of the burning semicircle, back straight as the warning hit the bridge. "Any more information on the activity?"

"Not yet. Stand by."

The chaplain's black lab coat shifted along the west gate, and Stew placed a hand on his knife, waiting.

N positioned his rifle toward the floor, held across his chest in a relaxed fashion as steady eyes surveyed their surroundings. He took a cautious step within the circle, suit crinkling stiffly against itself. Stew mimicked his form, his muffled footsteps carrying him behind the line of safety as the silence was interrupted, but not by the chaplain's voice.

The sharp tap of an invisible shoe paced by the western containment chamber.

The doorknob rattled once in its hold.

N raised his rifle, crinkling his suit as the doorknob rattled again.

Violently.

Stew watched the man exhale, and the shotgun fired with a crack.

The tapping ceased. The doorknob fell silent.

Cora was watching now, her welding shield up to survey the guards. The woman's leather sleeve dragged across her forehead, mopping a thick sheen of sweat. "Sounds like a level four."

The footsteps returned, twenty feet closer. Another shot cut the silence, followed by a deft reload, two shells bouncing against the ground.

"I believe you're correct, Cora."

Stew reached back for the old welder's arm, knees popping as the maintenance woman stood, grabbing a fistful of cast-iron scraps from the ground. The chaplain spoke, the radio slicing through the crack of the shot.

"Brace for a level four, likely malevolent."

Stew swore under his breath as N stowed his gun. Two knives slithered from his holsters as a powerful gust of air sliced from the sides of the bridge, extinguishing all copper pots at once.

Stew stood ready with Cora's arm in his grip.

N began to sidestep toward West Belfry, testing the waters. The bridge was silent, the surrounding windows giving the practitioners the feeling of being suspended in midair. Trapped in a tank with whatever pursued them.

The footsteps sounded again, only feet away, and Stew sprinted ahead with Cora in tow. Copper pots scattered against their fleeing feet, the remaining oil making a slick getaway as the three bolted for the exit. N reached the west containment door in four easy strides, the younger man plucking Cora's miniscule form from Stew's side as he did.

"Get her through!" the elder barked. Concern for the unshielded Cora outweighed sense as N fumbled for the keys, unlocking the door and slamming it shut behind them.

The pair flew through the small room, the chaplain permitting them to the other side.

Stew reached the interior doorway, skidding over the threshold seconds behind his companions, knees on fire. He forced the door shut, allowing himself a moment to breathe in safety, alone in the containment chamber.

Hands on his knees, he cycled the stale air in his helmet, managing a small smile.

Until he heard them.

Footsteps.

In the tight sterile space, the bulk of an entity collided into Stew's side.

The hit threw him to the floor. Seized under an invisible fist of whatever was locked inside with him, he sucked in his circulated air with short panicked breaths. The man scrambled on knees on fire, coming face-to-face with the chaplain in the etched glass of the next door, like a person praying for penance.

"You compromised the room!" she hollered, her voice muffled through the glass. "The space needs to go through decontamination."

Behind her, N wrenched his helmet from his shoulders. "You can't do that!"

"This will kill people. We cannot let it out," the chaplain rebutted, staring directly through Stew.

An assault came again, with unseen hands focused on kneading through Stew's protection like a wildcat. Back against the floor, the man slashed through the air with a knife, making no purchase as the entity shredded the plastic and dove against his skin.

Maybe I am too old.

The chaplain's tattooed hand rested on the glass, and Stew heard the familiar voice as if she stood next to him, her mouth moving on the other side of the glass without sound. The North Belfry's plaques flooded his memory, each name glinting, representative of someone he'd found behind the iron fifteen years ago, trapped in the cleansing properties of federal chaplains.

It was an unspeakable way to go.

It was proper this was how he did.

N pounded once on the glass beside the black-coated woman, professionalism cracked in the face of what was to come. "We will get you treated as soon as possible!"

"Don't bother!" Stew choked, kicking out his feet to make purchase against a solid mass, which flung into the containment chamber's wall with a thud.

A familiar tone echoed throughout the small room.

"Code Blue, Containment Chamber, West Belfry 7. Code Blue, Containment Chamber, West Belfry 7."

The creature joining him on this death march was clueless violent company. It ripped Stew's leg to the side, tossing him into the far wall.

He propped himself up, waiting for another attack, staring at the faces now watching him through the glass.

A set of bespectacled eyes joined N, the small maintenance woman peering through. "You'll be okay, buddy! You got your suit on. You'll be okay."

"I'll be *fine*," he said sternly, mostly to himself. Heart in his throat, he huddled into the corner, dragging his knees to his chest. "But next time, N, we cleanse before going for maintenance. I don't care if it takes longer."

There won't be a next time.

Stew did not need to imagine what would happen when the glass panes around him began to vibrate. He'd seen it all before. The light crept inward, cascading onto him from the ceiling as the chaplain's words manifested themselves, twisting the energy of the air into radiant light. His chest seized with indifference about the entity gouging his arm or the growing crowd of eyes observing through the glass.

Stew let teeth rip through his arm with the knowledge that nothing would cause him more pain than what was about to occur.

Awaiting the inevitable.

Cleansing white light seared his eyes, emanating from special seams in the room. They lined the entire hospital, a vein system of potential death and disfigurement for all at the hands of those who could wield them.

Stew would know.

He installed them.

Heat scalded Stew's skin for a mere instant before becoming too hot to feel, every nerve ending crackling inward from the tip like a million molten fuses set alight. His arm dropped from the air, exsanguinating through a hole in his suit as the entity dissolved with a shrill screech and the smell of burnt hair.

Fear overtook him.

And then Stew was dead.

Alone in a scalding sterile room.

North-West 7 Bridge,
The Cleanse, Fifteen Years Ago

A flash of white. Stew clutched the top of the key with an overwhelming surge of bone-wracking regret.

There was nothing to be done.

Blinding light flickered once from below like a spark on a gas stove. And he couldn't run. Part of him wanted to be as near as he could be.

To hurt, like they would.

But anonymous hands gripped his shoulders, dragging him from the bridge of West Belfry 7, ducking behind the unit entryway. Heat at his back, he was shoved behind the fire door by a plum-scrubbed individual as the blast consumed the occupants of North Belfry 7.

Another hand clamped over his, pressing onto his neck.

The scent of char assaulted his senses.

The screams next, of hundreds of people crying out, all at once.

The ones he let die.

And then, silence.

CHAPTER FOURTEEN

Unknown Place,
Unknown Time

Blood pressure dropped into 60 systolic, so we started norepi, now running 1.5 mics per kg per minute—"

Stew's mind worked at the pace of molasses as he realized he was no longer alone.

Clunk.

No longer in a scalding room.

"Respiratory got the tube? N holding C-spine. Count us down."

"On the count of three. One, two . . ."

Something scratched his back as the support underneath him grew soft, comfortable.

"Required two shocks for separate runs of aflutter to the 200s."

IV pumps screamed as drips transferred from one to the next, and he could not help but twitch, lifting his hand. A warm grip crushed his fingers like a vise, and he stiffened.

"On Prop at 50 for sedation with intermittent fentanyl boluses. Total 200 mcg."

"ETT 7.5, 21 cm at the gum, pulling good volume."

The beep of a button pad echoed distantly in his right ear, his arm attempting to escape from its stronghold.

"You're okay, S. Let the medication work."

Warmth flooded his limbs. If someone still held his hand, he did not feel it.

But he felt the eyes.

He felt the eyes.

So many eyes.

Angry eyes.

And he fell into the abyss once more.

PART 5

O, WHAT A THURSDAY

CHAPTER FIFTEEN

West Belfry,
Crowe Hospital Lobby, 05:46

Apple cider vinegar dissolves most supernatural stains. In fact, it's the only cleaning solvent that decimates 99.9 percent of devastation between planes of existence. All organically.

That was the first of many tricks learned in the Environmental Services department at Crowe Community Hospital.

O was far past this lesson—so far past she knew the exact frequency of chime it would take to chase a poltergeist from a recently used trauma room in order to get blood off the stretcher. She was aware of the power of dark moons and how to make potent cleanses from grocery store lemon and cloves, how to boil it so shadows fled. O could siphon stuck souls from reflective surfaces with cotton swabs and knock spirits from their death loops with a spritz of sterile saline and rosemary-infused Betadine.

O knew everything there was to know about the Art of Disinfectant.

Following a storied career cleaning the devastating messes in Crowe County's most gruesome traumas and surgeries and codes, O was ready to end her career within the neonatal intensive care unit on West Belfry's fourteenth floor.

Awaiting an elevator to the basement, O smoothed a pair of starched white pants. White struck many civilians as an odd color to wear when your occupation was being in charge of physical and metaphysical messes, but O enjoyed the classy look and never soiled her uniform.

The lobby at her back was empty in the early morning hours, and a small ding announced the arrival of her ride. Pinching crisp sleeve cuffs, the woman shuffled through the doorway in clunky orthopedic shoes, pressing B on the dial.

A half clock mounted above the elevator stopped at one, too old for a basement indication, before depositing her in a massive hallway of nothing but concrete. In a half hour, it would be bustling with people like a subterranean cityscape, with maintenance and Environmental Services relegated to this molehill beneath the belfries. It was a maze not many had access to without their training, but the days packed it to the brim quickly.

O preferred it as it was. Empty.

The hallway was windowless, all concrete, lit by bare bulbs marching along the ceiling. Pipes snaked through the fixtures like lines on a map, and O followed their rusted drips toward the EVS office.

"Hello, O!"

A miniscule woman, no greater than five feet tall, dragged an oversized maintenance cart in her wake. Her sagging face barely supported the loudest eye makeup one might ever conceive, the blues and oranges clashing brilliantly with her pink lipstick.

O tried her best to move through the conversation. "Good morning, Cora. What a delightful surprise."

"It is!" The small woman mopped her brow with a white cloth. A half-chewed cigarette danced on her lower lip, unlit and likely to stay that way. "You're here early. Are you here for the chaplain meeting?"

"Absolutely not."

Cora shuffled to replace the kerchief in her pocket with a laugh. Beyond her, the empty hallway stretched onward in two branches. One extended to the pathway of the belfries, extending in a web below each, toward the morgue.

The other was the true dead end.

Metaphorically and physically, depending on who you asked.

It was home to the chaplains, the only one besides the chapel on the first floor of South Belfry.

"I heard you received a promotion and thought—"

"In EVS," she corrected, pinpricks needling her palms. "I am in the neonatal ICU now. I hope to retire from there."

"Oh! Well, that's nice." The woman heaved her cart along. "Seems the chaps are in a tizzy this morning after what happened to S yesterday. I would steer clear."

The warning hit O like the broad side of a barn, spoken as nonchalant as the weather report.

"I heard it was awful."

The maintenance cart picked up speed over the uneven ground, as Cora appeared done with the conversation.

"Sure was! Horrific to see."

O gasped. "You were there, Cora?"

"Yes!"

"And you're okay?"

"Of course." The woman hit the elevator button, tucking the cigarette behind her ear. "Not me who got fried."

O's fingertips burned delicately beneath her nail bed,

and she took the time to touch a battered brass watch pinned to her lapel. The years of use had worn the patina to gray, but the small creature's second hand beat without hesitation against her palm.

Cora entered the elevator without further conversation, as was her way, leaving O standing in the barren basement to continue her routine. She attempted to put the conversation from her mind, taking a left at the fork to retrieve her cart.

By far, her favorite part of the day.

Environmental Services occupied the room nearest the elevator in West Belfry, and it was everything O hoped it would be, every day she worked. The room was the size of a football field, with plaster-coated walls that stretched infinitely, stocked with shelves upon shelves of supplies. O was hit by a wave of heat, from industrial washers and dryers operating at a distance. Their attendants appeared like small ants bustling in the space, and scents of detergent overwhelmed the woman.

From the linen to the cleaning to the scrubs and OR equipment, Environmental Services ensured the hospital kept moving. And it did its job well.

O hobbled toward the closest microcosm within the room, where cart supply lined a fleet of cleaning equipment by the left side wall. She pulled Cart 46 from the lineup like a child on Christmas morning.

Cart 46 was hers, every morning, and she inspected the equipment to be certain it was in top condition. Mop, broom, bleach, lemon-flavored dusting, trash bags. All were essential. But she loved the small touches, altered by Central Supply to accommodate her liking.

Apple cider vinegar in a glass spray bottle.

Three jars of sea salt.

Two large rosemary bundles she requested last shift.

Pine needles. Thistle. Beeswax chime candles and oils to dress them. A silver paring knife. Iron casket nails.

The cart danced with the air around it; all the ingredients fit together like a thousand-piece puzzle.

O was delighted.

And ready to begin her day.

Crowds of personnel parted around the cart on her way back to the elevator. Mere minutes welcomed the bustling with intense morning conversation, which absorbed into the concrete walls so they buzzed in a delicate pleasant way.

As the elevator carried O up, she recognized it was a hard atmosphere to leave.

The elevator opened on the first floor, admitting another beside her.

The company was human — at first glance.

The woman wore a light T-shirt and dark jeans, fabrics that attracted energy from the air like lint. Her hair was wild and dark as the fresh tattoos littering her arms wrist to shoulder. The effect could fool someone into thinking the woman was in her late teens, but by the wear to her hands clutching a tattered satchel across her chest and the graying raven hair at her temples, O deduced this woman was in her early thirties. At least.

A beat passed between them, and the woman stared unrelentingly at O's badge with dark tired eyes.

O turned from the scrutiny, delicately pressing the button for floor fourteen.

"Is it your first day?"

The voice chimed from the back elevator wall, but O's eyes did not leave the half clock of numbers ticking their way to the top of West Belfry.

"Far past my first," O answered, "but I am excited for a first of sorts, if that is what you're sensing."

The person's distorted form shifted in the metal door.

"Do you have psychic inclination, to do what you do?"

O became distracted by the warping reflection, which

made the room three times its volume, but she fell into her scripted response. "I suppose psychic is a term. Most of us are just born with anomalies in our eyes. We have extra nerve bundles, like a dog's scent ability but disseminated through—"

"Yeah, I learned all about that shit in school. You're like canine mantis shrimp."

The tattooed woman's reflection bent the wrong direction for a split moment in the elevator door. And in a blink, it was gone.

"I hear all Environmental Services are chaplains who fucked up and couldn't hack it. Is that true too?"

"We are trained similarly until we choose our professions at the end of our program. So no, not demoted."

"Were you?"

O adjusted her sleeves, silent and intent on the numbers climbing on the elevator panel. An urge mounted to leave at the wrong floor just to be rid of the woman.

"Did you clean up after the cleanse yesterday?"

O released a sharp burst of air, turning on her heel. "Who are you?"

The visitor laughed, a gap in her front teeth whistling with the force. The sound hung in the air, carefully placed strings missing the scattered imprecision of actual joy.

"My name is May, though I do suppose in here it's best to keep full names under wraps." The woman winked, repeating abruptly, "Did you? Clean up the emergency yesterday? I heard some nurses talking about it."

O eyed the visitor badge on May's chest with scrutiny.

"I did not," she replied.

The admission drew a pointed grin from the woman as the clock arrow stalled at floor twelve. "I heard it was an interesting job."

O stared as the doors shambled open. "That is a shameful use of the word *interesting*."

But May would not be shamed.

"How else would you describe the suffering of Birch-wood hired scum?"

The doors slid open to West Belfry 12 with a gentle ding.

The woman responded to the silence, jostling against O as she strode off the elevator. "I thought so. Have a nice day."

O coughed once as a stench wafted from the woman. Fetid and sharp, it cracked her senses like a punch to the jaw, lingering long after May's departure. The scent was pernicious, the way it fluttered around her collar like a swarm of beetles. And O displaced it carefully into the air with a single swipe.

As she dragged her cart onto the fourteenth floor, O went to great lengths to push the rot from her mind. Because today was going to be a good day.

West Belfry 14,
Neonatal ICU, 08:39

O performed her daily routine on West Belfry 14 with the vigor of a preschooler able to show off a sixty-four-color box of crayons at school — with the sharpener.

The woman pecked through her assignment room by room, attuning way-line frequencies for each patient with copper polish. Similar to a tuning fork, it left the tang of pennies beneath her nails, while lemon-instilled bleach wiped sigils counterclockwise into every surface, leaving a comforting scent clinging to her hair. Trash bags were exchanged and soap dispensers filled, all with intention and purpose of a person enamored with their environment who knew it was worth protecting.

The square-shaped neonatal ICU was bright and clean by design, one of the only units in West Belfry that did not show its age.

Mostly due to O.

New thistle exchanged every Friday in the door-ways of the rooms, with the linens refolded each evening to have three crisp corners. Two nights a month, O stayed after hours for dark and full moon banishment cleaning.

And to read stories to the children who would tolerate them.

She toiled quietly with efficiency born from knowledge of her craft, the clattering of her cart reassuring to the nurses who sat at their stations at three points of the square-shaped unit.

They appreciated her diligence even more on this day.

"You're spending an awful lot of time with my buddy."

The observation was made by an elderly nurse in plum-purple scrubs who watched O pin sprigs of rosemary to the cork ceiling of room 1459.

B wore age well, with emotions running rampant through the lines on her face and thinning hair done tidily in a bun at the base of her neck. She was sharp corners of a freshly done bed, if they suddenly transformed into a person, and also wore Birkenstocks to work.

In a clear case at room 1459's centerpiece was a spindly baby who was nothing but a cocoon of tightly wrapped hospital blanket and a wild crop of brown hair. He slept for now, but O placed a finger to her lips as she descended her ladder.

Beau was the thirty-four-week-old who'd come a long way from being born at twenty-nine weeks to a mother who never expected her pregnancy to take this turn. He was a wide-eyed imp, formerly a two-pound, five-ounce bundle of premature joy who could now theoretically fit in a car seat.

O came to know a lot about Beau in her time training for NICU.

For instance, she realized Beau did not know much.

She assumed he was uncertain of the date. He could not tell you where he was, only that it was too loud, too often. Beau was unaware of the weather outside his room and the fact that he missed his first Fourth of July home with his sister.

O knew Beau sometimes accepted the world with delicate ease, snuggled comfortably in his incubator. Other times, his body stopped breathing at the smallest inconvenience.

He was, as the nurses would say, "rude."

Beau was a strong name—a fact he was frequently reminded of when his brain's epicenter told him to hold his breath for too long and make nurses rush to his side.

Most important of all, O knew she wanted to protect Beau. More than most, she wanted him safe.

"My friend here did not handle yesterday's events well," O explained and quietly propped the ladder by the door.

The babe's monitor blipped above him as the hospital's energies ebbed, something B did not pay any mind.

"The rosemary is a little much."

O scrutinized the pattern of sprigs tucked into the ceiling.

"Do you think so? There was a woman I spoke with on the elevator this morning . . . left a foul taste in my mouth, talking about what happened to S. So I thought . . . I thought a little something to keep the rooms light."

B sighed as the child snaked a palm from his swaddle, nestling the small hand against his cheek. "Everyone's got an opinion on stuff that's not theirs . . . But a lot of people are feeling the loss."

O recoiled, migrating alongside the Isolette with B. "Flint and fire, loss. S didn't die."

The elder nurse took a low tone, waiting until O was close to confide.

"I heard he's stable for the time being, but I hear the chaplains are on edge. Between that and the possession on ten . . ."

O held a hand up to her friend, halting the speculation.

"Talk about opinions on stuff people shouldn't concern themselves with."

"You know about it?"

"Unfortunately." O took a seat in Beau's armchair, her hips popping in their sockets as she sighed. "It was my granddaughter."

"Oh no . . ."

O waved her hand again, an automatic gesture to keep from wringing her hands.

"She's okay, thank gods. But . . ." She swallowed hard, staring at the infant snuggled calmly in his blanket. "It's hard to say, B. She's been so . . . withdrawn."

"Well . . ." B began carefully, perching on the arm of the chair with a sigh. "I imagine if I had a demon or whatever it was fucking around in my head, I'd need some time too."

The twinge of a headache began between O's eyes. "Yeah, you're right."

"I know I am."

"I am trying to give her space. She slept over the last few nights because she feels safe there."

"She feels safe enough to be withdrawn and quiet. Give her time, O."

"Of course. And then the thing with S. He was with her that night helping, and now he's . . ."

She threw up her hands, at a loss for words, which B happily found.

"Crispy."

"Gods."

"Sorry, continue."

But O couldn't, cradling her head in her hands long enough for Beau to successfully free his second hand, placing both behind his head like he was sunbathing. The warmth of B's hand found O's shoulder, giving it a firm squeeze.

"We were always going to be worried about G, here," B said. "Having no inclinations was always going to be hard for her. But she has good intuition. And that will get her through."

"She's coming back tomorrow."

"Or, you know, maybe she's not all there."

O smiled, watching Beau sprawled in the Isolette, utterly content.

"Remember when we were worried about my grandson the most?"

B laughed, tension breaking into pieces in her chest like stars.

"Beau reminds me of him as a babe. All that beautiful hair."

"At least Beau won't date a Birchwood agent. That was a trip."

"Oh, B." O ran a hand over her face.

"No. He's back?"

"I don't know."

"What a mess."

"Very much so."

B leaned onto O's shoulder, her whole weight tilting the woman into the arm of the chair with a groan.

"They take after their nana, you know."

"Oh, yes."

The silence of long friendship consumed the room, leaving space for the gentle tick of O's watch and voices from the nurses' station down the hall, jovial and unaware.

"Let me know if you hear anything else about S. Maybe we can send his children some food," O mumbled as the way-line danced, fractals of light darting into the room and around B's head like fireflies. It was a comforting dance of functioning security, and she inhaled with purpose.

"I will." B forced a smile. "Jokes aside, I'm not going to say what happened to him doesn't make me nervous."

The conversation down the hall stalled as if running into a brick wall, leaving O's response barely audible as she forced herself up from the chair.

"It feels too familiar."

"I agree." B slid down the arm of the chair onto the cushion, exchanging places as O stepped over the way-line with her ladder. "Just know if the world tilts sideways again, I'm taking Beau and running right down the stairs and out the door. Too old for that disorderly evacuation nonsense."

"Absolutely. You and me, two old biddies out the door in a flash, Beau leading the way. Because we know better, don't we, Beau?"

O realized Beau did not hear much on account of his premature ears and inches of rune-etched glass separating him from the conversation. But he did blink once, and O took that as a satisfying affirmative.

CHAPTER SIXTEEN

West Belfry Basement,
Crowe County Hospital, 13:15

O exited the elevator into the basement of West Belfry. Uncharacteristically, for the second time that day.

Her lunch box encircled her wrist, with remnants of her break clattering within as she trudged on stiff knees to the fork in the hallway. The day was wonderful. She completed her tasks before noon. She even managed another visit to see Beau while his family visited.

That said, there was something she could not shake.

The fetid stench from the elevator followed her all day, lingering among the lemon and sharp pine. Like a plague to her senses.

So, she stood at the break in the basement hall letting the scent linger among musty drippings of old pipes above before she proceeded down the right-hand side of the fork in the road. On the way to chaplain headquarters.

Despite the rumors, O did not feel the instant cold coming from the bleak cement walls. There were no insidious whispers, no electric shocks to her mind. The hall was shorter than the stories.

But O knew this already. And it took no time to reach the plain wooden door at the end. A small brass placard was tacked into the entry, reading *Chaplains' Quarters. Please Knock.*

She did, raising arthritic knuckles to tap out a hollow beat.

A quiet rustle of clothing on the opposite side of the door preceded it opening with a groan. The person before her was dressed head to toe in a black button-up and slacks and dress shoes fit for a mortician. He had a face made of sharp angles, with sunken sockets that were consumed by reflective glass eye replicas.

Outside of work, this was Alfie.

His solemn expression cracked into a grin, staring directly past O with brimming enthusiasm.

"O. What a wonderful surprise!"

"Is it?" the woman questioned, wrapping her arms around the beanpole of a man with a fierce squeeze. "Better for seeing you."

"I'm flattered." He stepped aside with a hasty wave. "Please, please. Come in."

O shuffled across the threshold into a small room stuffed with a table, a couch, and more bookshelves than one ever thought possible. They lined the walls, overflowing from head to toe with ratty tomes and stacks of papers.

A microwave was crammed atop one, open with a lukewarm dish seeping the smell of old marinara sauce into the air, the entire room smelling of pasta and must. Across the room was a door leading to what O knew to be an on-call suite, with two cots and no leg room.

One other body sat nearby, buried in a pile of literature. The woman raised her gaze briefly.

She wore a similar uniform to Alfie, punctuated with a pansy pin on her lapel. Benign enough, the flower flexed powerfully into the room, pressing briefly into O's person like a nosy dog before retreating to its owner.

Chaplain supervisor — Beatrice.

"It's not often I know everyone in this office," O noted, closing the door gently behind her.

The supervisor did not look up from her work. "It is certainly a changing landscape."

"Do you want to sit?" Alfie asked, resuming his spot at the table, swarmed with books in identical fashion.

"No, thank you, A. I'll only be a moment. I'm almost done with lunch."

Alfie barely made contact with the chair before springing up, moving to the microwave to remove his dish. "Thank you for reminding me! Leftovers from this past Sunday."

O smiled as the man dug into his pasta, and repositioned her lunch box. "First off, I wanted to thank your team for helping my granddaughter the other night."

Beatrice spared a glance from the thick leather tome. "I didn't know that was G at first. But it became . . . undeniable, with her methods."

O was uncertain whether or not to be offended.

"When did she start?"

Alfie interjected through a mouthful of noodles. "Got a job three months ago in the ICU circlet. She was quite excited about it at dinner last Sunday."

"She's the unremarkable one, yes?"

O bristled. "I wouldn't say it in that way. She's very skilled in craft. Always very confident and controlled."

The supervisor's acknowledgment was scant but earnest. "She certainly contained the entity well. Expelled it without a cleanse, so that's fairly impressive."

"You were there?"

"I was."

"Do you know what entity it was? She's thinking . . . the only thing she mentioned to me was the name The End, but . . . that cannot be true?"

The woman gestured to the books laid out before her. Lore spread across the table without reprieve, scribed onto pages of volumes most hospitals could only wish to procure. "We're doing our best to deduce that. The only strand I have to go off is a creature named Alagor who has been a problem citywide, to this point. Identified itself as The End, but I don't believe that."

"Why don't you?"

"Because it is, frankly, impossible."

O moved to the table, looking on the texts for a brief moment before Beatrice flipped the page of notes over, looking at O over oval spectacles.

"What can we do for you, O?"

O cleared her throat once, taking a slow step away from the table. "I have a concern from this morning."

The topic removed Alfie from his pasta, and he wiped his mouth on the corner of his sleeve. "A concern?"

"There was this woman asking about S in the elevator. People are strange about Birchwood, so I didn't think anything of it. But she had this scent. And I have tried to forget it but am having trouble shaking it."

"Patient or visitor?"

"Visitor."

"Can you recall the scent?"

O closed her eyes, taking a moment to return to the elevator. To let the reek settle in her nostrils once more.

"Like . . . wet wood. Wood rot. And fish. It was decay. I know there were many rituals this full moon in the community, so maybe it could be residual from something of that nature. But I have a hard time shaking her demeanor."

The two ink blots sat with the information, Alfie more than his companion. Delicately, he adjusted one of his glass eyes, staring into the middle distance.

"I can't say I'm concerned about the scent per se," he admitted, "but I do trust your instinct, O. We can have our chaplains review the visitor logs with the guards, and if she's still in the hospital, we can find a reason for her odd behavior, at the very least."

"Thank you. That would mean a lot."

The reedy man smiled, returning to his pasta.

"Means a lot to us, if you caught something that's not supposed to be here. The thanks go both ways. Can we do anything else for you?"

"No, I should get back to my unit anyhow."

O retreated to the door, and Beatrice returned to her tome without goodbyes.

Alfie waved once, digging into his meal. "My best to Miss G. Is she accepting visitors?"

"She probably would for you, A."

He beamed.

"Splendid. I'll swing by after work. On official business first. But, I also have those trellises for her garden I promised. They're the smoothest I've ever felt. She's going to love them."

CHAPTER SEVENTEEN

West Belfry 14,
Crowe County Hospital, 13:48

O stood inside West Belfry 14 at the unit door, its fortified iron exterior riddled with infinitesimal inscriptions. She remembered the day these doors were placed, carved to life, behemoths that offered invaluable protection to every unit they oversaw. On each trip around the NICU, her hand found the cool black surface that sent miniscule vibrations buzzing to her knuckles. It was a reassuring sensation, a protected sensation.

Returning from lunch, O placed her ladder to the side, resting her hand on the iron companion.

And felt nothing.

She removed her hand from the surface like she'd received a shock, her fingers grazing the cool metal before setting her palm down once more.

Again, nothing.

O looked ahead to the first nurses' station, breaking into a swift hobble from the door.

The unit was quiet between care, nurses at the first station giving scattered nods in greeting, scribbling to catch up on their charts. The way-lines buzzed dully around each station, intact and secure.

"Someone, call the front desk," O instructed. "The front door is down. Request security to points of entry, please. Inform your staff."

One of the nurses reached for the phone with enough expediency that O felt comfortable continuing a cautious lap to the second care area. It was a duplicate of the first with two doctors speckled between nurses at the desk. Papers were spread across in a haphazard manner, consuming their attention as O examined the eight rooms.

All intact.

Halfway between the second and third point in the square was the room O needed to see.

The faint smell of rosemary wafted from Beau's room, a minor reassurance while O probed the way-line. Even at the distance, she saw the hairpin slit fractured across the bottom, causing the edges of the room to sway like a boat bent on capsizing.

O froze, feet from the threshold.

The smell unfurled in her nostrils, delicately at first. With each passing breath, it intensified, until it was as strong as in the elevator. The pestilent stench tickled just above her left ear, and O straightened her sleeve cuffs, reaching for the door.

B was the only person O saw.

She sat in the recliner by the lowered incubator, with her neck cracked forty-five degrees backward. Her ear bent into her shoulder blade, an ashen deadened expression that stole life from the lines of the woman's eyes.

The perverse horror raked O's soul.

O rushed forward, grasping for her friend. Searching B's tepid skin for a pulse. A rush of blood battered her ears, sharp sobs piercing the air as she struggled for breath.

The woman staggered, coming face-to-face with Beau's box for the first time.

Open.

Empty.

A chorus of sound screeched through the hall, screams shattering the serene day from everywhere and nowhere. Beau's room was plunged into darkness, black as pitch.

A deep siren grew from the bowels of West Belfry, cresting against her skull in a death rattle.

Red bulbs flickered to life, taking place of the hospital's fluorescence, lighting up the dark.

What remained of Beau's way-line was snuffed by the red mire, the stain of blood-tinged fog scattering the light around Beau's door like feathers before being swept away by gale force wind battering the hall.

Lowering of hospital security defenses happened quarterly.

Scheduled.

There was time to prepare. Time to plan. Time to brace the staff for what to expect and how to protect themselves and their patients from the onslaught of freed entities as the system reset.

This was Downtime.

Horrifically unplanned.

And no one knew what to do.

O limped for the doorway, the chaos she encountered dredged from the recesses of history.

Translucent figures tumbled from crawl space prisons within the walls. Their static humanoid shapes latched like leeches to a plum-scrubbed nurse bolting past. Her screams were swallowed by the alarm as they used their tendrils to rend her limbs from their sockets, scattering them down the hall.

Iron bars blockaded every window, etched by deft hands and searing hot to practitioners and family members bombarding the glass in hordes, frantic to escape.

They sought safety, but none existed.

Fear overflowed from the crowd in a thick mask of green, tinted black in the pulsating red light.

The hospital's beating heart.

O stooped at the doorframe, taking a long last look at B's slumped form before jumping into the chaos. Immediately, her shoulder was thrown sideways, knocking her hard onto the tile. Hip throbbing, O was brought eye level with dark jeans and fashionable boots slicked with viscera.

May leered down at O, her visitor badge blaring against her white shirt. The woman's face cracked in a clenched smile while the canvas bag in her hand let loose a tinny cry. It was barely audible, but O recognized the sound instantly.

Beau.

"He's not yours!"

O lunged for the bag, receiving a boot square to the chest.

With a single smirk, May darted across the hall, wrenching open the door to the stairwell, gone without a word.

Heat blossomed under O's eyelids, sucking wind through a straw. Staggering to her feet.

Another figure in plum scrubs flew from a neighboring room, their impact against the stairwell door muted as the alarm dragged itself to another crescendo. Lace-patterned moisture dripped from the ceiling, scorching anything in its path.

O tucked her chin, slamming gracelessly past the practitioner into the stairwell.

A metal rail hit her hand like sandpaper, the alarm screaming to O's elbow. O gripped the support, looking up and down the rusted edifice, which stretched eternally both ways.

Upstairs or down. Upstairs or down.

The woman threw her clicking hip forward.

Hobbling down two flights was lifelong, through sweltering heat pressing against her with every step, before she burst onto the twelfth floor.

A labyrinth of renewed chaos unraveled, and her sensible orthopedic shoes skidded on a dark puddle, inches from the stairwell door. Footsteps screeched around her while O steadied herself, blinking through the tide of nurses and patients who made a break for the stairs.

An escape from the madness.

O fought the current to the middle of the hallway, straining to empty her lungs. To breathe, though the air was thick enough to cut with a knife.

In and out.

In.

Hold.

Out.

There it was.

A carton of eggs left in a car trunk.

Fish picked clean by gulls on a summer day.

Putrescence, wafting from her left.

Broken tile slid beneath her as O tracked the carrion scent, coalesced on a heavy maintenance door.

It was distinct.

Worse, it was familiar.

O steeled her nerve for what she might find, shoving the door open.

Cleaning supplies were piled against the far corner of the dim room, concoctions of herbs and medical-grade tinctures stacked along shelves like soldiers. O knew them by memory like a favorite book, stocked beside tools tacked limply across a rack on the back wall.

U-bends and stiff buckets of oil pressed against the far corner, framing a young woman working dutifully to complete scripture on the peeling concrete floor.

She worked glyphs and sigils with white chalk around two props integral to her success.

A small maintenance woman named Cora, with makeup almost too loud to function, had been methodically filleted at the center of the circle. Her stomach poured its contents on the floor, and she stared lifelessly at the ceiling above as condensation dripped onto her forehead. Beside the corpse was unswaddled Beau, his limbs flailing amidst a small pile of liver and bile smeared in a triangle amidst the chalk etchings.

He was crying.

He was scared.

The empty duffel bag was discarded to the side, kitchen Tupperware strewn sloppily about the room.

O stood in the open doorway. She held her face in a practiced placid expression, marred by the fire dancing beneath her eyelids and the stabbing pain in her left hip. Fists hung loosely by her sides, she allowed the door to shut, claiming May's full attention.

"You're going to give him back!"

The alarm devoured May's laugh, but the light of it fell differently on the world, this time like confetti—joyful, scattering over the display in pyrotechnic sincerity.

May's eyes were on O like a prey animal, mania thinly veiled by lucidity. "Consider it an eye for an eye!"

O tensed as the woman completed the circle with a flourish and stood, throwing the chalk to the side. O moved around the perimeter of the room with delicate steps, trying to hold May's attention.

"Why?"

Beau whimpered.

May flinched, a blank stare settling on the infant while she matched O's steps, keeping distance.

"Because he needs to return. And he needs me to do it!"

The corners of the room dimmed, creeping inward. O's eyes adjusted as darkness hardened, encroaching.

Something in the room was listening. In a blink, the shadows crept over piles of supplies toward the circle.

O's eyes narrowed and she stepped forward to keep out of its gloom. "It's already here. Isn't it, May?"

May's glee dripped from deep blue circles beneath her eyes. She was a firework of a person, living days without sleep. Her arms opened wide, as if to embrace her good work.

"He never left! Alagor is patient and waits for what he needs."

The dark nipped at O's heels, pressing her forward with a chill that stung the woman's calves. The darkness crawled over the stone in a sheet of frost, finding cracks and heaving the floor upward. Beau's persistent whine devolved into a pained scream, swallowed by the alarm.

Time slipping away, O lunged for infant.

May was on her heels, fanatically responsive. The woman's weight landed hard on O's hips, jamming her into the concrete.

O slid through the bile smear as her opponent's cackle screeched, clinging to her legs in manic fervor. The older woman clawed at the floor, hands grasping for the edges of the room within the dark, throwing her feet at May's face as she lunged for the cleaning supplies.

May dug into O's thigh through the assault, climbing up her waist with fingernails like pitons as O shook one of the shelves. Supplies cascaded to the floor below, skittering over the circle. O lunged for a glass bottle nearest her, recovering the thin amber liquid before the darkness was able to take it.

With May's claws in her chest, O whipped the bottle around and pulled the trigger.

The first thing Environmental Services taught, the one O knew best: apple cider vinegar held immense supernatural flammability.

Both women screamed. Beau screamed.

"You bitch!" May shrieked.

She released O, hands flinging to her head. As darkness loomed upon them, opalescent steam spilled from the woman's locks, its cascade of smoke tumbling to the concrete in dense fog.

O loosed the contents of the bottle on every inch of May she could reach as she scrambled from the encroaching shadow. Steam hissed from May's body, brought to life by O's intention, sculpting the air around her to vibrant heat.

The elder EVS backed into the circle, scooping Beau into her arms, screaming disinfectant slang that captured the apple cider vinegar in the air and molded it, bending its steam inward like a turtle's shell until it clutched tightly to every inch of the woman like a wet suit.

"Stop! Stop!" the woman screamed, immovable under the influence as her darkness, the darkness she'd summoned, began to consume her.

O allowed it, eyes latched on May as the phantasm of lights wrought by the vinegar were snuffed. Inch by inch, the inky black ichor seeped over her body, sifting away skin in a real-time rot, peeling her body apart until there was nothing left.

With it went Cora's killer. B's killer. And all the strength O had.

The woman sank to her knees as a figure stepped into the circle. Swathed in darkness was writhing a shadow. Undefined. A tendrilled mass.

Its eyes latched on Beau while its limbs threatened to solidify, clawed fingers dripping from its tenuous form. The remaining shadow pulled into the figure in swells, siphoning warmth from the air as it took its first breath.

A heavy exhale followed, exposing a flash of color in its featureless form.

Pale green eyes snapped open, and it bent to stare at O and her charge. For a long moment, it was still, and O could feel its presence scouring the edges of her mind, probing for entry.

"There's nothing here for you," O challenged, any escape blockaded by the darkness whispering at her heels. "Alagor."

Its form crept forward toward the circle's center, towering over O where she knelt. The woman huddled into Beau, frantic to protect him.

The creature's strangled voice pierced the interior of her mind, as efficient as it was obscene.

"They say . . . to know a name is detrimental . . . in this facility."

Carefully, it stepped within Cora's carcass, siphoning her viscera into its form.

Within Cora's chest cavity, it solidified. Bent over, teasing clawed fingers through her entrails, its green eyes affixed to O's face, tilting its neck at an unnatural angle.

An angle reminiscent of B.

"Do you think that is true about me?"

Darkness beat against the circle barrier like a drum, cresting above O as the figure smiled with a mouth that stretched ear to ear. It stepped from Cora's body, dragging the shadowed darkness behind it.

O fell back, her spine curling against the energy that teased her pressed white uniform with its rot. Beau continued to cry; May's body fettered into the pulsating gloom.

The world was caving inward.

Well-known hospital flows, ones she cultivated and cared for, were indecipherable beyond the creature's scrim. Panic built in O's stuttering chest.

"What do you want?"

Alagor stepped closer.

"I want . . . this place. To burn."

It stooped in front of O, holding out a dripping clawed hand. At this distance, she noted its form shifting like tectonic plates of tar, molding itself into enough of a person to pass as one's shadow.

Its breath was a wave of stale eggs and seawater, and O's caught in her chest, coming in frantic gulps as Alagor's fingertips found Beau's hair, teasing his locks.

"I want to play."

The child fell silent under the creature's hand, his little chest still in O's arms.

Eyes wide, she wrenched away the inches she could, watching the babe's lips slowly lose their color to a lifeless blue tinge sweeping up his forehead.

"No . . . NO!"

Fire flared on O's eyelids, searing her gaze in a flash of white light that shot from the woman like a hailstorm and gained traction, slipping quickly from O's control.

Molten warmth gathered to a point at the tip of O's tongue, coating her throat, every crevice of every limb, with the instantaneous comfort of blinding heat. As if her entire person was wrapped in a wool sock.

This comfort was allowed a single ventricular twitch.

A fleeting moment.

Before it splintered across O's chest. A flash cracked through the room, the light searing outward from O's body like confetti. Alagor's dripping shadow lunged with a guttural screech.

O's spine cracked. A blast of molten light bathed the room.

A hurricane of tools flew from their holds, slamming onto the floor. Disinfectant dropped around them like grenades, exploding in fantastic pyrotechnic display, a shock wave that rippled through the room.

Chasing the dark.

O slammed into the door from the force, sliding to the ground with a final scream, the light ripped from her throat as fast as it came.

Residual heat seethed from toolboxes and shelves as O clutched Beau, struggling to right herself. The image of May's final moments clung before her in a mirage of heat, mingling in a thick green mire that congealed at the center of the room, where Cora's body sat smoking and charred.

The darkness was gone.

Alagor was gone.

O's eyes adjusted to a single light illuminating the room from above the mutilated workbench. Red light disappeared into the silence of the last alarm.

Beau spluttered once before his cry resumed.

Desperately, O rocked the blood-soaked babe as the color returned to his cheeks with flare, the tips of his hair wisping thin trails of smoke.

"You're okay," O rasped. "You're okay."

Her knees protested the movement, but O slid up the door. She leaned heavily against its searing iron form before the handle stiffened under her grip, locked.

"We're in here!"

The sounds of the room split her senses, potent and raw as O brought her hand down on the metal again and again, palm searing into the heated surface.

At her back, she felt whispers.

The creeping voices of creatures who existed just beyond what she could see, who were released when the hospital security went down.

Amidst those, she felt it.

She felt Alagor like pinpricks breathing down her neck.

Her hand came down on the door, increasingly desperate, until it disappeared beneath her.

O fell into the hall, clutching Beau close.

Her pristine white garment was marred by blood and bile. Gray and black garments gathered around her in a state of professional disbelief, their shoes shuffling around each other to get a better view.

O cracked open her eyes, a security badge emblazoned with S kneeling close.

The moniker was gone with another blink, standing in his place a younger man with a full auburn beard covering a serious expression. Without a word, he reached for Beau.

O shook her head, gripping the babe tight. "He's going nowhere but with me, out the front door with his parents to another hospital."

The declaration garnered the attention of straggling staff members who congregated from hiding, stepping numbly among ravaged bodies of deceased coworkers, the remains of their friends.

Patients and practitioners gathered like penguins in a windstorm, whispering about the woman in white and the baby she refused to return. On her feet, O met the young guard's gaze directly, and the crowd condensed to a suffocating circle, intent on hearing her words.

"I need to see the chaplains," she rasped loud enough to be misheard by half the onlookers. "Alagor is here, and we need to evacuate. Now."

PART 6

EVERYONE'S GAL FRIDAY

CHAPTER EIGHTEEN

West Belfry 6,
Evacuation Day, Unknown Time

The chaplains arrive with haste and say the children must leave. This is something I understand, as it is part of the emergency training provided by my own kind. To keep us safe.

It is not my place to say what the chaplains care about, but it is not us.

I remain near my hole, with one paw in the hospital and one back home as two foot coverings hurry through the door. They are larger than Alex's, and I am led to believe these are kin to the child.

I smell the green sludge around these elders but do not eat it.

Old fear is always bitter.

Familiar plush duck heads are exchanged for outside coverings. They have lights in their heels, and I do not know if this is for protection or for fun. The child jumps to engage them, giggling as they do.

This act informs me they must be for levity.

The large shoe coverings move quickly, stripping art from the wall. As they perform this business, I see the face of Alex pulling away the blanket that obscures my home.

Their kin cannot see me. They are aged and do not have that ability.

But they know Alex speaks to me.

"I . . . leaving," Alex says in my tongue, and the pronunciation grates on my glorious pointed ears.

I tolerate the assault on my language.

I tolerate the child reaching to touch my claw.

There is something I will miss about this Alex, and I bow my head.

"Will miss . . ." they say.

I do not know how to respond, but the child would not be an Alex if they did not come with a plan. Alexes typically do.

"Meet me . . . home? Have . . . bigger bed!"

The child bares their teeth the biggest I have seen, and it is this human version of joy that leads me to believe they are offering me employment.

I hesitate. Living under a child's bed is different. Negotiations are complex. In fact, there are usually none.

I pick a bed with green, and I feast. When the green becomes bitter, I leave.

Murmurs from my home warn of slayers forcing my kind to flee, and I am reminded of the situation's haste.

Alex looks on expectantly, and I complete the conversation.

"Will try."

I see human delight in the child's expression. Before I remove myself, they dive toward my face and mash their lips between my eyes.

My revulsion is barely contained out of respect for the child, and they are pulled backward by the owners of the large shoe coverings. What I know from research as a kiss makes my ears twitchy.

I slink into my hole, certain to close the way behind me so the hospital will not follow.

I will find Alex.

I will try.

CHAPTER NINETEEN

East Belfry, Crowe County
Emergency Department, 18:32

West Belfry cleanse in two hours. Please clear the premises. West Belfry cleanse in two hours. Please clear the premises."

"Sir, please return to your rig."

The chaplain's robes were trimmed in delicate silk, slithering against broken tile as he stepped forward. Peter stood eye height with the man, younger, driven, whose expression remained impassive while blockading the only double doors leading from Crowe's emergency wing to the hospital proper. His tone suspended in the air between them like a wet sandbag on fishing wire.

The paramedic's hand dragged down his face, attempting to adjust his exhausted features to something resembling friendly.

"Look," he said. "My sister is still in there, and I'm not stupid, okay? You and I both fucking know there have been deaths. The evacuation is winding down, and she's not out yet. I need to make sure she's okay. *Please*, Chap."

The chaplain's faraway gaze moved to Peter's left ear in response to his plea, speaking softly into the air. "I'm sorry. I cannot help you. If you don't return to your rig, I will have you forcibly removed."

The exit sign above the chaplain's head flickered with every syllable.

Peter paused, weighing the threat. "Well . . . it seems we're at an impasse."

Before deciding against his better judgment.

The chaplain's silken robes scraped against his skin like a branding iron as Peter lunged for the entranceway, slamming against the security bar. A sudden flurry of movement erupted around him as the way-line gently humming among the entranceway burst into brilliant red, searing Peter's palms as they wrestled with the door. The black robes enfolded him like a constrictor snake, prying him back with unprecedented strength.

"You're done."

Peter was tossed from the door, landing in a heap on a hard pair of shoes. His hands tucked to his chest, searing hot as the red way-line framed the ink blot before him, standing firmly against the entranceway with his faraway eyes, uncreased and unbothered.

"I need to get my sister," Peter choked, eyes swimming at the sight.

"I'm sorry. I cannot help you." The chaplain gestured calmly to the air behind Peter. "Remove him."

A flash of wolf gray yanked Peter to his feet, the paramedic's boot heels scuttling across the tile as his shirt bunched against his spine. The chaplain stepped back, their mute emotions following as Peter bucked ineffectively against the aggressor down EMS hall.

Empty stretchers were void of ire and indignation after hours of hospital diversion, and Peter slammed into each and every one as he lost sight of the chaplain and the doors.

"Get off me!" he shouted, hooking his feet against the trauma room, freeing his arm with a wild swing.

"Fuck! Why—!" the assailant hollered, his grip fumbling on Peter's arms as the paramedic's foot slipped from the handle of trauma room 5. "Gods, will you calm down? You're like a fucking wombat."

The paramedic's gums itched as he whirled on the aggressor. The voice was familiar as nails in a food processor and a lullaby all at once.

Clarence's fingers pressed firmly into Peter's shoulders as a thin stream of silver-hued blood trickled from his nose. Without a word, the man scooped Peter under one arm, heaving him down the hallway.

"That's not Birchwood's uniform. Who'd you steal that from?" Peter shook off the man repeatedly, only allowed steps at a time before his hands were on his shoulders once more. "Will you leave me alone? I'm going!"

"Can you be quiet?" Clarence hissed, passing clusters of plum-scrubbed nurses and doctors who all diverted their attention toward the scuffle. "Let's just . . . Come on, let's get you out of here."

Trauma bay antisepsis flooded Peter's lungs full force as he allowed himself to be led from the hospital. Clarence walked him away from the sliding glass doors before letting go completely. The sudden and overwhelming atmosphere hit Peter like a freight train. His feet couldn't stop moving, as if meant to outpace urgent thoughts strung in a lattice behind his eyes.

"All right, all right," Clarence said firmly. The man's hands opened to the paramedic, their movement blurred among the dense bunker air. "We weren't in a place to figure out what you needed in there. It wasn't safe for that. But now we can."

The words were lost somewhere in his neglected senses as the chaplain's silhouette stained Peter's vision, framed in the memory of crimson light that burned his hands fingertip to wrist. Heat coursed through his arms in jolts, and he stomped his shoe against the concrete, the sole of his foot numb to the shock.

Clarence's voice was on the periphery of his mind, muffled. "What do you need, Peter?"

The paramedic tensed, rocking onto his toes as he attempted to direct his feet to the sound. The man's vague outline clashed with the flickering of the way-line, with the shock of its warding and the door's hard steel.

The hospital caught up to him like food poisoning, biting at the back of his throat. "Salts . . . please. I have salts in my b-bag . . . b-back of the rig . . ."

Clarence's shadow darted around Peter, leaving him alone as if suspended in space. Lights blinked above him, embedded in the ceiling as gray mites leapt from passing practitioners he could not decipher. The paramedic gripped his side, huddling against himself before something potent cracked beneath his nose, assaulting his senses with a chemical blast.

The sting ripped Peter from his mind, catapulting him back to the ambulance bunker with watering eyes and a gag.

"Okay! Okay. Give yourself a minute, Pete."

Peter's shoulders sagged under Clarence's broad hands pressing into him from above. They pinned him to the ground, stymied his retching. The paramedic flinched, his neck twitching as Clarence's coarse fingers intertwined behind it.

He leaned his head into the man's hands, exhaling slowly.

The Birchwood man matched the breath, ignoring the landscape of people bustling around them as he did.

"That's good . . . The hospital's a lot right now. You're stressed, but you're safe. We can let this pass . . ."

Ambulances were crammed into parking spots with a line of impatient couriers stretching along the upper road. The rigs bore practitioners and insignias from neighboring cities, neighboring states, working around them in tandem. It was unprecedented times, and the demand on Crowe's staff was too much to bear alone. Reinforcements came in a flood, assistance converging on Crowe in a manner they'd pleaded for fifteen years ago. An anthill of activity siphoned patients into vehicles and off to secondary locations. On the road above, triage pavilions stretched a full block, crammed together in the open air of the stale summer afternoon to sort the rest.

The sounds of the city were gone, and something about that made Peter's fingertips sting. The sensation bit at his bandaged forearms differently than the hospital door's assault, a discomfort of unfamiliarity. The wounds pulsed with every heartbeat as he stared obstinately at the bunker wall.

Oddly enough, being crammed into the hectic garage with other rigs parked flush to their sides was a security.

Peter allowed his eyes to close, the rhythm of the chaos replaced by Clarence's voice.

"That's good. How are you right now?"

"Better . . . thank you."

His eyes opened to the furrowed brow of the man before him, closer than he'd been in a long time. The lines of his face were posed naturally in concern, a default expression for Clarence, with rectangular pupils fixed on him from a deep brown iris that continued like the depths of space.

This close, Peter noted gray roots peeking through Clarence's box brown dye.

"What do you need, Pete?"

A shaky breath escaped Peter's chest, and he brought his throbbing arms to rest around his stomach.

"It's my sister. She's in West Belfry. They only have two more floors to clear, and I have no clue why she's not out. We've gotten reports of deaths. The security system is being overtaken. I'm so fucking scared."

Clarence took in the information with a shift of his stance as a flood of people from the Emergency Department parted around them like the Red Sea.

When he spoke, his voice was soft. "I can go in and see if I can bring her out."

"Birchwood isn't allowed inside hospital walls."

"I'm not, um . . ." The man's fingers twitched on the back of Peter's neck. "I got sanctioned on Sunday and put in hospital interior for evac with Crowe Security. If I'm not dead by the end of it, I imagine I'll have to answer for turning on George."

"What the fuck does that mean?"

"Ace?" Henry emerged from the hospital, coming to a halt at a distance. "Is everything all right here?"

Peter gently removed himself from the proximity of the Birchwood man, suddenly uncertain where to put his hands. "I'm fine. You got my coffee?"

Henry held aloft a paper cup while his gentle eyes bored into Clarence. The gaze came with a warning shot as the elder's glasses caught the dim bunker light.

Clarence placed his hands in his pockets, retreating.

"I'll be back soon."

And with a blast of cool hospital air, he sped through the doors, out of sight.

The joints of Peter's fingers ached with an electrical sting, his breath coming in catches as he wiped his eyes.

Henry allowed his partner a moment of composure before holding out his hand. "Your coffee."

Peter reached for his cup, shuffling to rig 415 and slumping onto its back step. He cradled the beverage carefully, picking at the Styrofoam lip with a mumbled thanks.

Henry perched next to his partner with a sigh that communicated distaste. Maybe disapproval. Peter couldn't be certain.

Despite it, this was the closest to hope Peter had felt all day, allowing the fumes of burnt coffee to sting his nostrils as he scraped his tongue against his teeth.

"So, you tried to check in on your sister."

Peter took a slow sip of his coffee.

"Told you that might not be a great idea."

"Yeah."

"Said it might be tough for you to handle the inside in such an emotionally fraught time. You do remember, that's why I went inside to get the coffee?"

"I get it."

A low rumble of a storm tickled Peter's ears, announcing its approach over the not-far-off bay.

"Clarence is in there and being utilized for security. He's gonna check in on her."

Electricity danced on his tongue, ozone sharpening his words as his partner sat beside him. The silence grew in volumes as the PA above crackled to life.

"West Belfry cleanse in one hour, forty-five minutes. Please clear the premises. West Belfry cleanse in one hour, forty-five minutes. Please clear the premises."

The words fizzled into strands of static floating on the air, the insidious warning lingering like luminescent butterflies around their heads.

Henry nudged Peter gently, and Peter's breath seized in his chest. Every neuron fought to burst from his skin as the well-intentioned touch shocked his system, and he moved his feet to the concrete.

"Ace, Birchwood agents are pigheaded and resolute. He will find Miss G; there's certainty to that."

The reassurance did nothing, but Peter forced a nod for his partner's sake.

The chaos of evacuation was immense. Streets adjacent to the belfries were closed completely, save for emergency vehicles tasked with whisking patients to receiving hospitals. Trip after trip, Peter was less interested in the chaplains and less intrigued by the impossible streets. News vans appearing at the Birchwood perimeter held no interest, and the sky threatening to open with sheets of rain faded from concern.

Ten hours later, his care narrowed to one person, and he sat up with hope as the Emergency Department doors slid open once more.

Waiting.

Relying on Clarence.

Carefully, he relaxed his shoulders while crumpling the empty coffee cup to mulch.

"H," Peter asked quietly, "does this time look better than North Belfry's fall?"

The older man sighed a tired answer, watching the wave of people hurry past.

"Oh, yes. Last time we were caught completely off guard."

A flicker of lightning danced on the wall with the shadow of their rig, a tenuous roll of thunder quick on its heels.

Peter let it reverberate in his chest, the patter of rain bringing goose bumps of a different kind under his bandages. "So, you think we'll get everyone out in time?"

A slow roll of thunder consumed Henry's silence.

**East Belfry, Crowe County
Ambulance Bay, 18:55**

Clarence took up the entire entrance of the Emergency Department, the top of his head scraping the doorway as he entered the ambulance bay. His brutalized face was solemn, cracking when Peter caught his eye.

As Clarence stepped aside, Peter caught sight of a plum-scrubbed figure in heavy isolation attire, hiding in the Birchwood man's shadow. Curly brown hair poked from beneath Gigi's sterile scrub cap as she ripped off her face shield, dashing from the doorway.

Peter was on his feet in a flash. "Hey!"

Gigi crashed into a full-throttle hug Peter barely managed to absorb. Damning the shock of agony from his arms, Peter squeezed his sister as tight as he could manage, kissing the top of her head before holding her painfully at arm's length. The only recognizable feature beyond her protection was a pair of deep brown eyes misting above her mask. Carry-on bags clung under her eyes, but she was here and whole, allowing Peter to release an unsteady breath.

"Are you okay?"

Gigi swiped at her face with the sleeve of her gown.

"Of course not. But we're almost done, so I'll feel better soon." She looked him over with a sigh. "Your arms look like shit, Pete."

"I'm getting the rabies series. It's . . . just a little pain." Peter grimaced, allowing inspection of the bandages before dropping his arms to his sides. "Besides, this is not about me."

"You taking something for it?"

Peter rolled his eyes. "I'm gonna."

Gigi paused before smacking his forearms.

"Fuck! Stop it!"

"It wouldn't have hurt as bad if you just took some meds," Gigi countered, hesitating a beat before smacking them again.

Peter cringed, catching Clarence above his sister's head with a smile the Birchwood man didn't attempt to hide. Gigi followed the distraction, and while Peter couldn't be certain what look she sent the man's way, Clarence immediately cast his eyes to the ground.

She returned her attention to Peter with an expression that made him straighten his spine.

"I'm happy you're here," she began slowly, quirking an eyebrow as Peter's face flooded uncomfortably with heat. "But I gotta say, Clarence is not the person I expected to see."

"He was the only one I could find who could get past security into West Belfry. People are dying, G. I needed to make sure you were able to get out."

Gigi's forehead creased, dragging the corners of her eyes downward.

"They aren't holding me hostage, Pete. We're just waiting on a couple more patients, and mine is pretty fucking ill."

"You know I'm an ALS rig." He hit the side of 415 with pride. "We can take whatever patient you have and hoof it. You won't have to come back. We can go to Nana's together after, watch from a distance . . ."

A gentle sound interrupted, finding Peter's ear through the protests. The paramedic's eyes wandered to a copper timepiece pinned to his sister's gown, the gentle inscription facing out as his voice faded into the ether around them.

The siblings sat in the moment, listening to the isolated tick in the chaos of another flood of patients and emergency personnel pushing past, scrambling for their transports like the rebel evacuation of Hoth. The pulse through his arms slowed to keep time with the little watch, and Peter's breath fell into rhythm with Gigi, steady and slow.

She lowered her voice. "I'm taking care of Stew Michelin, Pete. We're waiting on air evac; he's too sick to move by ground. M volunteered, and they needed someone else, so . . . I'm sticking it out."

Peter's judgment was swift. "That man is not worth staying behind."

Gigi's eyes came to rest on his own with paralyzing sadness. In the corner of his sight, Clarence stepped from the doors, inching toward their gathering by the ambulance to keep out of the way. His gray uniform gave him wide berth from the rest of the crowd as he stood feet from Henry, both men doing their best not to overhear the conversation.

"You know he was one of the security personnel with me on Monday." She fiddled with her bun, securing flyaways as she spoke. "I feel like I owe him a fighting chance."

A lazy grumble of thunder trailed after Gigi's words, and lightning played against the bunker wall, making shadow puppets of them all.

"And I'm actually the best to be in there right now," she continued. Her smile wrestled its way past tears. "I don't have anything too special about me and . . . you know that's always been hard. But the hospital doesn't hurt me the way it hurts someone like you. And I got M and Alfie up there with me. I can do this."

For a person who never lacked words, the words Peter managed were hard won.

But it can still hurt you.

Was what he wanted to say.

"I'll be here when you're done, okay? You meet me back here after he catches his evac. We go together. I'm not leaving without you, all right?"

"Sounds like a plan." Gigi smiled, an expression that did not require approval but appreciated it all the same.

A suffocating embrace hit Peter like a freight train, and Gigi spared his arms for a final hug.

Lightning flashed across his eyes with a single image, a moment in time fifteen years ago, as he watched the city of Crowe fall into darkness. A curly haired child sat huddled against their nana on a loud floral couch behind him, and he did his best to spare her from any fear. Did his best to be brave.

In this moment, he wasted no time on bravery, returning a ferocious hug. The protective gown crinkled uncomfortably between them, and Peter's eyes burned.

"West Belfry cleanse in one hour, thirty minutes. Please clear the premises. West Belfry cleanse one hour, thirty minutes. Please clear the premises."

Gigi found her brother after too long, her smile earnest and tear stained.

"So, what about Clarence?" she whispered.

Peter released her with a grin. "You can fuck off now."

Her laugh met his ears, and she backed toward the door with a wave.

"Love you, Petey."

Peter raised a hand in parting, watching his sister hasten through the slithering doors.

"I love you too."

And just like the memory, she was gone.

CHAPTER TWENTY

Unknown Place,
Unknown Time

Stew's eyes roved the sterile landscape of a room somewhere in the guts of Crowe County's West Belfry, looking for whatever dragged him from the recesses of his sedated rest. Or maybe from a dream. Or a nightmare he couldn't escape, somewhere between sleep and waking among a cacophony of beeping, the voices of strangers. The foreign hands he wrestled out of instinct and lost himself to, among the sting of antiseptic wash.

It all hurt.

Everything.

Everything was on fire except his mind, which screamed nonsense without sound, tennis ball ricochets of half-formed pleas. No one listened. Because he failed to speak. There was no speaking. He couldn't find his mouth.

But he would find pieces. Somethings. Now, his elbows announced their jagged selves, digging into soft padding below while his new fingertips gouged the substance for purchase. Muscles strained for nothing, sinking back as frantic reality played among the darkness, stretching beyond his capacity to see.

Except a single shape.

Drifting, in the corner of his eye.

Hello, Stew.

The beam of fluorescence flooded red, as Stew raked his gaze to the right, to the source of the sound, a grating voice that trembled from a half-formed figure slumped into where a sterile sheet of white met another.

A corner . . . A wall!

His elation was struck down by the figure's presence, formed from dense clay and dripping globs of resin from its features. It was humanoid at best. Pale green eyes were the only defined feature as it reached for Stew, its fingers twisting delicately in the air before it.

I wanted to see you before I begin. In earnest.

The dense fog wove around the sodden being, Stew's observations half-formed and numb, watching its shadowed form wrestle to its feet. He was acutely aware of the waves of pain crashing against him as he struggled to understand why this thing was here. Why a rough laugh from the being hit his senses sideways, stunned him in fear.

If you escape, I will come for you. We have a blood debt now, you and I.

A faint hiss sliced Stew's ear. Building louder and louder, it set his temple on fire before pounding it like a fist as it tumbled into the expanse of thoughts and pain. Screams. Dozens, hundreds. They were familiar and wrenched his senses side to side like a rabbit in a bloodhound's jaws. Shadowed beings crept before him, seeping from the walls and cascading into the floor in waterfalls of crimson viscera.

Remember?

People. Friends. Faces violated by memory and fear. Their eyes bleeding, chins dangling from their skulls in pleas that overflowed every crevice of his mind. Jagged limbs trailed on the air like wedding trains. Their vacuous mouths suspended in time, repeating unforgotten words, desperate bargains.

Fluorescence savaged his eyes.

And he was back in the formless space of white-washed walls framing the solitary figure before him. Its teeth were acrid, bared, and unmoving.

So many people are longing to see you, Mr. Michelin.

The voice tore from his mind, leaving Stew abandoned, thrashing against strangers once more.

PART 7

NATHANIAL TAKES
FRIDAY FROM HERE

CHAPTER TWENTY-ONE

Evacuating West Belfry 8,
Unknown Time

Nathanial maintained his post in front of room 829. Stressed.

"What's happening?" he barked from the door-frame, heels digging into the bright way-line as it faded to its pale glow.

Through a flurry of practitioners, Nathanial watched Stew Michelin thrashing within the confines of his bed. A glass dome obstructed the view, affixed from side rail to side rail over the bed frame with portholes constructed into either side. Every inch of the thick glass was etched with symbols he could not understand.

But Nathanial saw enough.

Stew Michelin was wrapped in bandages along the lengths of his arms, his face, his head. They all wept a blackened liquid that mingled with excess viscera, combining through his dressings in an alarming purple hue. His eyes were barely visible beneath the clouded glass exterior, but Nathanial still saw frantic sclera, white and wide.

Terrified.

Familiar plum-scrubbed nurses worked to soothe the patient back to his mattress through the opened portholes. M tightened soft restraints, and G3 worked the room. Navigating a tree of IV pumps, she adjusted the drips. A blond woman in blue scrubs silenced the breathing machine screaming discontent from the head of the bed. A reedy chaplain obstructed the respiratory therapist's path, his spindly fingers and thinning gray hair visible beneath his dark robes, silent and still.

Moments stretched on, forcing Stew to the bed, tense but sedate.

They seemed to have it well in hand, though Nathanial was uncertain how helpful their efforts would be to the last patient leaving Crowe County.

"What happened?" he demanded.

The chaplain raised his distant gaze to Nathanial for a brief moment of eye contact that made the guard's right knee buckle. "He saw something during the security blip."

G3 examined the chaplain over the bed, wrestling with the expression on her face. "Something, A? What something? Something bad?"

"After that reaction, I would assume so," the man responded with a delicate frown. "If I am going to be honest, there is not much left in this hospital that is not nefarious. But at least this will protect him."

He slapped the glass case gingerly, like a new car hood made of tissue paper.

M was less delicate, closing the portholes with a finite snap.

"We appreciate the honesty, Chap. It's rare."

Nathanial nodded his agreement, the only sense he could add to the conversation.

The chaplain informed him at the beginning of evacuation that the glass could protect Stew from anything—from *more* than anything.

Cleansings.

Demons.

All would be halted in their step.

Famously, this glass protected the children's playroom, a safe house advertised as something to keep out all the hospital's bad. However, as reassuring and impressive as the hospital owning this tool was, Nathanial could only picture his boss as a storybook princess.

Half-dead, waiting to be saved.

"West Belfry cleanse in one hour. Please clear the premises. West Belfry cleanse in one hour. Please clear the premises."

Twenty-four hours of lost sleep clung to Nathanial with blurry vision and nausea. He dragged a rough palm over his face, bringing the space before him into temporary clarity as the excitement faded within room 829. The unit was a large intensive care unit, with thirty rooms that circled a central nursing station. Stew's alarms chimed at his back, punctuated by a rotund doctor stationed beside Nathanial, who committed bravely to small talk and clearing his throat on a regular schedule.

"So, what are your thoughts?"

Nathanial blinked slowly at the man, introduced as Doc R. "I'm sorry?"

The red-faced doctor laid his hands over his knees, smiling.

"Your thoughts."

"Yes." Nathanial was short. "My thoughts on what?"

The doctor waved his hand at room 829 with an infuriating smile that tap-danced on Nathanial's one remaining nerve.

Doc R cleared his throat, thirty seconds on the nose.

"Do you need a lozenge?" the guard snapped, leaving the previous question to die.

As far as his thoughts on the evacuation went, he had no good response.

He remained acutely disturbed by the imagery of Stew Michelin laid to rest in a glass coffin.

And he had no faith in the success of their mission.

"Base to Birchwood One, signal six."

Apple-crisp diction crackled to life on his radio, jolting him from his thoughts.

A foreign voice echoed from the unit's main door, responding to the radio's request.

"Birchwood One to base. Eighth floor, same patient remaining. Awaiting evacuation. You got an ETA?"

Nathanial squirmed, his eyes on the gray-clad shadow who'd returned G3 to her patient after whisking her away without a word. On loan from Birchwood, he'd arrived with a bruised mug, mean expression, and an inability to sense when he wasn't wanted.

Even when Nathanial stated, very clearly, "You are not wanted."

Some people just can't take a hint.

The radio response echoed over the empty unit between them. "Base to Unit Five and Birchwood One. ETA five minutes for heli evac. Delayed due to storm. You are the last in house. We will hold cleansing as long as we can and let you know when to move."

"Birchwood One to base, copy."

Nathanial locked eyes with the Birchwood man, answering in quick succession, "Unit Five to base, copy."

We are the last ones left.

The Birchwood agent spoke loud enough to be heard from the door.

"Five minutes is a long time."

Loud enough for the hospital to hear.

The security system's crimson lights crashed around

them, overtaking the quiet fluorescent glow. The oval unit faded into the distorted hue. Like a mirage, it grew distant and hazy while an alarm swelled from the building's depths, vibrating through Nathanial's kneecaps.

The guard peeled his eyes through sleep-deprived paranoia, watching the unit come to life through the sights of his rifle.

Two shadows floated from beneath a nearby nurses' station, slithering along the baseboards. A stack of charts launched off the same desk, papers spraying across the center of the room. Nathanial dug his back into the doorframe. His ears twitched at the approach of something he could not see. The haze distorted his vision, forcing him to squint into the far end of the unit, the tip of his finger teasing his trigger. Static frayed Nathanial's nerves, his radio's malfunctioning music sizzling beneath his chin.

G3 arrived at Nathanial's shoulder, drawing his attention. She removed her shield, peering into the red-bathed unit, tight brown curls plastered to her forehead by sweat.

"What are you looking at?"

"I don't know . . ." He lowered the barrel of his rifle to stare down the miasma.

Every joint seized with the alarm's persistent yowl, and Birchwood One's eyes probed the doorway of 829 from his post.

"What's out there?" he yelled.

Nathanial responded, his voice screamed hoarse, "I hear something, but I can't see it!"

Footsteps paced the center of the unit, consumed by the alarm.

Shards of tile broke from the ground.

The red mire drifted around Nathanial's feet. Its tendrils seeped across the unit, obscuring upheaved desks and shattered chairs.

The footsteps grew with it, heavier, louder; they cleaved the floor in two until a humanoid figure moved past the door half-dressed in a single sheet, every step a foul chore. Four mottled limbs twisted around a stretched trunk like putty, its mouth dangling past its sternum from a thin string of skin. The creature dragged the mire with it, red steam hissing from its hunched back in a trail that rotted the ceiling above. Tiles shattered in burnt heaps at its feet.

The creature owned no features, except a gaping jaw that swung open with each step, a vacuous hole.

Nathanial raised his weapon, finding the head in his sights. He reached for a purple rabbit's foot on his belt, giving it a squeeze while muttering to the nurse.

"Get in the room, please."

G3 backed into the stillness of 829 as the creature froze directly ahead, its slackened jaw swinging gently beneath its body.

Nathanial locked eyes with the Birchwood man, and he raised a cautious hand, beckoning him. A silvered knife in the man's gloved hands glinted through the gloom like scales on a fish.

At first, they did not move.

Out of fear or want of a fight, the guard couldn't be certain.

Then Birchwood took a step toward 829.

The creature's head snapped forward.

Birchwood froze, while its blackened maw unfurled a reedy tongue that danced on the air, mere feet before him. Nathanial's heart stalled, seized muscles keeping the creature in his sights.

Only the tongue moved, flitting lazily among the haze.

Before it lunged, a staggering step twisting its lumbering form forward. Birchwood flew into the hall, ripped from view by the force of the creature as the rifle kicked hard against Nathanial's shoulder, scattering its shot where the being once stood.

"No!"

Stew's heart monitor spasmed behind him, a discordant rhythm tying Nathanial to his post despite agonized cries from the hall.

"What was that?" G3 appeared beside him once more. "Where's Birchwood?"

Before he could answer, the nurse shoved past. Without a backward glance, she plunged toward the entrance of the unit where the screams split the air.

"G!" M shouted, rooted to the threshold as Nathanial was, staring into the abyss with wide eyes.

The radio on his lapel stuttered between alarm swells, static muddling every syllable. "Birchwood—Unit—ive. Proceed—helipad. Lock—holding —you're clear."

Nathanial whirled on the remaining occupants of 829, palms slick on his rifle. Chaplain held up the wall, a protective way-line light seeping from his fingers while the lady in blue troubleshot a fritzing ventilator and Doc R supervised.

Birchwood's screams fractured his eardrums through the mist's symphonic warp. And worse, he heard no sound from G3.

Clenching his rabbit's foot, the guard peeled himself from the door, rubber-soled shoes sturdy on the broken linoleum.

"Stay with him!" he directed M like he had authority. "I'll get her back!"

The unit outside 829 hit him like a pyroclastic cloud. Sweat gathered on his spine, and he wiped his hands on his vest before sprinting to the entrance with new security on his rifle. Outside the way-line, the alarm weighed his feet like cinder blocks, pushing past cleaved flooring as he rounded the corner.

A fluorescent starburst lit the entranceway. Like minutes before, the bellow of the alarm faded mid-yowl, leaving silence as the deep hum of generators kicked on around them.

The hospital's steady light bathed the situation before him in grim reality.

G3 knelt by Birchwood One, a silver blade poised in the air over the guard as he lay splayed across the floor. Whatever furrows of fear the nurse held in the red light were chased away now, stern attention focused directly on the man.

He was chewed to a pulp, cradling a macerated arm to his chest while his pant leg exposed a julienned thigh, pulsing waves of dark blood onto the tile. If he wasn't the color of oatmeal, he might not have allowed the nurse to drag his belt from his pant loops. But he no longer had that fight.

Nathanial charged the scene, snatching the knife. "Why the fuck did you run out of the room?"

G3 shot a look of scorn that withered Nathanial's insides, though she relinquished the weapon without protest. "Someone had to help, and it certainly didn't seem like it was going to be *you*."

The back of his neck tingled uncomfortably under her scrutiny before she broke eye contact to attend to Birchwood.

Safe to say, Nathanial did not win that staring contest even in technicality.

Belt in hand, she wrapped it around Birchwood's upper leg.

"I told you not to stay, Clarence," she muttered, leaning into the tourniquet to pull it taut.

Birchwood gritted his teeth, his fingers dug into his side.

"I-I . . . get it."

The nurse continued, pitching her voice the lowest it would go. "I can't get the paramedic to talk to me, but getting him to worry about me is pretty much the same thing, so I guess I'll stay with his sister in the collapsing hospital."

"Wanted to make . . . sure you were okay."

"You're *unhealthy*, Clarence."

Clarence?

G3 shed her nursing fleece, packing the material against his side to hold steady pressure, similar to her never-ending chastisement. "And now look where we are. You are now my second fucking patient."

Nathanial observed in silence, rifle trained on the ground. The Birchwood man sucked pond water, his chest rising in weakened attempts of will, but it was clear he was fading quickly.

G3 turned, her voice sharp.

"He needs to get to the ED. Now."

Nathanial cleared his throat, addressing the Birchwood man with uncertain authority. "Are you okay to walk?"

"Probably."

Probably . . .

"Base to Birchwood One, Unit Five. Do you copy?"

Nathanial looked to the elevators, mind fraying as he leaned into his radio. "Unit Five to base. Request repeat of previous message. Downtime fucked with the radio."

"Roger that, Unit Five. Expecting helicopter evac imminently. Proceed to helipad. Cleanse pending. We will hold as long as we can."

So close.

Nathanial pushed a hand through his sweat-drenched hair, slicking it away from his eyes.

"Unit Five to base, copy that. Unexpected delay. Birchwood One injured by level four. Sending down to

West Belfry lobby. Please look to receive." With a brief glance at G3, he muttered, "Stay with him a sec."

Long strides carried the guard into the unit, clocking the practitioners clustered on the threshold of Stew's room. Its solitary way-line flickered faintly by the chaplain's hand, and as he neared, Nathanial clocked the respiratory therapist rebooting the ventilator, listening to the conversation from afar.

"Are they okay?" M asked, shoving her glasses to the bridge of her nose. "When does our ride get here?"

"About a minute. The Birchwood fella is hurt pretty bad. Need someone to go down with him while we bring S to his ride. Medevac will take our respiratory therapist but will not be able to accommodate other passengers. So, rest of us will ride with S to deliver him, take the stairs back down quick as we fucking can. They'll hold the cleanse while we do. Hopefully."

"Stairs?" Doc R grumbled, resting his hands on his knees with a sigh.

"The elevator might be unreliable with the security going on and off like this. So we will play it by ear," Nathanial stated. "Now, who's going down with Birchwood?"

Silence stretched among the group as the practitioners exchanged a collective look.

The purple rabbit's foot played between the guard's fingers as he remained too aware of time ticking away.

"Come on, let's make a decision here. Chap?"

The man in black shook his head, thin and reedy. His glass eyes probed Nathanial like they contained real vision, cutting him to his core. "You will need me to maintain security in case events go awry. I am afraid I must stay."

"M?"

"I volunteered for this." The elder nurse spoke brusquely. "And I'm not leaving G all on her own in this hellhole."

Nathanial gripped the paw, serious eyes falling on Doc R as the aging practitioner flexed his knees. "How 'bout you, Doc?"

"I think . . ." He cleared his throat on cue. "I think I might be needed for medical orders."

M plowed headfirst into rebuttal.

"I think we're past that, Doc. We have all our drips running, and if shit goes south, there's nothing we're going to do anyway. We can maintain care."

Nathanial watched the doctor's face shift, his jovial redness dissipating slowly with each of her passing points.

"You're an ER doc, and he's going to need a trauma workup. It makes sense to send you down to take care of him," the guard began. "You've done enough up here."

The corners of the doctor's mouth twitched once. He trudged toward the entrance on stiff hips. "I'll make certain they don't zip you in here, lads. Let's get him out."

A heavy pause consumed the room, and Nathanial examined his group, all staring past him like they saw something he didn't.

Unsettling and comforting. Uncomforting. No, that's not right.

"That's settled, then. Rest of us will head to the roof. Anyone taking up issue with this plan should tell me now."

The silence was an anchor, broken only by M darting into 829 to arrange the bed for transport.

Nathanial met Doc R at the unit door, with his hands in his pockets, taking in the scene. Birchwood's skin was sheet pale, leaning on G3 heavily for support.

But they were standing.

Nathanial could work with standing.

Shifting Birchwood to Doc R was rough, done in only enough time for Nathanial to call their ride. Pulling a ring of keys from his belt, he flicked deftly to an iron key with five teeth, jamming it into the slot near the elevator.

The keypad shuddered beneath his hand, delivering the elevator promptly.

"Hurry. Before the lights switch again."

Birchwood limped forward, shuffled into the space by Doc. The wounded man's eyes wandered to G3.

"Thanks. Be . . . safe."

The nurse nodded beside Nathanial, raising a blood-doused glove. "Says you."

The man spared a faint smile, and the door shut.

"Hold your breath," Nathanial cautioned, and G3's arm tensed beside him, watching the elevator dial tick down floors.

Seven . . . six . . . five . . . four . . . three . . .

The lights above flickered once; a warning shot across the bow that caught G3 mid-breath.

Two.

So close.

One.

"West Belfry cleanse in forty-five minutes. Please evacuate the premises. West Belfry cleanse in forty-five minutes. Please evacuate the premises."

The elevator found its hold below, and Nathanial exhaled. Daring a glance at the nurse, he found her brow digging trenches between her eyes, fixated on the dial.

She stayed that way for a moment suspended in time, blinking rapidly behind her face shield before closing her eyes tight.

Words formed in the back of Nathanial's throat, of encouragement or condolence, dying on his tongue as her eyes opened and she corrected her posture with a roll of her shoulders. The change in the nurse was immediate and palpable, and a hint of nausea flipped his stomach as she caught him staring.

In the normal world, on a normal day, he would try to ask her for breakfast at Mary's Diner after work. Maybe pancakes. Pancakes to discuss how she was holding up with her demon, why she knew Birchwood agents by name, and how she went home at night and forgot this place enough to plant flowers in her garden.

Maybe we still can.

"You okay?"

Nathanial cleared his throat once with a stiff nod. "We should get going."

But now is not the time.

CHAPTER TWENTY-TWO

West Belfry Elevator, Heading Toward
Helipad, Forty-Five Minutes Until Cleanse

Despite M's preparations, the elevator did not accommodate them graciously.

The chaplain positioned himself next to the elder nurse, both working at the center of Stew to keep him calm as the metal box shuddered upward floor by floor.

G3 squeezed at the head of Stew's bed, titrating medications as they were needed.

Nathanial clutched the small purple rabbit's foot, catching G3's eye with a frantic heart as the elevator shambled its course. He looked askance, toward the elevator dial, where a brass needle ticked to the next number on its half-moon clockface, steadily toward HP.

Finger on the side of his rifle, he mumbled a third prayer.

"Blessed be thy name. In thy hands I place my soul, to guard or garnish for your taking. To honor thine gods and trust thine purpose."

Nathanial did not count himself a religious man.

"In thine greatness, amen."

But in times like this one, it was best to not take chances.

The white-lit space flickered with the journey past each floor, and Nathanial forced a breath, patting the wall once in encouragement.

As if sensing fear, the elevator shuddered to a halt, its clock needle stalling between floors nine and ten. Wailing alarms reverberated against the metal walls, wracking his skull.

The practitioners froze in their tasks, shifting their attention to Nathanial.

Crimson pulsed from above, obscuring their eyes in shadow. Inhuman.

M spoke sternly from the corner. "Do you have a way to get this moving?"

"Absolutely."

Why am I lying?

Balancing the rifle, Nathanial clumsily flicked the iron override key once before he jammed it into the lock.

If that lady catches you in a lie, you don't get to worry about the hospital killing you. She'll do it herself.

All eyes were fixed on his movements.

Two more floors, he reasoned, keeping a steady hand on the wall. *Two more fucking floors.*

He turned the key, and the elevator lurched sluggishly to life. It stuttered, as if uncertain whether it would listen, before lurching upward. The speed buckled Nathanial's knees, and a shaky breath escaped him as the red lights transitioned to white.

His radio returned to life with a crackle under the sound of the fading alarm while he forced a smile at the group.

"Well, that sucked. Huh?"

No one smiled back.

The final heave of the elevator rocked his core, arriving at the top of the belfry.

Sunlight poured through the antique doors opening to a gritty rooftop where a behemoth awaited. The helicopter was set down in a skilled manner on West Belfry's slanted roof, the rotors moving relentlessly as jumpsuit-clad practitioners slid the doors open, hitting the gravel below.

The roof was unaccommodating, taking every one of them to move the bed where it needed to be, heaving Stew toward his salvation and its crew.

Nathanial shrank into the background as Stew's medications were transferred, his breathing machine was switched, watching the task without a single spare thought.

They did it; they got him here.

And even as the chaplain's deft fingers pried open the glass case, throwing the heavy blankets to the ground and exposing Stew in his broken state, immense relief washed over Nathanial like a cool shower.

Stew transferred to the helicopter's stretcher in a single heave, leaving the gutted carcass of a bed glinting in the setting sun, exposing Stew's face to the world for the first time since lockdown began. His features lit in a cascade of pink and purple, filling his pale features with life as the chaplain escorted the stretcher until it was secured.

Nathanial watched his partner disappear, tracking the helicopter as it rose into the air, the bird fading into the summer sky. For a moment, there was respite from the building below, the professional dread of their escape abated by this immense success.

A tap on his shoulder refocused him.

G3 removed her shield and gloves, tossing them to the gravel. The chaplain remained a soundless shadow behind the group, but with a reassuring presence in this time and place.

Nathanial forced a breath, arranging his shoulders so they weren't hunkered by his ears. Under their expectant gaze, he felt too young to be there, too young to be making these decisions.

"All right." Nathanial looked to his company. "That was great. Really superb. We should, um, we'll get going, yeah?"

M clapped her hands once, leading the charge to the elevator. "Absolutely. With the helicopter gone, I'm sure they'll start the cleanse on time."

Nathanial readied his weapon, following with the override key.

"They said they would hold."

M spared a single look back, moving from Nathanial to G3. The guard shifted beside the younger nurse, who appeared at least as confused as he felt by her mentor's assertion.

"You don't think they'll hold it?" G3 pressed forward, walking at the older nurse's side.

"Of course not." M spoke with certainty, watching the two as Nathanial recalled the elevator with his key. "They're tuna fisherman who don't care if they catch a couple hundred dolphin. So long as they get their quarry."

The chaplain closed the distance, a frown tugging on the corners of his mouth. There was unspoken certainty in his expression, but of what, Nathanial could not tell.

M surveyed the group, reaching out to squeeze G3's shoulder. "But we will be all right. We will make it out, just like last time. Just got to hoof it, okay?"

"What about the stairs?" G3 spoke quickly as reassuring fluorescence of the elevator interior greeted the group.

The chaplain moved into the space first, his glass eyes distant and appraising as he placed his fingers on the metallic walls. "I'll hold the lights as well as I can for our ride, G. I believe we will be better suited here than the stairs. Faster. If everyone would like to board?"

M let a small smile slip, releasing G's shoulder to stand in the back corner opposite the chaplain.

Except, she didn't.

Immediately, the elder nurse's face contorted as she was lifted inches from the ground. Into the air of the elevator threshold

A horrified beat extended in time as her body hung there. Before she flew through the air directly into the chaplain. A deafening crack of the chaplain's head ricocheted off the back elevator wall, and the transportation shuddered in its hold, giving a single moment's pause where M detached herself from the chaplain's huddled mass. She scrambled for the door as red light assaulted the space and G3 rushed for the pair.

"Molly! Alfie!"

Neither could beat the building's timing.

The nurse's shout pierced the air as Nathanial caught G3's waist, hauling her back. The elevator doors slammed shut, consuming the elder practitioners before barreling downward at a speed Nathanial felt through the sandy rooftop.

The dial above the doors clicked down and down, landing on the second floor.

And staying there.

The alarm took its place, rattling from the depths of the building below. Once. Twice. It reverberated through the elevator door, siphoning through Nathanial's mind as he held G3's arm. Waiting for something that would not come.

Nathanial released the nurse with mumbled apologies, scrambling for the override lock. He jammed the override key to the right, pressing the elevator button.

Nothing.

He did it again.

Again, nothing.

Any success of the evening shattered at their feet, standing among the sand and gravel crunching against West Belfry's roof.

Nathanial retrieved his key ring slowly, turning to observe his companion.

G3 stared at the metal doors. While the dusky surface was nonreflective, she seemed to see something within it. Slowly, her hand reached to grasp a small pin on her lapel, the little watch he remembered.

Nathanial watched her hold the clockwork heartbeat, with profound loss embedded in the creases of her face.

He knew it well.

But they couldn't honor it. Not now.

Gently, he touched her shoulder.

"We need to go."

"But, Alfie . . ."

"G."

G3 removed her attention from the door, looking through him. Her expression was long, riddled with sorrow.

But she was listening.

"I'm so sorry," Nathanial said, surprised by how much he meant it. "But we have to go . . . I . . . I hope we can find them on the way down."

G3 removed the watch and ripped her protective gown away, knotting it among her fingers. Her gaze fixed on the floor dial, watching the stagnant arrow as she let the gown fall to the sandy floor.

Quietly, she followed Nathanial.

"I hope we don't."

Nathanial opened the staircase with the five-toothed key, looking down into the concrete depths bathed in red. In that instant, he agreed. Wherever M and the chaplain were taken, he was certain they would not be the same when they were found.

West Belfry Staircase,
Unknown Time Until Cleanse

Nathanial navigated the concrete stairwell. The alarm echoed infinitely down its steps. A metallic handrail vibrated to his elbow as he grasped for purchase, rusted metal peeling off in his palm. And they proceeded downward. Downtime thickened the air around them to sludge, exchanging effortfully in Nathanial's lungs. Every muscle in his legs agonized with each step.

G3's grip on his shoulder kept him present.

"Shadow to your left." Her finger aimed over his shoulder at a landing between floors. Which floors, he was uncertain.

He'd already lost count.

Heeding the warning, he gave wide berth to the scrim of energy pressing into the stairwell corner, watching the apparition disappear from sight in a momentary flash of white. The hospital tried to regain its composure before surrendering again to red.

Nathanial's grip strangled his rifle as a series of footsteps echoed from floors above in the waning alarm.

G3 leaned forward, one step above his height.

"We aren't alone," she whispered.

Oddly, this phrase was not reassuring.

"We need to move faster," she added.

Neither was that.

Nathanial spared a moment for his companion.

"I . . . understand the concern. But I worry if we move faster, something will get the jump on us."

The steady footsteps continued to descend from above, a bookend to floor nine greeting them at the landing below. The floor's wrought iron door bent across the landing like an origami figurine, folded off its hinges.

Nathanial caught G3 with his arm.

The nurse's eyes grew to dish saucers as they exchanged volumes with one look. Nathanial began to lead them forward, readying his weapon to navigate the felled door.

Peering into floor nine was a Dalí painting, ratcheted to ten.

Bodies littered the ground like leaves.

Gouges dug into each person in uniform fashion, cracking their chests open like birdcages. Their faces smeared into the ground in piles of mincemeat matter, unidentifiable at best. The air before them was a familiar mist, wafting the acrid stench of warm flesh and iron toward the stairwell.

G3 gagged, pressing her nose into the crook of her elbow as she straddled the remains of the door, inspecting the scene before her. As she cleared the barrier, a scream shattered the air, and Nathanial jumped in tandem with the nurse on the other side of the landing. Hastily, Nathanial tucked himself against the doorframe, gesturing G3 away from the opening.

"I know what that is," she whispered, glued to the door as his eyes probed the floor.

The screams preceded their owner out of the mist.

A hulking form consumed the doorway, shuddering into their sight. The writhing creature was an amalgam of the dead, a mass of distorted limbs, assembled from scraps. Its scream pierced Nathanial's ears, and he clapped a hand over one as dozens—*hundreds*—of discordant sounds tumbled from the creature's mouth like someone slamming their hands onto a synthesizer. Nathanial pressed his back against the stairwell wall, locked on its talon-clawed feet, which made no purchase against the ground as it shambled two steps.

And stopped, turning its oblong head to the two crouched in the doorway. Nathanial stared directly into its milky white eyes, before it tossed another scream to the charred ceiling.

The creature pivoted toward them like a tortoise, and suddenly Nathanial was moving with the nurse's arm under his as she dragged him over the decrepit doorway in three bounds.

A chill sat deep in his bones while the stairwell tilted beneath him, tripping on the steps before coming to an abrupt halt in front of the eighth floor door.

Nathanial wretched with his hands on his knees, winded as he exhaled slowly toward the ground, unable to comply with G3's continued pull. The hospital's red hue swirled in his vision, tilting the concrete platform as he attempted to right his senses.

"That was—" He pursed his lips to push the sting down his throat. A scream echoed from above, eaten by the alarm from a floor away.

A gentle hand rubbed circles along his back as waves of sickness crested.

Nathanial tilted his head to G3, her own lips pursed as she breathed heavily through her nose. Her attention was consumed by the staircase, her hand's soothing course between his shoulder blades almost reflexive.

She spoke above the alarm. "Something similar used to live at my nana's house. Peacefully enough in the far corner of the basement, but that sound . . . it's horrific."

The warmth of her hand disappeared as he stood, breaking with a single pat on his shoulder. Nathanial found his words, cheeks stained red beneath the security system's glow.

"You didn't want to call Birchwood to get rid of it for you?"

She seemed unimpressed by the question.

"Unnecessary. We named it Mortimer. Nana kept it well fed. And besides, if it's a nice entity, why not keep it around?"

Nathanial took a beat with her answer, dissecting it like it might be a joke, though she appeared entirely sincere. Just as he was opening his mouth to ask what in the fresh hell semi-corporeal entities ate in suburban homes, she held up her hand.

"Wait, wait . . ."

Preoccupied with what type of practitioner allowed their grandchildren to listen to those screams at night, Nathanial was oblivious to the staccato footsteps echoing from a flight above, drawing near with intense speed.

G3 shoved in front of him just as he caught the noise. She bounded down the stairs two at a time as the footsteps built behind them, their invisible assailant in pursuit.

Nathanial kept pace with his gun aloft, sprinting past floor seven before the toes of his shoes scraped the cement steps. Pressure bunched his shirt against the back of his shoulder blades, and his feet left the ground as the cut of his uniform tightened under his arms, suspending him midair.

"Help!" He slung the silvered butt of his rifle into something solid and unseen.

A screech pierced his right ear, jerking him backward in a windup before he was flung down the flight of stairs.

Abandoning his rifle, he crumpled as a shock tore through his right leg. Writhing against the concrete landing, he clutched his knee and a guttural scream tore from the back of his throat. His assailant persisted, closing the distance fast, and rusted metal grated against his back as the same grip tangled the fabric of his shirt, lifting him effortlessly from the ground. Nathanial's vision swam as he slammed into the wall, the world fading and returning abruptly as his head ricocheted against concrete, falling to the ground in a heap.

G3's words barely pierced through the haze as he viewed her amidst blackness and blur.

A plum-scrubbed woman swung his rifle like a base-ball bat, a fly swatter, the silver plate glinting in the red light. The footsteps caused the platform to tremble, sharp as they evaded the nurse, who cut into the air with frantic abandon.

"Shood'it!" Nathanial slurred, covering his head as an invisible footfall landed inches from it.

G3 planted her back against the wall, fumbling the weapon to barrel side out. Her finger found the trigger, squeezing.

"It's not shooting!" she screamed, wide-eyed. The reddened bulb above floor seven shattered across the landing.

"S'a two-stage. Pull harder! And put it 'gainst—"
Too late.

A deafening shot ricocheted through the staircase moments before the warning, the rifle kicking back hard into G3's shoulder. Nathanial winced as she flew into the wall, stunned and shaking her head. She staggered, reaching for his arm to abandon the fight.

Nathanial fumbled to be a help, his vision pulsating with the searing pain coursing down his right side. His cry was swallowed by the alarm, a rusted stair rail drag-ging along his side as he stumbled down another flight beside G3, slung over her afflicted shoulder. A placard for floor six flooded his vision, and G3 fumbled colorfully through swears, grabbing for his key ring.

"What are you doing?"

She shouted to be heard. "During orientation! They told us about a dome on the pediatric ward for emergen-cies! We might be able to make a call out!"

Nathanial laughed deliriously. "That's . . . that's bril-liant!"

"Which key?"
Nathanial blinked, heart in his throat.
"The one with . . . six teeth!"

"Who has time to count!"

The footsteps gained, intensely near as G3 forced the key in the door, tumbling through to West Belfry 6. Hard linoleum hit Nathanial's back, pulsing down his leg as he dragged his eyes into focus.

Ears ringing, he turned to the woman beside him, who untangled her support to observe their surroundings.

Right, right . . .

The throbbing in his leg pulsed in maddening opposition to the rhythm of the alarm as Nathanial observed the sixth floor.

At first glance, nothing made sense. An onslaught of light scorched his eyes with a disco tech of malfunctioning way-lines sputtering from brightly colored patient rooms. They flickered without rhythm or purpose, punctuating the space with uneasy protection. The nurses' station was bathed in the glow, mutilated by the strobe.

A clattering metal train carried itself above the madness, clacking along its track dutifully through the cacophony of noise.

Being one of the floors they vacated first, the pediatric floor was thirty hours into the complete anarchy of no hospital control, and it showed.

Nathanial's arm shifted without his say, and it took a moment to register it was G3 helping him to his feet. Blood flooded his leg, beating against his skin as he attempted to bear weight.

"Can you walk?" she asked, a grim echo of his words to the Birchwood man.

Nathanial let loose a stubborn nod, accepting the help. "Should be good . . ."

Proceeding down the hall revealed each room to be in its own state of disarray. Beds were flipped, wallpaper sliced, light fixtures ravaged. The under-the-bed creatures left when the children did, their spaces shuttered closed from their side. It robbed the unit of their residual warmth, so Nathanial's ragged breath escaped him in clouds of frost.

A translucent person missing half its skull paced this stretch of hallway, the rut it was wearing uninterrupted by the belfry's new chaos. G3 navigated slowly along the carnage of the narrow nurses' station, paper charts shredded to confetti.

"What did this?" she asked, careful to keep her voice low.

Nathanial shook his head. "There are . . . so many things contained in this hospital . . . it's hard to tell."

The glass dome bubbling from the farthest wall stalled further questions.

Nathanial grimaced as G3 quickened to an unbearable pace. In the frantic steps necessary to cover ground to the bubble, optimism had time to be born and die.

Gouges punctured the shell's exterior, intact but weakened.

A temporary safety at most.

Key in hand, Nathanial held it up to the playroom lock and paused. The opaque metal was shattered, hanging limply from the sealed door. Exchanging a glance with G3, he scrutinized her reaction, eyes shut in a moment of disbelief before her lithe hand reached out for the door, pressing it open.

The air of the playroom was crisp and fresh like an electric shock to Nathanial's core.

He inhaled deeply.

Wooden weaponry and painting supplies were dropped on the carpet, leaving green paint to ooze over the worn play rug. The guard dutifully allowed himself to be helped onto a beanbag chair in the middle of the room before G3 closed the playroom door, dragging a plastic chair in front of it so it stayed shut.

The first to leave. And left in a hurry.

As the door fenagled shut, Nathanial leaned into his radio, its static fading in the playroom's silence.

"Unit Five to base. Do you copy?"

No response. His heart pounded in his throat.

He tried again. "Unit Five to base. Do you copy?"

Silence drilled into the dome before finally, "Base to Unit Five. Good to hear your voice."

Nathanial cackled, relief hitting him in a manic wave.

"Unit Five to base! Did you receive Doc R and Birchwood?"

"Unit Five, we have received them."

Nathanial paused, G3's eyes burning holes into the nape of his neck.

"A . . . a nurse with moniker M and a chaplain were taken down by the elevator. Did you receive them?"

The radio filled the space with gentle static, and Nathanial's eyes rested square on a puddle of green paint inches from his boot heel.

"Unit Five, that is a negative. No twenty on M or the chaplain."

G3 sat cross-legged in front of Nathanial and his beanbag throne.

He watched her expression carefully, the sadness beginning to creep its way in. "Base, consider the two missing and under duress. Work on getting the chaplain ID'd."

The woman raised her hand, tugging once on her bun. "Alfie . . . his name is Rosewood."

Nathanial's face fell, repeating the information. "Rosewood is his name."

The radio spoke beneath them, G3's absent gaze fixed on his. One hand clenched the watch ticking by her badge.

"Roger. Unit Five, we recommend departure from premises prior to cleanse in T minus fifteen minutes, forty-five seconds. We will hold the gate open as long as we can, but when it goes down, it will not be reopened."

Nathanial's heart sank to his stomach, but he spoke brusquely while he could. "Understood."

And the static returned, gentler within the playroom walls.

Accessible.

Nathanial let his hand fall from the radio, gripping the rabbit's paw on his vest as he spied a wooden shield and sword discarded on the rug.

The weight of looking at his companion was too much to endure. "I'm sorry."

G3 shook her head. "If they can get out, they will. They're both so powerful and just . . . so intuitive."

She blinked quickly, a smile gracing her features.

Forced. Fleeting.

Nathanial winced, intense pain coursing to his hip. "During the exorcism, M really seemed . . . to know what she was doing, so I don't doubt that . . ."

G3 braced her shoulder with a firm grip.

"I'm scared."

She cleared her throat as if to rid herself of the words.

Nathanial rearranged his leg and leaned forward quietly. He held out an unsteady hand.

She stared at it.

Nathanial's stomach flipped once as he watched the nurse watching his hand. In this moment, he wished his branding wasn't so rough, that the skin had settled in a softer way.

And then G3's hand joined against his square palm. A small comfort settled in his chest as her thin fingers intertwined with his, a small moment of warmth.

Nathanial sighed a shaky breath of stale cigarettes and Extra gum into the crisp air of the play space. "I'm scared too."

The echoing sentiment was met with a smile from his companion.

He liked making her smile.

Now's not the time.

He squeezed her hand once. "In the . . . in the meantime, w-we won't survive a cleansing if we get caught here. We should—"

Bells.

Nathanial raised his gaze over G3's shoulder. To a solid black-and-white harlequin. A clown whose black-gloved hand tapped softly on the glass, moving a wrist of rusted brass bells with each twitch.

Are you fucking—

G3 whipped around, immediately scrambling over Nathanial's leg at the sight. Searing pain shot to his ribs.

"Jesus fuck!"

"I'm sorry!"

The creature stalled the conversation with another shake of its wrist, leaving Nathanial to fall silent, clutching his leg as the clown flung itself forward, gripping its stomach in mimed hysterical laughter.

Like a flower seeking sunlight, it unfurled, squaring off with the dome's etched glass.

Its painted face was a muddled splotch of white grease paint, blackened around the mouth in an exaggerated grin that disappeared as its jaw slackened. Teeth jutted like acrid tombstones from fetid gums.

Pale yellow eyes fixed on the pair, sunken into its skull as they twitched in perpetual motion, jumping from Nathanial to G3 like fleas.

The guard pulled the lone knife from his belt, heart stuttering beneath the gentle static of his radio as he lamented the loss of the rifle.

The creature's eyes widened, clocking the threat.

It closed its mouth in an exaggerated frown, pulling

the corners of its lips to the ground. Nathanial froze, transfixed, as a delicate dance carried the creature two steps forward and one back, the music in its head bringing it closer and closer to the entrance of the dome.

The clown stopped before the door, lowering its gaze to both practitioners at once.

Its lips dripped thick tar onto its ratty diamond collar.

Staring.

G3 squeaked as its right hand rose to the glass and waved. From his beanbag, Nathanial watched the gloved hand tease the doorknob, bells jingling gently with each exaggerated attempt.

Once. The doorknob must have burned it.

Twice. The doorknob was too slick to grip.

A performer's rule of three allowed purchase the third time, sunken eyes wide with surprise.

Its blackened tongue ran delicately over the jagged smile as it pressed the door open.

The pink plastic chair skittered along the floor, an ineffective barrier.

G3 huddled beside Nathanial, and he could feel electricity through her grip, coiled for action as the clown planted itself in the entry.

Its jingling hat scraped the doorframe as it stared down at the practitioners. G3's trembling was fierce, kinetic energy confined to a single body as she clenched his hand.

Tap.

The clown took a step forward, but that wasn't the sound Nathanial heard.

Tap.

The alarm fell silent, allowing the guard to pick up a percussive familiar sound.

Footsteps jolted toward the playroom from the hall. In the same instant, the clown lurched forward.

Before it could make purchase, the harlequin was hauled backward by its tattered costume, heaved down the hall. A length of translucent blue light towed the clown in its wake, sprinting for the nurses' station with clicking footsteps from the stairwell.

The clown's black shoes scuttled frantically against the ground, bells jingling in pronto, clawing at the iridescent shape holding it hostage.

Nathanial was pulled from the beanbag by G3's frantic force, following quickly on its heels.

He held fast to his knife as G3 kept pace, inches from the clown's grasp as they poached an opening.

The flash of translucent blue gave them that chance.

In decisive action, it slammed the clown onto the desk. Black-and-white chunks flew from its ethereal form and scattered into the air where the incorporeal viscera hung suspended at eye height.

Nathanial's leg seared, the cloud of dismembered clown brushing his face as G3 forced him forward at the pace of the clattering train, through the door and down the stairs as quickly as he could travel. But Nathanial was not allowed to stop. G3 kept him moving at breakneck pace, a tunnel vision of fear as they hobbled down staircase after staircase. The ticking clock on her lapel was enough to let them know they were running out of time and had no room for error.

They passed floor five.

Four.

Three.

Two.

Two.

Two . . .

"W-wait!" Nathanial panted, stopping them on the landing.

G3 halted, the pounding alarm swelling louder from below the lower they went into West Belfry.

"We've passed this before."

"What do you mean?" she demanded.

Nathanial extended a hand, placing it against the second-floor placard. "We k-keep passing this floor."

"That's absurd."

"Is it?" He leaned against the wall to steady his leg.

Agony was now his constant companion, the bent leg on fire, straining against the stitching of his trousers. Sweat dripped from his forehead in what he thought might just be the pain before remembering Downtime cut off the vents to the outside world, and the environment around them was becoming unbearably hot.

G3 watched him with panicked eyes, shifting in her sneakers.

"How do you suggest we get out, then?"

Nathanial wheezed an answer, holding his chest. "We get to the elevators? Maybe we can override . . . to get to the first floor."

G3 took a lingering look down the last flight of stairs.

"You're certain we're repeating?"

"Yes."

A pause suspended between the two where something worked behind the nurse's eyes.

Considering her amount of trust.

After one alarm cycle, she conceded.

"Fine. But if it doesn't work, we try the stairs again."

Nathanial nodded, carefully removing himself from the wall.

"Fair."

The second-floor door scraped open, red light illuminating the hallway before them. Nathanial stood as if at an altar, staring into its emptiness, the ceilings and halls vast in their abandonment. With a faltering hand, he palmed his knife.

The alarm was absent from this floor, leaving only pulsing red light in its wake as Nathanial dragged his leg behind him, leaning heavily into G3 as he gestured the way.

"Patient transport elevators are down on the left."

"I know."

Her answer was near silent, the lack of alarm deafening.

Nathanial turned off his radio, persistent static mounting as they proceeded down the hall, blinking the red haze.

Finding the elevator bank was quick work. It sat a short walk from the stairs in a mournful state. Removing his keys from his pocket, Nathanial gestured to the center set of doors, which hung open, the sight seizing his breath.

A blackened pool congealed on the center of its metallic floor, dragging a slug trail of viscera out the door and down the hall that disappeared into the haze. The cabin's darkness hit him with a wave of vertigo as G3 paused before it. Her fingers pressed into his side to keep him aloft, the ticking of her watch persisting.

The deadline for escape loomed over their heads.

"Could they still be alive?" her quiet voice asked from his side.

Nathanial allowed himself time to answer, every nerve prickling along his limbs.

He stared along the trail of blood, pressing his gaze into the miasma until his head swam at the thought, whispers sliced into his skull as the radio continued to flicker in and out of silence. Fragmented words shouted from the hallway's void, barely audible and infinitely enticing.

He straightened himself, ready to lie, to take the open elevator if it would run and never turn back, to convince her there was no way they survived. To convince her to leave with him.

But there she stood, with unyielding judgment, voluntarily the last in the building to give *his* friend a chance at escape.

"This looks like a single trail." He formed his words slowly. "We know the chaplain was injured, so maybe . . . M could have pulled him out to hide. She could still be alive."

Without pausing to think, he turned them in the direction of the hall.

And they pressed forward.

West Belfry 2, Hallway, Unknown Time Until Cleanse

Nathanial closed his eyes, his feet stumbling along the blood trail. A faint scent of cigarette smoke unfurled before him, preceding the warble of a gentle old melody, and he craved nothing more than a long drag.

The flat portion of his silver blade pressed to his chest as G3 tugged them through the hall.

Slowly, he felt himself humming the same tune, off-key, from somewhere deep in his throat. For a moment, he was entirely at peace, and the hold on his blade became lax.

"What's that song?"

The answer to his question was immediate. Concerned.

"What song?"

Oh.

Stock art hung from the walls, their pictures necrosed and feathering from their frames as the practitioners neared the cafeteria, where the blood river bent out of sight. Nathanial was consumed by the art, their delicate decay.

A field of flowers melted down the wall like Escher clocks. Transfixed, his gaze corrected rapidly as G3 pulled him along, opening his eyes to a forest of bodies in the hall before him.

Each swung idly in no breeze with their toes scraping the floor, necks at unlivable angles. Their uniforms were antiquated, purple scrubs, solid black, and wolf gray, but rang with grotesque familiarity. Each deadened gaze seared into his neck, though on closer inspection their eyes were closed.

The echoing melody faded, chimes finishing the verse before it started anew.

Nathanial clocked G3 at his side, noting concern as he struggled to ignore a body rotating over her shoulder.

"Hospital's playing tricks." He leaned into her as she adjusted her support. "Take the knife. I dunno what my head's doing."

The silver left his hand like the severing of an appendage.

"What are you seeing?"

"Grisly nonsense."

Without faltering, the song restarted with the skip of a needle, and they rounded the bend.

G3 poised the weapon in her free hand, shaking as they stood at the threshold of the cafeteria. The room was empty, chairs piled in corners, tables pushed away. A vending machine buzzed idly to their right, though its innards were long dark.

Goose bumps stung Nathanial's skin as he stared into the vacant room, trying to blink away the sight at the end of their trail.

But it wasn't a trick of the hospital.

Pinned to the wall was a slumped mass of black robes, the reedy chaplain's feet resting firmly on the ground.

His body stood tacked into the drywall, the lifeless husk of a practitioner who, not an hour before, had busied himself protecting Stew.

No less than five kitchen knives jutted from his stomach, holding his form aloft.

Nathanial allowed his eyes to linger on the being for the briefest moment before settling on another.

M knelt in the center of the room, plum scrubs soaked, bloodied with wire-rimmed glasses out of reach on the floor. Her back heaved with labored breath, hands planted against the tile.

It can't be real . . .

Nathanial stumbled as G3 darted away. She managed two steps before skidding to a halt as M lurched once, sitting up with a gasp.

G3 poised the knife toward her friend as M shambled to her feet a limb at a time, revealing herself to the room with an unsteady sway.

Her plum scrubs were split down her middle, intestines spilling from an open stomach into a swinging pendulum of entrails writhing to the floor. M's keen eyes were harsh, creased at the corners as she took full deep breaths.

Nathanial staggered forward, his hand reaching for G3's shoulder.

"We need to go. We . . ."

He limped forward, his hand outstretched.

His hand . . .

Nathanial fell through open air, missing his companion by inches. Tenuous footing threw him to the ground, off-balance as his mind skipped like the record needle restarting the plague of a song.

A hum issued from the back of his throat as the predatory violin melody circled his thoughts. Vaguely, he wondered what they needed to do with such urgency.

What he needed to do with such urgency.

Why do we need to leave?

Nathanial became abruptly aware of how comfortable he was against the tile, even before a warmth pressed against his cheeks.

Why do we . . .

Searing pain brought the scene at hand to view with intense clarity.

M was close, too close, huddled and screeching as she flailed for a familiar knife lodged deep in her back. G3 was closer. On top of him, her knee digging into his broken leg with the expression of someone who'd just realized their oven was on all day. Clumsily, he made an attempt to shove her off, the maddening sensation crackling up his spine.

"What'd I do?" Nathanial slurred, the hospital alarm chasing the song from his head with its angry bellow.

"You tell me!" G3 shouted, hauling him to his feet.

Watch out!

He blinked sluggishly, his mouth gulping.

Out loud! Speak!

"Watch —"

M's hands were on G3 before Nathanial could utter the warning, grasping the nurse by the throat. Nathanial fell back, the cafeteria jilting under his feet as M flung her across the room. G3 slammed into the body of the chaplain, into the back wall with the sound of a muslin rag doll.

Landing, unmoving, on the floor.

Satisfied with the result, M turned her attention to Nathanial.

With limbs of lead, he stared at the remnants of the elder nurse faltering toward him, G3 in a heap at the chaplain's feet like an effigy in prayer.

A foreign hand raked broken nails against his scalp as M's grip closed on his hair, forcing his gaze to her distorted form.

"Birchwood filth," M's corpse rattled, and she jammed her knee into his chest. "What remains of my host enjoys this . . . immensely."

Nathanial recoiled, the scent of rot overtaking his addled mind, struggling for clarity.

"Y'ur . . . disgusting . . . I'm . . . I'm sorry, M . . ."

The stern expression staring him down did not falter, the absence of M's typical wire-rimmed glasses almost disturbing enough in its own right, but there was something else to the scorn. It was scorn from a man named Gregory on West Belfry 10.

Nathanial's heart stalled at an abrupt realization, seeing directly to the entity occupying M.

One he'd already met.

"Alagor. . ."

Nathanial gasped, the strain of his ribs pushing inward under her knee as it jammed against his sternum.

Inches from her face, Nathanial managed a toothy grin, blinking through a haze of pain to lock eyes with the specter. "Wha'? 'Fraid of your name . . .? 'Fraid 'cause you don' know mine?"

M's intestines recoiled, and Nathanial was certain he'd made a mistake.

"I have nothing to fear." She punctuated her speech with a dig of her knee. "After this cleanse, I'll be back again."

Another dig into his chest.

"And again."

In his gut.

"You fleas will release me. Or I'll take every inch of this place first, on my way out."

Nathanial's resolve stymied with every assault, black dots competing with the red in his vision until M stabbed into his leg. His throat split in two, a scream spilling from his mouth without his consent as his vision flashed black.

He felt the cold floor make hard contact with his head as he muttered prayer after incoherent prayer, slumping completely into the tile as his leg agonized him with pulses of heat.

Heaviness flooded his chest as he pried his eyes open for a moment more, his mind seeping into the broken linoleum. The pile of plum scrubs across the room caught his breath in hitches, G3's stillness emptying his limbs of any fight as he watched her desperately for movement.

Please get up.

The threat of a fingernail danced along his fluttering eyelid.

"You're going to die here, Nathanial."

Please.

Blackness consumed him.

"And so is she."

PART 8

GIGI'S FINAL TURN

CHAPTER TWENTY-THREE

ittle one.

The voice was a snake bite, and Gigi steeled herself against the familiarity as its venom seeped into her thoughts.

It was M's voice.

Gigi pried her eyelids open with impossible effort, the blurred form of her mentor visible like a mirage across the room. Entrails poured from M, writhing against Not-Stew's chest. Jaundiced skin stretched in wax paper folds over her jutting bones, deepening the shadows around those blackened abyssal eyes. Her knee dug into his sternum.

And a deep smile split M's pallid features.

She moved to his stomach.

Gigi sucked a breath, testing her aching limbs as warm words danced along the inside of her skull.

Stay down, G. Take a minute.

And she might have.

But M moved her knee to the guard's leg next. His auburn hair was soaked to his scalp as it dropped against the tile and a dark pool seeped from beneath him, a slow spill of blood in Downtime's red light.

He screamed.

Gigi forced her hands into the tile, the jagged floor painfully familiar, the situation painfully familiar.

Take a minute.

Uneven breath stuttered rebellion from her lungs, shoving the instructions down as far as she could.

Tick. Tick. Tick.

M's eyes landed center mass as Gigi staggered to her feet. The creature wearing M's skin left Not-Stew's leg, and a soft gasp escaped his lips. Moments later, the sound crashed against Gigi's ears in maddening desynchrony.

Gigi's legs were lead as she trudged toward the pair without a plan, sinking into the floor with every step. The short walk to M felt infinite, and whatever inhabited her mentor knew this, abandoning the guard for new quarry.

The creature latched onto her shoulders, and Gigi recoiled under its grip.

M stared, recognizable only in the shadows of expression. It was a visage of her former self, puppeteering a grab for emotional real estate.

Gigi's throat was dry and cracked, but she attempted to speak. "Hey, M."

The inhabitant mimicked M's wry smile. "Hey, G."

The rot of fetid flesh coiled inside Gigi's nose as her mentor's intestines grazed the tips of her shoes. This close, Gigi noted one of M's eyelids was ripped in two, while her jaw clicked with sweet words rasping from the depths of her throat.

Hot tears pooled in Gigi's eyes, overflowing in a stinging mass toward the corners of her mouth.

"I'm sorry this happened to you," Gigi said thickly, the salt biting her tongue. "You do not deserve this, and I'm so, so sorry."

The entity stared through her with M's eyes, jagged fingernails dancing along Gigi's shoulder blade.

M's head tilted, speaking sweetly. "You . . . caused this to happen . . . This should have been *you*, Gigi. The moment chance brought you to my room."

"Your room . . ."

"Yes." It smiled, showcasing cracked teeth dangling in M's mouth. "We have played together before."

Gigi's heart leapt into her throat, pounding her ears as the image of Gregory stared through her with those same eyes.

The eyes now watching her from her friend's skull like a rabid animal. Hunter's eyes.

Its grip forced her close so the wood rot burned her nose. Decay seeped into her mouth.

"Think of all the suffering you would have negated. Think of all the people you would have saved, taking me from this place."

Gigi gripped the watch on her lapel, the accusation landing with a choke, fighting M's proximity. Sweat poured from her curls, shellacked to her cheeks in the stagnant crimson air, and her grip slipped against the woman's arms.

Spit clogged the back of her throat, desperate to inhale air not clouded by rot.

That's not true.

"It is." M spoke with unmatched certainty that dug doubt into Gigi's will. "Alfie would still be alive, if it weren't for you."

No . . .

M flashed a smile.

"The cleanse will not stop me. I will be back. Until then, we will have some fun, little one."

One arm coiled around Gigi's, the miasma around them slowing each motion as M swung her other up, plunging her nails into the nurse's jaw from below.

Gigi hung suspended for too long, her shoes scraping the tile below, her fist clenched around the copper heartbeat in her hand.

Before time caught up.

Agony shot through her skull, the warm wet seeping down her throat as foreign nails scraped against her teeth. They hooked her jaw, throwing Gigi to the ground. The nurse felt a scream shaking from her throat, sounds warbling into the air as the next onslaught came. The corpse placed its knees on her chest, depleting it of air before gripping the sides of Gigi's head, drawing her close. A jagged nail traced the nurse's eye, her nose, her mouth as it seeped blood onto her chin.

Tears coursed through the viscera, and Gigi gripped the watch on her chest, inches from the beast.

Fear nothing.

But she felt fear. She felt it in every ion of her being, coursing through each limb, pulsating from the wound filling her mouth with blood.

Gigi's grip held on the watch, mind racing as intestines flung around her head, the open cavity of M's stomach vacuous and deep.

Within reach.

Fear nothing.

Gigi mined for the feeling of snow. It whipped the smell of pine into her senses and the warmth of a yellow Victorian's dimly lit interior that siphoned away the defeat colonizing her bones.

The house sat in Crowe, atop a small hill overlooking the city, overlooking the Sticks, with a view of Persephone Tower embedded on the horizon from its window seat, with the four belfries of the hospital reaching skyward amidst a stretch of slate-gray city.

Where people thrived among the weird and awful and wonderful.

Where Gigi thrived among the weird and awful and wonderful.

Where she promised she would return after this was all over.

She turned the copper watch in her hands.

Twice.

Three times.

It opened its mouth to speak again, and Gigi reared back, spitting the blood into M's face.

Fuck this.

In a single stroke, Gigi ripped the pin from her top, burying her hand deep inside M's abdomen.

The gentle tick disappeared as Gigi's hand sat plunged into an abyss of roiling intestine. Bowel coiled around her wrist, tugging her close as M cleared her face of blood, gritting her teeth.

For a terrifying moment, it did nothing.

The corpse opened its mouth to speak.

And then there was smoke.

Billowing from every orifice, pouring from M's eyes, nose, mouth, gut, cascading to the floor like an ashen waterfall as the corpse split the sky with a scream.

Gigi shoved the pin farther, catching against something dense inside her friend, searing hot to the touch. Jolting backward, the corpse scuttled away with smoke tumbling from its twitching gut, crackling char consuming her body from the inside.

Sudden alarms shattered the air, clearing the fog in Gigi's head.

The corpse howled beneath it, spindly hands digging among the entrails coiling at its feet, wading through burnt flesh for the assailing trinket.

"I'm so sorry, M!" Gigi blinked, wiping her face as she stumbled to Not-Stew's side.

She shook him once, the force of it splattering blood from her jaw over his wolf-grey uniform.

But it made no difference, with the state he was in.

A wince twinged the corners of his mouth, while shallow breaths pushed timidly at her hand. An ache began in Gigi's chest as she counted breaths through the touch, feeling his respirations in six seconds, multiplied by ten.

Forty.

The red lights flickered.

We won't get far . . .

For a camera's flash of time, the fluorescence was back, exposing the corpse running her intestine for the copper trinket buried within. Distracted. In pain.

Gigi looked to the door as the red crashed around them once more, the corpse's shriek cutting into her mind like a bell.

Might as well die trying, Winsted.

"Come on!" Gigi heaved Not-Stew from the ground, dragging him along jagged tile in a desperate bid for the hallway. "We have somewhere to be!"

The guard's eyes fluttered, weak in an uncoordinated attempt to assist as they staggered into the hall, hitting every wall on their way.

Red and fluorescent light wrestled for control overhead.

"Wha' . . . happened?" Not-Stew mumbled, the scent of his blood overtaking the zombie's char.

Gigi limped under his weight, eyes fixed on the elevators through the briefest glow of fluorescence.

"We have a chance to leave, so we're leaving!" she cried. "But we need to move!"

Something in her words brought the guard online, fumbling for his keys.

The confused alarm swelled from below, fractured and stuttering.

"It has to be near the cleanse." Gigi darted for the middle elevator door, which hung open, white lights covering the puddle of chaplain viscera on the harsh metal floor.

M's scream at their backs stalled.

Before growing to a steady hollow screech that forced Gigi to glance at steady footsteps dragging behind them.

M lunged through the cafeteria doors, her innards trailing smoke that stained the ceiling tiles. The woman landed on all fours, her body arching against the tile.

It laid there like a funeral pyre, smoldering against the blue lineoleum.

Before it slowly shuddered to its feet.

Taking one step. And another.

Covering ground at the pace of a rabid dog.

Not-Stew jolted against Gigi's shoulder, stumbling from the sight.

"Why's it burning?"

"Just get in!"

Gigi flung her companion into the elevator as the white light punctuated the corpse jolting in their wake, emphasizing its skin splitting with each jerking step.

Heart in her throat, Gigi ripped the keys from Not-Stew's hands, jamming them into the override slot.

The elevator doors slammed shut just as M's mangled fingers pried through the gap, closing over the corpse clawing the other side.

Not-Stew sank to the floor, pulling Gigi with him under his weight. The air of their new space was thick with the remnant scrim of Downtime heat, a sickly-sweet scent of blood rising to meet them where they sat. Gigi's jaw pulsed toward her temples, her heart rate felt in every pinhole constructed by the corpse's fingers.

Fluorescent light seared the nurse's retinas, and she blinked slowly to adjust while Not-Stew lifted his head.

His eyes were unfocused as they assessed his own carnage, deep red staining the wolf-gray uniform. It seeped through his clothing like a fresh river into the chaplain's stagnant blood below.

On the door, a foot from her head, the pounding of M's hands consumed the small space.

Above, there was gentle crackling music from the elevator speaker.

The warbling of gentle violins.

Gigi reached a trembling hand for the panel of buttons, depressing the button for one, which flickered fainty under her thumb.

"Please . . ."

The word left her without permission.

And the elevator plunged into darkness.

Dim red lamps swelled to life, and with them left the sound of the corpse against the door.

The change was sudden, permitting the sound of M's ragged breath just beyond the barrier.

Gigi stared at the elevator door, grasping for Not-Stew's arm.

The corpse continued to pant, its breath throttled and coarse, growing louder as the red lamps continued to pulse above.

Not-Stew squeezed Gigi's arm in a weak pulse of recgonition, but she did not look to her companion.

Her gaze fixed on the crack in the elevator door as a figure overtook the space.

It cut the elevator in two with its shadow, and a pinprick of white was visible from the other side of the door.

A single eye, bloodshot and unblinking. From a corpse whose eyelid was cut to their scalp, staring directly at Gigi.

Its voice crackled from deep in its chest.

"I see you."

Gigi tumbled into Not-Stew as the elevator shot upward, the dial whirling with its movement.

Three.

Four.

The box shuddered to a halt.

Gigi quaked, fixed on the doors as they twitched once.

"Wha's . . . happening?" Not-Stew gasped, his grip on her arm unrelenting.

Gigi blinked back tears, poised beside the guard as aching words shoved themselves from her mouth.

"Alagor wants to play."

She shielded him against the wall as the doors sprang open.

A translucent spindly figure floated feet from them at the opening, turning to the light of the elevator with its arms outstretched.

The doors slammed shut, and the lights flickered again, rocketing the elevator to nine.

Not-Stew struggled to pull his legs from view as the doors revealed a bloodstained corridor with beds embedded deeply in plaster walls. A crawling figure shrouded in hospital gowns lapped a deep pool of liquid at the crossroads of the hall.

Gigi stretched quietly to the panel, pressing the button to close the door. Black dots danced in her vision as she tried not to breathe.

The doors slammed shut, no thanks to the button, bucking upward floor by floor like a rodeo bull.

The elevator rocketed to ten.

To eleven.

To the helipad.

It stopped.

Gigi's fingers wrapped in the coarse fabric of Not-Stew's sleeve as he gripped her forearm. Neither spoke, watching the door, waiting to see if it would open to the roof. If they could make a run for it. But, it didn't.

The button for floor two lit up the small space, so bright it illuminated the shadows of pallor beneath Not-Stew's beard.

And they proceeded downward.

Slowly.

Deliberately, toward The End.

Red light encroached from all sides, and a stringy tune crackled from the elevator speakers.

Not-Stew's uneven breath stuttered against Gigi's arm, and she sank against his clammy form, a pit in her stomach.

"I thought I would live longer than this," she admitted softly, watching the dial arrow marching down floors.

The violins crackled from the speakers.

Not-Stew's gaze was unfocused, eyes heavy.

So pale . . .

"S-same," he croaked with a strained smile. "Shoulda stayed in . . . sanitation."

Gigi pulled her legs to her chest, surveying him. The uncomfortable sweat began to go cold on her skin, causing chills to sneak their way onto every limb.

"Chasing sea serpents from the sewers probably sounds pretty good right now."

The corners of the guard's mouth twitched, and Gigi noted crow's feet under his nearly invisible eyebrows. She kept her attention on him with all the force she could muster, deliberately ignoring the elevator's inevitable descent.

"What's your name?" she whispered.

"I, um . . ." He lost his words, shuddering. "Nathanial."

"Nathanial." Gigi placed her chin on her knees. "I like it. It suits you."

The guard's mouth aimed for a smile, landing on a hiss as the elevator locked in place with a jolt, the number two glowing on the dial above.

Gigi paused, listening to a renewed steady knock echoing through the metal box. Red light filtered from the second floor, and she did her best to ignore the shadow of the predator playing with its prey moving in front of the crack in the door.

The guard's hand was loose on her arm, the five-pointed star branded into his palm gritty against her skin. He swallowed effortfully, forcing his words.

"Y-yours? What's your name?"

Gigi felt the lifeline in Nathanial's unsteady question, his slow breaths punctuating the sudden silence as the song above faded in its final chorus of bells.

The record skipped and skipped.

And skipped.

"Gigi. My name is Gigi."

Nathanial took a beat, his speech broken by clumsy consonants.

"G2 really . . . wasn't sm-smart, huh?"

She smiled, the corners of her eyes stinging as her jaw raged with last words.

"No, Nathanial. Not really."

The elevator door shambled open by mere inches, exposing burnt entrails writhing like stop-motion snakes. Mousy brown hair was glued to M's scalp by sweat and flesh, and a cobblestone texture patterned her limbs.

M's fingers pried into the gap, making a show of wrestling the door open inch by inch.

"Come out, little one. Your friend looks so tired."

The words issued from somewhere in the air, a disjointed echo scratching through the atmosphere around their heads, no longer feigning the voice of her friend.

Nathanial reached for Gigi's hand, the prick of tiny claws tickling her thumb as a purple rabbit's foot pressed between their palms. Gigi supported him, holding the trinket steady.

His eyelids fluttered in a way she both recognized and feared. But she asked anyway.

"Do you think it will help?"

Nathanial's head fell, and his grip went slack against her own.

Tears stung trails into her cheeks as the firm weight of Nathanial's chin rested on her shoulder

The man's breath was shallow, almost nonexistent.

M heaved ragged breath into the small space so the young nurse felt the heat of it wafting over her. Stale.

Holding on to Nathanial's hand, Gigi rubbed the charm with her thumb, observing her mentor's corpse.

"You afraid of rabbits' feet, Alagor?" she asked numbly, holding it aloft. "Does the power of bunnies compel you?"

A sudden hum crashed against Gigi's ears from beneath her feet. Searing light ripped through the space, illuminating the second floor behind M with a heat Gigi had never before experienced. She crowded against Nathanial as it poured through the elevator door, watching the corpse wrench itself away, staggering into the hall with a shriek.

The elevator slammed shut, drowning in a raw chime that now emanated from every crack and crevice of West Belfry.

The cleanse.

Gigi's eyes moved frantically from Nathanial to the elevator pad. Her mind ran a mile a minute, ten seconds of thought bringing unbearable heat in its wake.

Go to one? Gate's probably down.

Snatching the key ring, she threw herself against the override slot, allowing a moment of debate before jamming the *HP* button under her thumb and snapping it in half.

Let's go, Winsted.

Radiance tickled her skin, building to a stinging burn as the elevator shot upward. Small flames ignited in bulb sockets, the fires illuminating the elevator dial.

The elevator sprang open to the sandy roof, which illuminated from the box in a blaze of light. Gigi grasped Nathanial under his arms, heaving them into the night. Fresh air stung Gigi's nostrils and she hauled the guard over the fine gravel, muscles seizing from the strain as she hurried for the center of the roof.

Toward the empty hospital bed abandoned like the coffin it still had a chance to be.

At least it's a pretty one.

Hands shaking, Gigi ripped the radio from Nathanial's shirt, screaming the last of her voice into the static. "We're on the roof! Whoever can hear us! Unit Five is injured. If we survive the cleansing, send help!"

Heat blossomed insidiously under Gigi's feet as she abandoned the radio for the etched dome. Her hands were practiced and frantic, throwing it open with all her force and seizing Nathanial by his shirt. She stuffed him into the bed in piecemeal fashion, angling deadened limbs one after another unceremoniously under the protective glass.

She spared no time sliding into the bed beside him and bringing the glass dome down tightly with an inaudible click.

The first cleanse was visible miles away, and Gigi remembered it well. Curled on the window seat with her brother, the curated radiance shot into the night sky. Its beacon was sharp and scattered, the frantic effort of a group of people who were untrained, who lacked precision and timing for the sake of efficacy.

This time, the light shot into the darkening sky in a carefully constructed beam. Hand on Nathanial's wrist, Gigi counted his pulse with her eyes on the sleek phenomenon, refined one hundred times beyond its predecessor. She noted the delicately carved runes responding within the glass, lighting inches from her nose as the confined air thickened around them.

She imagined they were in a cloud during a thunderstorm as a lightning bolt gathered strength.

And for a moment, it was silent.

It was beautiful.

Before it wasn't.

The cleanse pulsed into the sky from below, the entire hospital trembling as radiance crackled through every crevice, through the perimeter of the roof and the open elevator doors. The stairwell door ripped off its iron hinges, and Gigi closed her eyes in an attempt to ignore the bed beginning to inch uphill, across the roof.

Images of M nipped at her thoughts while the air inside their coffin became unbearably hot, the warmth of Nathanial's blood brought to a boiling point through his uniform. It fluttered in wisps of steam to the air around them.

The heavy scent of singed flesh filled the case as heat seared beyond the dome. Gigi pulled Nathanial away from the glass, jamming the toe of her sneaker against the side to leverage him off it.

The guard slumped heavily in her arms, and she trembled under his weight while the dome atmosphere gathered like a storm, white-hot. In that moment, loneliness gripped her chest like a vise, and Gigi pined for the gentle tick of her watch.

There was no one here with her.

If I die —

The bed was bucked by the force of heat, rocking violently onto its side with a final burst of light. Gigi clung to Nathanial as they hit the pavement, tumbling across sand and glass and jagged cement. The cleanse died in a moment of respite before the bed crashed against Gigi's back. Glass bit her from every angle as she lost hold of Nathanial, slamming into the lip of the roof.

Darkness followed.

PART 9

THE TUESDAY AFTER

CHAPTER TWENTY-FOUR

Seventy-six deaths are confirmed during the evacuation of Crowe County Hospital's West Belfry. On the international stage in infamy and acclaim, stories of survivorship and bravery shine through unparalleled resourcefulness. Rallying together, practitioners of Crowe County Hospital evacuated West Belfry."

Nathanial rested his head on a crushed pillow in a room that smelled vaguely of bleach and thyme. Two hospital beds were crammed together in a South Belfry office space, which was outfitted for patient overflow after the chaos of nights before. A small TV balanced precariously on a dresser before them, an *Out of Order* sign tacked across its screen. If it were operational, Gigi was certain a man named Daniel would be informing them of the news in her place.

Instead, she flicked the corner of the *Crowe Gazette* and continued reading.

"Council members of Crowe County are convening in private chambers to discuss the fate of the hospital as a whole and how best to keep its doors open in service of the seven boroughs of Crowe County. At this time, sources within Birchwood Services indicate the West Belfry's demise was a similar source to what felled North Belfry fifteen years ago. This being was identified and will remain anonymous during preliminary stages of police investigation in collaboration with Birchwood Services.

"The courage of two practitioners who survived the cleanse—"

Nathanial held up a hand, waving off the rest of the reading. "Don't wanna hear about that."

Gigi placed the newspaper to the side, flopping a large picture of West Belfry onto her companion's legs. The picture was grainy, as most of the belfries were, with a white light piercing the night from every window.

"That's fine," Gigi croaked. "Hurts to read, anyway."

Though she had to admit, it was nice to have the time filled.

Since they were rescued, she remembered vague flashes. The helicopter hovered overhead, its searchlight dim compared to the cleanse. Its practitioners hit the jagged roof, and Gigi felt herself moving. And then the memory stops.

Nathanial didn't wake up on the roof, but Gigi was unaware at the time. Scattered fluorescent lights and blurred faces were all she knew before waking up in the South Belfry.

Gigi decided she didn't mind not knowing the rest.

As it stood, there was plenty she would like to try to forget.

Dawn filtered into the room from a single window to their right, illuminating every shadow on Nathanial's face in a hazy golden glow. A gaunt expression hid beneath his auburn beard as a bag of blood trickled through an IV taped clumsily to his forearm.

A singed rabbit's foot was clenched loosely in his hand, and his thumb ran over it slowly as if trying to claim some of its luck.

"I think your paw might have run out of juice." Gigi yawned. Propping her chin on the heel of her palm, she leaned onto his bed. "It did its job pretty well."

Nathanial's chuckle came from deep in his chest, rattling fluid that still sought to escape his lungs. "How do we get the mojo back? You bathe it in moonlight or something like that, right?"

Gigi attempted a smile, the expression foreign. "I think you just gotta go to the 99-cent store and buy a new one. Single use."

"Seems pretty wasteful." He matched her expression, eyes softening at the corners. "You seem tired."

Gigi blinked slowly. "Nah, I'm good."

"You sure?"

"Yes."

"You lying?"

The sun's steady rise with its peach wash brought the skeleton of West Belfry into sharp relief. It rested like the bones of a felled giant as the dawn feigned unnatural peace in the empty windows and abandoned infrastructure.

Gigi's fingers twisted in the edge of the *Gazette* on Nathanial's leg, watching the building come to life. "I'm just thinking."

"A dangerous task."

She looked to Nathanial, nausea clamping her throat as he tilted his head into the morning sun, letting his eyes close. The image of him unmoving on the roof ran constantly through her thoughts.

Gigi allowed herself a moment to clock his chest for the telltale rise of life, her attention fixed on every facet of the man, how the scent of hospital soap and a lone cigarette Gigi had snuck him at midnight clung to his skin. Fresh pine tacked in a swath above his bed dropped needles occasionally into his curls.

In this moment, there was comfort to that.

A beat passed, and her bandaged hand reached for a menu at his bedside.

"All right, no more clear liquid diet." The words scraped from her throat like sandpaper. "What do you want your first solid meal to be? My brother said he'd bring us whatever we want from Mary's."

Nathanial's beard twitched, cracking a tired eye. "You wouldn't happen to like pancakes?"

"Of course. What do you take me for, a monster?"

"Not anymore, no."

Gigi smiled, holding the menu for him to peruse. "Pancakes it is. Now I want you to think hard because this will be the most difficult decision you make in a very long time."

Nathanial's eyes were dull but focused, his mouth twitching in amusement under his beard. His attention settled on her with a force that struck her square in the chest.

Gigi basked in that look, pointing to the breakfast section with a serious flick of the menu.

"Do you want blueberry or chocolate chip?"

ACKNOWLEDGEMENTS

Before the curtain goes down, I want to recognize the friends and family who supported me in this writing process. You overwhelm me with love and support. I'm forever lucky to have you all in my life.

To my writing teachers: Ms. Michaud, Ms. Dillon, Mrs. Thompson, Ms. Francis, Mrs. Capozzi, and Ms. Davis. Please know you made a little person's life full of magic and possibility. I think of you often.

And to all the medical practitioners I've had the privilege of working with throughout my nursing career. You've made me who I am today. I'm better for being part of this career, and I hope I managed to carve a piece of its terrible beauty onto these pages for you. You are, and I cannot understate this, amazing.

TORY TALLBERG

was raised in Stratford, Connecticut, where she lived with a penchant for exploring places she shouldn't and a special love of all things strange. She has been a thespian, special effects makeup enthusiast, seamstress of mediocre garments, hiker of beautiful spaces, and a bedside nurse for six years. When not on shift, Tory can be found trying most things at least once, accompanied by her beautiful menace of a German shepherd, Darcy. *Crowe County Hospital* is her first publication.

 Instagram: @torytallberg

www.ingramcontent.com/pod-product-compliance
Lightning Source LLC
Chambersburg PA
CBHW030139310726
48970CB00005B/1502

9798986155111